Novels by Annabelle Lewis

The Carrows Family Chronicles:

Charlotte McGee, Book One

Titan Takedown, Book Two

Carrows Justice, Book Three

The Bad Penny, Book Four

Fisher of Men, Book Five
(Available Fall 2019)

The Bad PENNY

BOOK 4

THE
Carrows Family
CHRONICLES

ANNABELLE LEWIS

This book is a work of fiction. People, characters, places, events, and situations are the product of the author's imagination. Some historical names, celebrity names, and actual venues appear in the novel in order to place the story in a historic or modern cultural perspective, but these names are used in an imaginary context and do not suggest that any of the incidents ever happened.

Contact Annabelle at annabellelewisauthor@gmail.com

ISBN-13: 978-0-9993368-5-4
ISBN-10: 0-9993368-5-1

First Edition

Publisher:
PePe Press

Cover Design:
JD&J Design LLC

Editors:
Susan Stradiotto, The Write Prose

Interior Designer:
Pikko's House

Chapter 1

Eyes glazed over, Charles Carrows looked at the enormous amount of food he received in his Denny's Grand Slam breakfast then into the laughing brown eyes of his sweetheart, Angelica Renner.

"You told her you wanted to try their most popular item, Charles." Angelica smiled as she poured honey into her oatmeal.

"Yes, well, it's been a long time since I had the metabolism of a teenager. Wow, I don't know where to begin." He spread the melting butter on his pancakes with his fork.

"I'll take one of those links," she said, reaching over and spearing one.

"Hey, backup. How do you know I'm not going to want both of those?" He reached over and grabbed a blackberry out of her fruit cup, popped it in his mouth, and chewed.

"It's okay, darling. If you want more, I'm sure they'll be more than happy to oblige." She took a bite of the sausage.

"Oh, my God, these are so good, have you ever dipped them in syrup?" She reached over for the decanter.

Sitting in the large booth, the sun shining on them, Charles was incredibly happy sharing another breakfast with his wonderful girl. That they had been together for nearly a year was a testimony to their love. Angelica had moved into his new home in the Carrows Las Vegas Casino only last month. It was one of the happiest times of his life.

"What did you think of her so far?" Angelica whispered, referring to their waitress, Catherine, as she limped away from a nearby table. "Didn't I tell you she was special?"

"She seems very capable. Quick, funny, easy going. I see why you like her." He said through a mouthful of eggs and toast.

"I've been in here about fifty times and every time I see her I get to know a little more about her. She's just so memorable, Charles. Sometimes I think about her all day after I come here for breakfast."

"Now you've peaked my curiosity. What is it you would like to do for her?" Charles sat back and took a sip of coffee.

"All my life I've just been a regular person, a good person, trying to do the right thing, and we've talked about this. Sometimes people are put on your path for a reason. I believe that. I think that me bumping onto Catherine's path, and then onto yours, in a weird way, brings us all together."

She wiggled her shoulders and leaned across the table. "And see, now that I know you, and I know what a kind and generous man you are, and since, I know how *extremely capable* you are about things, I was wondering if you would do this for me, as a favor I guess."

Charles responded to her overt flirting. Her eyes twinkled at him knowing the effect she had on him. He smiled and considered throwing down a hundred and taking her out of the diner to somewhere private but contained himself. "One of the things I love about you, Angelica, is your wonderfully warm heart, so, of course, if it's important to you, we'll do what we can to help. What exactly did you have in mind?"

Angelica launched, and Charles happily listened while he ate. She amused him and the speed of her thoughts, the whirl of her intelligence fascinated him.

"Okay, so did you know that this is only one of her jobs? She's been working here, for like forever, and she's a great waitress. I asked her why she hasn't gotten a better paying job somewhere else on the strip, but I think I may have hurt her feelings because that question hit a nerve. Her hip, I mean, her limp, is really pronounced, and she told me that she was born that way, and that she just wasn't sexy enough for the glam jobs on the strip, but no one seemed to mind here. All the walking and being on her feet is incredibly hard on her, too."

Angelica inhaled. "But she has a son, and she's a single mother, so she said she does what she does for them to survive. The thing is, she's like one of the most *positive* people I've met who's been given such a difficult hand. So, speaking of hands, it turns out we both love poker, and she told me she's pretty good, but she can't afford to gamble, so she stays clear of the casinos. I asked her if she thought about becoming a dealer, you know that way she could maybe be off her feet too, but again, I think I embarrassed her because she told me that the big boys were all looking for the best-looking girls to attract the players. That's a load of crap, which of course, means it's true."

Charles smiled at her as she took in another lungful of oxygen. Her boundless energy exuded, her spirited optimism contagious, he thought she could sell ice to Eskimos. Familiar with her process, he patiently listened while she continued.

"Soooo, she's been getting by, and I watch some of the people here when I come in and the way some of them treat her behind her back. Some people are nice and tip well, but some people are rude, and stare, and I just want to smack them for not noticing how hard she works, while being so upbeat. So anyway, last year she had to take a second job, at night, to cover some unexpected bills that her son got them into. Charles, really, this is such a sad story. Her son is twenty-three now, and he's on the autism spectrum. One day, when he was twenty-one, he and some of his friends, I guess he has some friends who are on the spectrum like him but pretty high functioning, and they went into this health club—Strongfit, do you know it? So they go in there, like thinking it might be a cool place to meet some girls, and they get a tour from this one girl who was apparently very, very good at her job, and the boys kinda goad Catherine's son, Matthew, that's his name, into joining the club. So he was in way over his head, and long story short, he signed a contract for three years which he can't get out of and can't afford."

"Didn't the gym realize he had a disability?" Charles said, chewing on a piece of bacon.

"I have to believe they knew that something was different, but they just didn't care. They got him to sign up for their premier package too— the most expensive contract they have. So, he goes home and tells his mom, and Catherine calls them right away trying to explain that he really didn't want the membership, but he didn't know how to say no. She told them that he didn't have any money to pay for it, and they basically told her to pound sand. They didn't care. As long as he didn't have a legal guardian who needed to be consulted and had full rights as an adult capable of entering into a contract— then as far as they were concerned, the contract was legit. The fact that he's so horrified and embarrassed by the whole thing— having his mom getting involved with the manager and stuff, and the fact that he won't even use the gym, makes no difference to them at all."

Angelica's eyes filled with tears, but she quickly moved to compose herself, putting a hand over her nose. She took a sip of water, and in a very quiet voice she said, "So, here is Catherine, now in the hole each month, saddled with this stupid contract for three years, limping away over there, with a *goddamned smile* on her face, waiting on people, while she's so much more deserving than all of this."

Charles reached over to take her hand. She asked, "So, what do you think, honey? Can we help her?"

"I love you, Angelica. Of course, we'll help her. If I'd met Catherine on my own, I might want to help her. But if I can help her and make you happy at the same time, then I can't think of anything in the world I'd rather do."

The smile he received from her was payment enough. It was a beautiful thing. Her aura sparkled. She radiated with health and sexual energy.

"Oh, I knew you'd say that. Thank you. Really. We're doing the right thing here. She deserves a break. I know it."

"I believe you. Like I said last year, you have good instincts, and I've come to rely on them. We make a very nice team."

"I agree." She smiled and looked around the restaurant, her hair in some kind of up-do barely containing the heavy dark tresses. "Charles, do you ever worry about playing God over people's lives? I mean, since I've met you, I've seen you, and your family, do some pretty outrageous things. I know you've done so much good, but I worry about the people you're making as enemies. Do you worry about that?"

"From time to time. My family, my friends, I don't want anyone to get hurt, and now there is you. Even though I tried to disguise you from the people we were playing, I knew you'd be vulnerable being attached to me. It's why we try to keep a low profile. Or as low as we can, in a city with our name on a casino."

"I get it. I just worry a little too. Sometimes. Not a lot. Oh, this is going to be so much fun! I can't believe I'm going to be able to reach out a hand and help her. It feels sooo good!"

"It does. That feeling will never go away. My family was built on the backs of people willing to take incredible, sometimes illegal risks, and I guess we haven't changed all that much. But I like to think that we do more good than anything else. The money's there. There's more than enough for everyone, so it's nice to be able to help others. But, again, what exactly did you have in mind?"

Angelica grabbed a piece of bacon off his plate and chewed, contemplating him with adoration in her eyes. "Charles, I would not wish any companion in the world but you," she smiled.

"Hamlet?"

"No. Keep studying."

Shortly thereafter...a letter was sent.

BAACH, MCKENZIE & BLAKE, P.A.
Baach Tower
7200 San Pedro Drive
Beverly Hills, CA 90213

Mr. Howard Mitchell
General Counsel
Strongfit Corporation
72 South Walker Drive
Chicago, IL 60601

RE: Contract between Strongfit Corporation and Mr. Matthew Cox

Dear Mr. Mitchell,

This law firm represents Mr. Matthew Cox (client) with regard to the above-referenced matter. Mr. Cox entered into a contract with Strongfit on December 9, 2015 for membership in your gym/club in Las Vegas, NV on 9000 Paola Drive. Since that time, Mr. Cox and his mother, Catherine Cox, have written you asking to be released from the contract for the reasons outlined below. It is our understanding that you have denied them release from the contract and they have retained this firm to seek a legal remedy.

Mr. Matthew Cox was of legal age, 21 years old, when he walked into the gym on Paola Drive. He and his friends were given the tour by an employee by the name of Kelly O'Day. Ms. O'Day apparently did an excellent job convincing our client that if he signed a three-year contract with Strongfit, his life, in all areas, would be greatly enhanced. This included but was not limited to: his strength, fitness, physique, skin, and overall looks—which Kelly O'Day assured Matthew would result in his ability to attract the opposite sex. "His dating prospects would skyrocket."

Mr. Matthew Cox, as has been previously explained to Strongfit by Catherine Cox, his mother, has been diagnosed to be on the autism spectrum. He is on the higher end of the spectrum, however; and so has no legal guardian who would need consultation before legally entering into a contract. That said, Mr. Cox is a vulnerable individual. He was greatly influenced by the "unbelievably cute girl who seemed to really like me" who encouraged him to join your gym.

Regrettably, Ms. O'Day and the general manager, Mr. Brian Roberts, who eventually walked our client through the contract, did not take into consideration the full implications of the situation.

That our client had no job and very little money did not deter them from encouraging him to enter into their "Premier Elite Package" at a cost of $400 a month for a period of three years. This contract would require our client to pay $4800 per year and $14,400 over a three-year period.

After entering into the agreement, our client's mother, Catherine Cox, immediately contacted the club to explain that her son did not fully understand what he was signing and should be released from the contract. Even after she presented medical documentation of the diagnosis, Strongfit refused to let him out of the contract. The General Manager helpfully pointed out that her credit would be destroyed if her son failed to meet his obligations. Not legally her obligation, nevertheless, it was stated. Under duress, Catherine Cox, a single mother, was forced into retaining a second job in order to make the monthly payments.

Mr. Mitchell, we would like to remedy the situation

imposed on our clients with the following demands. Immediate release from the contract between client and Strongfit, reimbursement of the $4800 paid to Strongfit by Catherine Cox to date, reimbursement of late fees which were incurred due to my client's inability to pay at the absurd rate of $50/day which have accumulated to $1500, and $10,000 for her family's egregious mis-use by your organization.

We also need to make clear our intentions that if this settlement is not accepted, we will immediately proceed to litigation in the Nevada courts. Baach, McKenzie & Blake has been fortunate enough to recently retain the services of Jessie Waltzer, who will be handling the day to day of this case in the State of Nevada. We have instructed Ms. Waltzer to make this case her top priority and full-time job. You might expect that Ms. Waltzer, who is an extremely thorough and zealous young attorney, will, every day, until we ultimately meet in a Las Vegas courtroom and request a trial by jury, be in contact with your firm requesting preparatory documents such as operations manuals, sales manuals, training manuals, general ledgers, customer demographics, customer information, complaint discovery, profit and loss statements, tax statements, and the collection of depositions and such so as to ascertain the full picture of the Strongfit organization.

When we meet after the jurors are seated, I will be requesting that they award all legal fees incurred by our firm during the litigation process, and real and punitive damages against our client. Ms. Waltzer is currently billing at \$400 per hour. My fees are much more considerable, and I will happily release that information to you should you request it.

I would like to make certain you are under no illusion that we will enter into a settlement agreement for anything other than what we asked. We feel certain that you will agree it is fair. We believe the courts would also appreciate our fast settlement rather than taking up their valuable time. If you choose to deny our settlement request, please factor in the following: I will personally, in perpetuity, with the full weight of our firm, seek class action litigation against Strongfit for other customers who have been coerced into signing agreements that they could not afford.

One last item for your consideration before making a decision, is the recent, personal relationship Catherine and Matthew Cox have entered into with another Baach, McKenzie & Blake client who is highly respected and represented by our firm, Mr. Charles Carrows. Mr. Carrows has graciously taken a personal interest in the well-being of Catherine and Matthew Cox, and he too hopes for a morally respectable and speedy outcome. Catherine Cox is now an employee of Carrows Casino in Las Vegas.

Thank you for your consideration. We look forward to hearing from you by the end of the week.
Sincerely,

Oliver Baach
Founding Partner, Baach, McKenzie & Blake

Chapter 2

Carrows Casino in Las Vegas was similar to the one recently opened in Atlantic City and had an extremely luxe, private, and clubby atmosphere. By Vegas standards, it was purposefully small, so the guests wouldn't have to travel miles through endless corridors cycling past retail stores to reach their destinations. Gated, the imposing facade looked more like a grand hotel in Italy with an old-world sophistication. Only twelve stories high, the membership-only destination had a reception entry with a massive grand staircase extending up the first three levels of casino rooms, restaurants, and bars. The all-suites hotel had a rooftop club with a patio and pool, and the grounds contained a larger pool with cabanas, tennis courts, a garden restaurant, and a spa. Security was extremely tight, ensuring no one without a membership would be allowed into the casino or hotel without prior authorization.

Invitations had been issued for a grand opening celebration to be held in mid-December. It would be attended by the Vegas elite, the moneyed membership of both the Atlantic City and Las Vegas casinos, some celebrities, the Carrows family, and their special guests. On that very special list were the Renner family from San Antonio, Texas—Dr. Patrick and Natalie Renner.

Arriving the day before the big event, Angelica had been extremely proud as she and Charles showed them around. Her parents had expressed their awe amidst the grandeur of the lobby. The atrium had been transformed into a winter wonderland created specifically for the opening. Warm blue and white lights highlighted the partially muraled walls turning the area into a fantasy of forests and meadowlands. A three-story natural spruce tree blended into the scenery of the lobby but with the open plan of the atrium, the eye was drawn past the center chandelier to spruce trees lining the above stories filled with white and blue lights.

Angelica had been thrilled that the Carrows family had been so warmly welcoming of her parents. They'd all dined together their first night, taking the time to get to know one another. It was a gratifying show of support for the blossoming relationship between she and Charles. After dinner they'd made arrangements to meet the next morning for breakfast.

"Well I thought it would be fun if we all wore Christmas colors tonight," Charlotte said pointedly to Carey that next morning.

"Well I don't," said Carey. "I'm not wearing red or green. I'm going with a gold lamé St. John gown."

"That'll look great on you, obviously. I wasn't going to force you to wear red or green, it was only a suggestion," Charlotte said, fork in mid-air, stopping to reassure her prickly sister.

"I have no complaints," Angelica smiled, purposefully interrupting the forever quarreling siblings. "I can't wait to get into that Zac Posen dress. I can't tell you how much fun I had shopping with you, Charlotte. Thank you so much for taking me, and for having all those dresses pulled in advance. My God, I didn't know people could shop like that like. It beats running over to Macy's."

Charlotte shrugged. "I don't typically use a stylist, but I thought it might be fun for the big night to have some help pulling it all together. I'll stop by with the jewels after I finish dressing. Carey, did you want to meet us up at Charles' or down at the reception?"

"I'll meet you up in the room and we can all go down together. We can do the red carpet as a group before we split up and mingle." Carey sat back and sipped her coffee.

"I don't want Angelica walking the red carpet tonight." Charles made a small gesture of regret towards her. "We talked about that."

"I know," Angelica rolled her eyes. "I understand. I need to keep a low profile for a while. So just the three siblings, and Alex and Harley, of course."

"Harley doesn't want to do the red carpet either. I think it should just be the three siblings unless Alex feels strongly about walking it with us?" Carey looked over at

Alex who seemed startled that they had brought him into the conversation.

"Ah," said Alex. "I can safely say that I would be delighted if I could opt out of that. I can't think of anything I would rather do less than smile and pose on a red carpet. I know you girls will more than satisfy their appetites, and Charles can stand in for the guys."

Charles smiled. "I don't mind. It's all part of the publicity. The Carrows machine at work. I'm wearing classic black tux by the way. So, Charlotte, not a stitch of red or green for me either."

"Okay, okay, I just thought it would be a fun theme with Christmas and all."

"Patrick, Natalie," Julia turned to them. "Would you like to walk the red carpet with Henry and I?"

"Yes!" said Natalie Renner. "I've never walked a red carpet before, and this will be such a glamorous event. It's not every day I get to wear wonderful evening clothes and rub shoulders with famous people."

Angelica was happy that her mom was as excited about the opening party as she was. They'd always had an easy relationship and it was fun to watch her around the Carrows.

"I know what you mean," Julia smiled. "I'm tremendously excited we secured so many cast members of the Vegas casino movies to attend. Charles, your Jacqueline is a dream. It's truly wonderful how she has pulled so many of the incredible details together. It should be such a fun night." Julia referred to Jacqueline Dunn,

Charles and Carey's personal assistant, who had helped organize the event with the help of the Carrows public relations machine.

"I agree," said Charles. "She's invaluable. The cast members were well-compensated, I can assure you. But I'm sure they'll be a terrific asset."

"Do you think Brad Pitt and George Clooney are coming?" Natalie whispered, her fist clenched in a ball of hopeful expectation.

"They are not on the list, but if they should decide to crash the gate, I believe an exception will be made," Charles smiled. "I hope you don't mind your beautiful daughter not walking the carpet tonight," Charles asked Patrick and Natalie.

Angelica's mom and dad had been coming around about understanding the Carrows' way of doing business. After she'd told them the story of her hired activities for the Carrows the previous year, they had been quite alarmed. They were appalled that she'd been brought into a possibly dangerous and certainly unsavory situation that forced her to change her identity. They'd also thought it was outrageous that the Carrows had given her a car valued over a hundred thousand dollars as payment. But not long after Angelica told them about what she had been up to, she and Charles had gone to San Antonio for a visit. Her mom and dad knew, of course, who Charles was, but they'd said they worried that he and his family's vast wealth had used her badly. During the visit, however, they softened. They witnessed her and Charles' growing love and made peace with it. Charles was a gentleman, and his explanation of how much he respected their daughter went a long way toward making them feel better. Angelica was grateful for all of this.

Now, being brought into the Carrows inner circle, and socializing with the family, Angelica enjoyed watching first hand, her parents being swept away by the Carrows' collective charm and wildly exotic lifestyle. That the Carrows family was deeply supportive, and that the union was blessed by her parents made her extremely happy.

"I understand," said Patrick. "I appreciate why you would want some distance between last year and tonight with all the press. But you must assume that you and Angelica will be photographed together some time in the future. You are a celebrity of sorts."

"I know. You're right. I just think we should be cautious with any of the bigger press releases. We'll want the pictures from tonight widely distributed, but the other stuff, we'll just have to take those one at a time."

Angelica shook her head. "I don't mind, really. As long as we can get some private pictures of all us together while I'm wearing that Zac Posen, I'm fine."

"We'll be sure to take lots of photos," Natalie said, beaming at her. "Oh, can I take pictures? Is that allowed?" Natalie looked at Julia.

"I'm sure its fine," Julia answered. "As long as it's discreet. But we might consider asking permission first from some of the celebrities. They can be funny about that stuff."

"Hey, for what we've negotiated with some of them,

shoot away," Charles laughed. "Really, they'll love it. Just not around the tables, or the money, only in the bars or the reception. The casino is off limits to photography, for everyone. That's serious business. We're hoping people will leave tonight with some sobering regrets, if you know what I mean."

"Well, I set a limit for myself," said Patrick. "I brought a thousand dollars to gamble with and once that's gone, it's gone. I don't mind gambling, but if I sit down at a poker table with someone like George Clooney, I may end up losing my shirt just to stay at the table."

"Oh, darling," said Natalie. "Once you lose your shirt I'll take over. Mr. Clooney and I will bring it home."

"Mom! You don't even like to play poker." Angelica smirked then smiled.

"I do too. I've played my share of that game with you and the girls. I know how to play. Sort of."

"Nobody plays as well as your daughter," said Charles. "Which brings up a point. Angelica could pose a problem at the tables. If she sits down and starts taking all our guest's money, they might think something is rigged. I'm sorry, Baby, but maybe you should stick to roulette or something you're not so damn talented at."

"Fine. I get it. No Photos. No Red Carpet. No Poker. Yeeesss, Zac Posen. I'm still totally cool," she said dreamily.

"That must be some dress," said Charles. "I can't wait to see you in it."

"She will be stunning," Julia said to Patrick and Natalie. "You have an incredibly beautiful daughter.

Don't you think that she and Charles will make lovely grandchildren?"

Angelica smiled at her parents' somewhat shocked expression. She wasn't quite sure she was ready for children, but Julia, Henry, and oddly, Petunia were doing their best to convince her. As a card player, she knew a pack of charming Carrows was hard to beat.

Chapter 3

Charles had made the practical decision to live in his hotel and casino for the first year as the project would be a priority for the family. While not exactly a traditional dwelling, it suited his lifestyle, so he and Angelica had made it their home.

Named the Italian Suite, their home opened to reveal a beautiful, oval shaped, cream-colored room with cream and brown sofas and chairs elegantly illuminated under a barreled ceiling design with a grand chandelier. At 2,500 square feet, it also boasted two bedrooms, a small kitchen, and dining area. The innovative ceiling designs in each bedroom were warmly lit and the cream bedding accented the Italian brown cashmere walls in the master bedroom.

That evening, Charles opened the door for Charlotte and Alex to enter. "Charlotte, you look wonderful, come in. Alex, as usual, you've cleaned up nicely," he said facetiously.

"Thank you, brother." Charlotte swanned into the

suite wearing an Oscar de la Renta, floral-embellished ball gown in cardinal red. She raised a hand to where her long black hair was pulled up revealing ruby and diamond Cartier drop earrings that danced as she looked around the suite. "Where is your lovely girl? Can I go back and help decorate her with some small baubles?"

"Head back. She said she won't let me see her until she's all put together. She's waiting for you."

Charlotte left them as Charles led the way to the large marble bar with a deeply engraved wooden back and mahogany colored fabric lining the walls and furniture. "How about we get a drink and take in some air on the patio while we wait for the ladies," he said to Alex.

"There's a plan. Make mine on the softer side, though. It's going to be a long night."

"How was the nanny that Jaqueline hired for the girls? What was her name?" Charles asked putting cubes into crystal tumblers.

"Dawna. I can't recall her last name, but she seemed to be up to the task. Energetic. Jacqueline told me that they originally met at the gym on the track. I guess they're both runners. Dawna works for an agency here, so she thought of her when we decided we should bring the girls. Glad it worked out."

Charles handed him a glass of ginger ale, and they made their way over to the balcony and out into the cool Las Vegas night.

"Ahh, nice out here," Alex said as they looked out onto the Vegas strip from the ten-story balcony. "Thank goodness both the kids gave us a break this morning and slept in. It's going to be a long night." He took a sip of the drink and continued. "Our suite is really great, Charles. And the butler staff has been incredible. They seem determined to make sure Petunia has everything a reigning princess might need."

Charles laughed, "I told them to spoil her rotten. She's a top VIP at this event. Really glad they're both here. I don't get to see my sister and the girls much." Charles put his hand in his pocket and craned his neck looking down into the parking lot below.

"Are you and Angelica thinking about taking any next steps in that direction?" Alex said, his eyebrows raised over the rim of his glass.

"I don't know yet," Charles answered evasively. "The last year has been amazing, and I really love her. But she's younger than I am, and I don't want to rush her into anything. She's only twenty-five. I thought maybe we could travel together a little after we get this place off the ground and before we open London. Maybe spend some time wandering around in Europe. She's really interested in going on a safari, either in east or southern Africa. It wasn't something that was on my top ten list, but I'm warming to the idea. We've been looking into arranging a private safari. I don't suppose there's any way you guys would be interested in joining us?"

"Well, that depends on when you're thinking about going. Maybe. I've never been to Africa. Have you?"

"No. I haven't. We don't want to do any hunting,

obviously, but there's so much to see. I think if we do go, we'll need at least three weeks to do it right, but at minimum, two. I know that may be hard to swing with work, but Angelica's really getting excited about a vacation, and so am I. I've been so busy getting this place in order. It's been a brutal push to hit this holiday opening, but we made it. There's still a lot to finish-out in some of the rooms, but the bones are in place. Macchi & Macchi's been an ace on the security front. I have you to thank for that." Charles raised his glass to Alex.

"No problem. It's all part of the Maachi & Maachi business. We've already got you in the brochure, so to speak." Alex turned toward the door. "Dang it's cold out here." He walked inside.

Charles followed. "How is your family? Your mom, I hope she's doing well. How are Isabella and Finn?"

"Everyone's great. We try to get together on Sunday at Mom's for dinner. It's Petunia's favorite part of the week. The bigger and noisier, the better for her. She told us yesterday that she thought it was time we get a baby brother for her and Lily. She said she wanted to be just like you and Carey and Charlotte. A couple of sisters and a big brother to look out for them." Alex made himself comfortable on a sofa.

Charles laughed. "Oh yeah? That's awfully sweet. Maybe you should listen to her. Are you going for round three?"

Alex groaned slightly. "The thought is nice, but we're just enjoying Lily so much right now, and they're not kidding about the sleepless nights. It's a lot of work. I don't think Charlotte would mind though."

"Well, there's not really a rush. You have time."

"Yeah, but Petunia's nine now and if she's going to have a relationship with another brother or sister, we need to have one before she's in high school. I don't know. So, maybe. We'll have to see."

"Mom and Dad would love it. They've got grandchildren on the brain. Did you hear that comment Mom made at breakfast?"

"Yes, I did, Charles, and I think it's important that we focus on *you* procreating rather than us. Maybe you could take a little of the pressure off."

Charles gave his brother-in-law a chin jut and stood. "What's important right now is to get ready for the grand reveal. Here they come."

Angelica stepped into the room wearing her Zac Posen. In brilliant blue silk, it was a halter-neck trumpet gown with a squared halter neckline, fitted bodice and trumpet skirt with the pleats falling from mid-thigh. There was a straight hem falling to the floor with a train at the back accompanied by Graff blue and pink sapphire and diamond chandelier earrings. With her auburn hair side parted and in a low loose bun, she looked young, fresh, and lovely.

"Angelica," Charles said going to her. "You look beautiful. Really beautiful. I understand now why you were excited to wear this dress. It's perfect for you."

"Thank you. The jewelry really sets it off. I'll have to

thank your mom for loaning it all to me," she smiled at her wrist admiring the pink and blue sapphire five-row palmyre bracelet.

"Mom does have a lot of nice pieces she's acquired over the years. I'm sure she's happy to see them getting some use," said Charlotte. "She was especially glad that you would be wearing them, Angelica."

Angelica appeared humbled by all the adoration. "Are we going to need a bodyguard walking around tonight? Between your jewels, and mine, and I'm sure Carey's and your mom's and everyone else, there's going to be a lot of money hanging off earlobes out there."

"Security is tight and in place," said Alex. "Just relax and have fun and let them do the worrying."

They perked to someone knocking at the door. "Speaking of," said Charles as he walked to open it. "Look who the cat dragged in. Hey guys, come on in."

Carey and Harley entered. "Hello everybody," Carey said, making a bee-line for the women. "Angelica, you look wonderful! Oh my God. That dress fits you like a dream. Love the earrings too. Those are Mom's, right?"

Angelica put her hands up over her ears. "Yes. Charlotte thought they would look good with the dress, and your mom said she didn't mind."

"Oh, I'm sure she didn't. Glad to see them put to good use. What do you think about me?" Carey said, giving a turn.

"I thought you were going with the gold lamé?"

Charlotte asked, gesturing toward her full length, bright marigold gown.

Carey ran her hand slowly down the side of her body showcasing the tightly fitted gown with a trumpeted skirt and body contouring seams. "Well I was, but Angelica was going on about her Zac Posen dress, and I remembered I had this little number tucked away. I thought I'd wear it instead. And this color gave me an excuse to wear all these fabulous Buccellati gold and diamonds. I mean, aren't they just perfect?" She splayed her decorated fingers and wrists lightly over the bare chest of her strapless gown and swung her hips and shoulders in a playful manner.

"They certainly are," Charlotte said, angling her head and examining the ensemble. "No one is going to miss you tonight, that's for certain."

"What? Are you jealous over there, *Mommy* with your old Oscar dress?" Carey challenged.

Charles interrupted, "Guys! You all look great. Carey, you look great, and so does Charlotte. So, stop." He shook his head and turned to Harley. "Carey told us you didn't want to do the red carpet so why don't you and Alex escort Angelica down and the three of us will follow. We'll do the press line and meet with you later." He walked over to Angelica, took her hand, and gave her a kiss on the cheek. He lingered by her ear and whispered, "If it was a competition, you'd win, baby. You look incredibly beautiful. Have a wonderful time, and remember what I said about losing gracefully," he said with a wink.

The Carrows children each said their goodbyes and

watched as their significant others left the room.

"Man, Carey," Charles turned on his sister. "It's not a competition to see who looks the best! We're a family. Now let's get out of here and crack the proverbial bottle on this ship. We've worked hard and it's time to celebrate. I'm proud of *both* of you. Take my arm, Carey, and play nice, you hear me?"

"Whatever, Charles," Carey said as Charlotte rolled her eyes and the three of them left the room. "But you *know*, I look the best."

Chapter 4

Dawna Hook was a runner, and a nanny, but only recently so. Several months prior she had registered at a nanny agency and completed their interviews and background checks. Dawna was ambivalent about the children, but not about the money. It was not a terribly lucrative job, but it served a greater purpose— to pass as a legitimate nanny and get hired by Jacqueline Dunn to take care of Charlotte Carrows Macchi's children.

She and her partner knew Jacqueline was the personal assistant for Charles and Carey Carrows. They also knew from her social media information that she was a runner and they went to great efforts to locate her gym. In Las Vegas, for most of the year, runners worked an indoor track when it was too hot outside to run. They successfully located her, and Dawna made it a point to develop an easy friendship, relating her love of children and her job as a nanny. What Dawna and her partner didn't know was whether Charlotte would bring her own nanny to Las

Vegas, but Dawna made sure she impressed Jacqueline with her love for children. It was an investment of time and effort and a risk, but one that they were willing to take. It paid off.

When the time came, Jacqueline asked her if she was interested in babysitting for her boss's nieces. She told Dawna she'd checked out the agency, and since everything looked good, she thought it would be a perfect fit to hire her to babysit Petunia and Lily.

Dawna and her partner knew about the Carrows Casino opening. Everybody in Las Vegas did. With that information, they predicted that there would be a grand opening celebration. What they hoped, was that Petunia would come to Las Vegas for the celebration, with her family. That it had so far gone exactly to plan was a minor miracle, but now employed, and firmly ensconced into the Macchis's suite, Dawna took the next carefully prepared step of the evening.

After receiving a short tutorial on the evening's expectations from Charlotte Carrows Macchi, Dawna and the children said their goodbyes to Jacqueline, Charlotte, and Alex. Dawna immediately called the front desk.

"Hi, this is Dawna Hook. I'm the nanny for Charlotte Carrows and Alex Macchi. They just left for the event and I'm taking care of their children, and oh my gosh, I totally forgot my asthma medicine at home and my brother is going to bring it to me. So, I know there's a lot of security and stuff so I was wondering if you would let him in and bring him up to their suite, so he can give me my medicine? I don't want to bother the Carrows with this. I'm so embarrassed that I forgot it! I was just so nervous tonight because it's such an important occasion and all. I'm so sorry to trouble you with this, but would you be able to help me?"

The staff was very anxious to be of help to the Carrows family, and they did just that. Not more than fifteen minutes later, a knock on the door announced the arrival of Dawna's partner and his security escort. Dawna opened the door and threw her arms around her guest who was holding an asthma inhaler in his hand.

"Oh, I can't thank you enough for coming to my rescue! I was so nervous I was going to create a scene, and on a night like this too! Oh, please come in and sit with me for a minute, I'm so rattled right now!"

Security, sensing that the two of them actually knew one another and that a small bump in the evening had been averted for the family, left them to attend to their business and returned to the party.

Dawna shut the door, looked at her partner, and said, "Okay, David, you're in. The ball's in your court."

David Torres Cordoza entered the luxurious suite and spied his daughter, Petunia Carrows Macchi, on the sofa working on some craft with a loom and rubber bands. She looked up questioningly as he approached, and they locked eyes for the very first time in their lives. David had a slight moment of parental stirring as he took in his daughter's lovely brown hair and eyes and the scattering of freckles across her nose and cheeks. Adorable, really. He hoped she'd be cooperative.

Chapter 5

Petunia had heard the exchange at the door and felt a small worry. She turned to look as the man and Dawna hugged. Sitting on the long purple and pink sofa in the main room, she jerked back around after they saw her watching. She pulled her legs under her as she heard them walk toward her from the entry. She made a quick grab for her phone on the coffee table and slid it next to her under a big purple pillow.

"Hello, Petunia," the man said as he and Dawna walked to stand in front of her.

"Hello," Petunia said, picking up a rubber band and threading it with her hook.

"I'm a friend of Dawna's. She invited me up here so that I could meet you." The man stood, smiling before her.

What was he doing here? He wanted to meet her? Petunia felt a small sense of alarm that something was wrong.

"I'm actually an old friend of your mom's. My name

is David. David Cordoza. Has she ever mentioned me to you?" Wearing a dark suit, he put his hands in his pockets and smiled at her.

"No. I don't think so." Why was he looking at her like that? She glanced at Dawna who smiled, too. Didn't she say she was calling her brother? Would it be rude to bring this up? Her parent's trusted Dawna. She should be polite.

"Well, I knew her a long time ago, before you were born," David continued. "We went to NYU together. We actually met in an art history class. Does your mom still like to draw?"

He seemed to know something about her mom. "Sometimes," she said.

"When we dated, she and I used to bring our sketch pads and sit in the park and draw. She was pretty good, but I don't think she really loved it. More like a hobby for her. I, on the other hand, have spent most of my life committed to art and I'm not trying to brag or anything, but I think I might be pretty good. I left some of my drawings with your mom. Did you ever see them?"

Petunia was confused. What was this about? He dated my mom? This was one of my mom's old boyfriends? "I don't know." She shrugged.

"Well, that's okay. Maybe we can draw something together later. Do you draw? Do you like art?"

"Yes, I love to draw, and I have all these crafts that I do, too." She held up the loom to show him the colorful rubber bands strung together.

"I see. What is that called that you're doing there?" David cocked his head.

"It's called a Rainbow Loom. I make bracelets, and snowmen, and bees, and flowers. All kinds of stuff."

"I see," David walked over to the coffee table in front of Petunia and picked up a few of her finished pieces. "Wow, this is really impressive stuff. You made this?" He smiled, holding a snowman.

"Yes. I did."

He continued looking at the snowman as he said, "So I understand you have a sister now? Where is she?"

"She's asleep in the other room." Petunia grabbed a purple rubber band and placed it around her hook.

"And her name is Lily? She has a lovely flower name just like you."

Why was he talking to her? She glanced at Dawna who sat down in a chair across from her. David sat in another one, next to her.

"Are you going to the party tonight? Are you meeting with my mom and dad?" she asked, trying to be polite.

"No. I'm not really dressed for the party. I'll bet your mom and dad were all dressed up pretty fancy. This is an exciting night for them, isn't it?" David crossed his legs and glanced around.

"Yes. They had on tuxedos and my mom had on a beautiful red Oscar dress. We took pictures with my phone."

"Oh, you have a cell phone? Can I see the picture?" David held out a hand, excited.

She scooped her iPhone out from beneath the pillow but suddenly felt nervous about sharing the pictures. She looked at the phone and then glanced at the two of them.

David put out his bottom lip and nodded. "It's okay, you don't have to show me. I'll bet your mom looked really pretty. She was always a pretty girl."

"You dated my mom?" She squinched up her face and rolled her phone in her hand.

"Yes. We dated for quite a while. We actually lived together in her house in the West Village. I'm pretty sure you guys still live there. Is that right? She had this wallpaper in her room that was kind of light green on the top, over the wainscoting on the wall? I'll bet you have the room right down the hall with the long bathroom in between your room and another room? I'll bet the other one's Lily's room now. Is that right?"

Petunia was amazed that he knew what her house looked like. And he said he used to live there? All of the sudden she felt a lump in her throat. She looked back and forth between the faces of the adults staring at her.

"I think I'm going to text my Mom and let her know you're here. Did you want to see her?"

David held up his hands. "Yes. I'd like to see her, but don't you think we should wait for a little bit to give them time to get their pictures taken on the red carpet and stuff? They're probably awfully busy with the press and the reporters. You don't want to bother her right now, do you? I know she'll be anxious to see me. I was just down the street, so I thought I would pop by. I thought I might catch her before she went down, but I must have just missed her. Let's just wait for a little bit and then give her a call, okay?"

Petunia didn't know what to do. Her mom and Alex *were* busy and she knew that it was a really important night. She looked over at Dawna for support, who nodded and said, "I think that's the best plan too. Hey, let's make some popcorn and maybe watch a movie or something while we wait. What did you want to do this evening?"

Did she mean he was going to stay the whole night? "My mom said I could stay up late. I wanted to watch *Despicable Me.*"

"Oh, that sounds good. I haven't seen it yet," said Dawna as she got up. "I'll go make that popcorn and be right back."

Laying her phone carefully beside her and turning back to her loom, she scooped up a handful of rubber bands and discarded the unwanted colors nervously, fully alert to the presence of the strange man in the chair across from her. She kept her head down and swallowed hard as she grabbed a rubber band and yanked on it to stretch it out.

"Petunia, did you say you have some drawing pads? Maybe some pencils? I'd love to show you how I draw. Maybe we could draw something together." He gestured around the room, swiveling his head and looking for supplies.

"Oh, okay," she said as she popped up and ran to the other room to grab her backpack. When she got to her bedroom, she was breathing hard, suddenly worried that she had left her phone in the other room across from the man. What if he takes it? Her heart fluttered in her chest as she ran back into the main room. Thankfully he was still sitting in his own chair and she spied her phone on the sofa where she'd left it.

She got down on her knees and glanced toward the kitchen where Dawna had gone. She started removing supplies from her bag and loading them onto the floor. David surprised her as he got onto the floor and crawled over to look at the spread.

"Wow, cool, these are really nice drawing pads," he said. "The paper is super conducive to the lead. Oh, and look at those pencils! That's high-grade pigment there. Those leads will draw beautiful pictures. Do you mind if I take one of these sketch pads and draw something?"

This was interesting and seemed pretty safe. She shrugged and scooted a bit away from him, her back pressed against the sofa. "No, go ahead. My mom tells me she loves my drawings, so we go to the art store and try all their different pencils and pens. She said that she wants me to take some extra art classes too."

David pulled open the cover of a pad and saw a drawing of a landscape. "Did you draw this?"

"Yes, it's from my aunt's house on their farm in New York. We go there all the time."

"It's really good. Really good." His bottom lip extended, he nodded his head as he flipped over to a new page in the sketchbook. "You should definitely continue with your studies. You have some talent, Petunia." He took a black charcoal colored pencil and began to draw on a blank page.

"Okay now, watch me," he said as he sketched. She watched as his hand flew quickly through the motions in seemingly random strokes but quickly revealed an adorable puppy. "Voila! A puppy! Did you see how I did that? I learned that trick in school. Do you have a puppy at home?"

She sat on her knees and leaned forward on her hands to get a closer look at the drawing. "No. We don't have any pets, but I want a dog. Mom says we might be able to get one soon. She thought maybe my sister should be a little older before we get one."

"I see. That sounds sensible. Here, let me show you how to draw this puppy again. This time, I'll draw a line, and then you draw a line where I show you, and we'll do it together."

Petunia inched toward him and was engrossed in the duet as he calmly explained where to draw the lines and what to look at while they were drawing. In short order, they had a near replica of the first drawing and David ripped it out of the book. "Now we need to sign the bottom of the picture as the co-artists and give the portrait a name. What should we name it?"

"Let's call it Puppy."

"Just Puppy?"

"Okay, how about Puppy Cakes!"

"That sounds perfect. Let me just write the title in the corner and I'll put my signature on it, and now you do the same," he said, handing it over to her.

"There, now we have something that we did together. You can keep it and remember me when you look at it."

Petunia was engrossed with her creation and was beginning to feel more relaxed sitting on the floor among the drawing pads and familiar supplies scattered around them.

Dawna came back into the room with a huge bowl of popcorn and some napkins and said, "Hey that looks great. Should I get the movie started?"

"Sounds like fun," said David. "*Despicable Me*. Isn't that a movie about a man who falls in love with little orphan girls and they want him to be their daddy?"

"Yes," said Petunia. "It's one of my favorite movies. It's so funny."

"Alright, let's get it going." David got up and grabbed a handful of popcorn from the bowl on the table.

Crunching, he gestured with his full hand. "You've seen this before? Why is it your favorite movie?"

"I didn't say it was my *favorite* movie, I said it was one of my favorite movies. I have lots of favorite movies." She added some color to one of her drawings with a pencil.

"Well, what about this one makes you like it?" David took his chair again and looked at Dawna who sat next to him with the remote.

Petunia had to think about that for a moment. "I guess I like that the girls found a daddy. And that the daddy found the girls. They're a family."

"You have a dad, right? Alex Macchi, he's your dad?" David squinted at her.

"Yes, he's my legal adopted dad." She nodded.

"Your adopted dad? Does that mean you have another dad? A real dad?"

No one ever talked about her real dad with her. She was slightly unnerved that this man was asking her about that particular subject.

"I guess so. He's my biological dad. My real dad is my dad. Mommy and he got married." She scrambled back on the sofa and grabbed her loom.

"That's nice for you. I'm glad you have such a nice dad. Did they ever talk to you about your real dad—about what happened to him?" David popped another kernel into his mouth.

She felt this was private information because it was a serious subject, and everyone got very serious when she brought it up. She didn't know if she should be talking about this with him or anyone. She shrugged, "He's around somewhere, I guess." She grabbed a large pink pillow and put it on her lap and placed the loom on top of it. Her eyes glanced again at the phone, wishing she could use it.

"Do you ever see him?" David asked with wide eyes.

"No, I've never met him," she offered, unable to help herself, suddenly drawn into the vortex of this fascinating aspect of her life.

"Do you think about him? Would you like to meet him?" He leaned forward.

She didn't know how to answer that. When she was little she thought she wanted to meet him all the time, but then after Alex, she didn't care as much, and her Mommy said Alex wanted to be her Dad, and she wanted that, too.

"I suppose so." She grabbed another rubber band and held it.

"What if I told you that I know him, and that he would like to meet you?"

She snapped her head up. Another person who actually knew who her father was? She thought he was a secret. Did her mom tell him? Her heart beat faster.

David leaned forward resting his arms on his legs, his hands clasped between them. "Petunia. I want you to look at me. I want to tell you something that might be a little hard to believe and might be a bit shocking. I told you earlier that I knew your mom in college. Well that was true. We loved each other. We actually dated for a long time. And Petunia, I didn't know about it until many years later, but when we were together, your mom got pregnant, and you were born. I'm your father, Petunia. Your real biological father, and I've always wanted to meet you."

It was like a bolt of lightning hit her. She jumped up and stared at him, and tears sprang to her eyes. Completely caught up in the emotion, she stared at the two adults sitting across from her and didn't know what to believe.

"Petunia," said David, getting up.

She couldn't help herself and began to cry harder as he approached her, but then he stopped moving.

He put his hands up. "I know this is shocking. Listen, it's going to be okay. I've wanted to meet you since I first found out about you, but your mom and your grandparents didn't want me to. I didn't even know you existed until about three and half years ago. I found out when I saw your picture in the newspaper in New York, and I called your mom and asked her if I could meet you. I met with her, and then your mom and I decided it would be too confusing for you, so I agreed to stay in the background. But, Petunia, I made a terrible mistake, because I've wondered about you ever since. Like you've wondered about me, too, right?"

She put her hands over her face and began to sob.

"It's going to be okay. Don't be afraid. Really, I'm not going to hurt you. I just wanted to meet you. Your mom and Alex will be back soon, and you'll see. It'll be okay, I promise." He walked toward her.

With fear, and anxiety, and shock, she said, "I want to call my mom. I want my mom."

David crossed the room and touched his daughter for the first time of their lives. "Petunia," he said softly, "I'm so sorry. I didn't know another way to meet you. And I wanted to meet you so much. I wanted to get to know you. I'd like for us to have a relationship if you'll let me. I know it's a lot, and it's probably too much for you to understand everything right now, but it's going to be okay."

Just then Lily started crying loudly, too, and Dawna and David looked at each other.

"I'm going to go check on Lily, Petunia. I'll be right back," said Dawna.

Petunia watched Dawna leave the room. She didn't want to be alone with David. She grabbed her phone and ran into the dining room crying and shaking as she tried to pull up her mom's number. Unfortunately, it rang to voice mail and she remembered that her mom had left her phone in the suite with instructions to call her dad's number if anything came up. In frustration, she yelled loudly to David who had followed her. "How do I know you're really my dad? Why didn't you come to see me?"

"I did want to see you. I'm seeing you now." David rounded the table slowly toward her. "You were just too young to get involved and we had to make some decisions without you. Your mom and I decided it was for the best, but like I said, I made a mistake. I should never have agreed to the plan. We were wrong. You deserved to meet me. You deserve to know who your real dad is."

"I have a real dad. He adopted me!" She wailed, trembling.

David, close, stopped walking. Tears ran down her face as he said, "Yes! I know he adopted you. That's okay. Really. Your mom and I decided that if she ever got married that her husband should be able to adopt you. I only ever wanted what was best for you, so I agreed that was a good plan. Your mom said you could meet me when you were an adult, but in the meantime, she didn't want me involved in your life. Mostly because I was living in Brazil and that was just too far away. But I live in the United States now, and maybe I made a terrible decision tonight to come over for a visit, but I knew you were in town and I had to meet you. Finally. You needed to know that your real dad was out there, waiting to meet you, *wanting* to meet you. Maybe it was stupid. I'm so sorry if this is too shocking for you. I just couldn't wait any longer."

David reached out a hand to touch her again as Petunia heard Lily wailing in the other room. She ran past David to see what was happening. She got into the room and saw Dawna walking with her trying to calm her and that seemed normal, but everything was just out of control.

"She won't calm down," said Dawna. "Does she have a pacifier? Do you think she might be hungry?"

Petunia wiped at her face, but the tears kept flowing. "She doesn't like her N-nuk. Sometimes my dad sings to her and she calms down."

David had followed her into the room and the three of them were drowned out by Lily's cries.

"So, this is your sister? She's awfully pretty. I mean, I'm sure when she calms down she's prettier," David said loudly above the crying. "Does she have the same color eyes as you?"

"N-no. They're turning green."

David nodded. "Yes, but yours are brown, like mine."

Petunia had sobered up slightly when she was distracted about the welfare of her sister, but now she again had to face the situation in front of her. Something inside her made a snap decision, and she once again looked to her cell phone.

"Are you calling your mom again?" David said, his hand extended like he was going to take the phone.

"No, I'm calling my dad," she said, keeping an eye on him and backing up.

David seemed very hurt by this and hung his head. "I'm sorry about all this Petunia. I really am. Let's go in the other room so you can call him without your sister crying in the background. You don't want to upset them even more. You know they'll leave the event and come up here right away, don't you? You know that you'll ruin their evening. This big Carrows event that's going on that's so important to your family. You'll ruin it if you call them right now. Why don't you wait for a little while longer? Let's talk. Just talk and visit. Please give me a chance, before they come up here? Please."

She was so torn up with guilt and uncertainty about how she should act, she hesitated. But her emotions got the best of her and she made a decision. She pressed Alex's number and said with a wobbly voice, "Daddy, you need to come home."

David shook his head. It was done.

Chapter 6

Answering the phone but immediately alert to the sound of something in Petunia's voice, Alex put the phone to his ear and walked away from the group of people he was speaking with. "Petunia? What's going on?"

"There's a man here who says he's my father...and he said he wanted to m-meet me...and Lily's crying...and I'm sorry, but I want you to come home." After the rush of words, she broke down, sobbing.

In horror, Alex's hand flew to his mouth, and his eyes frantically searched for Charlotte. He grabbed Harley and pulled close to his ear. "Get security and follow me *now!*" He turned back to the phone and said to his daughter, "Honey, honey, are you okay, are you hurt? I'm on my way. I'm on my way. Is the man still there, did he hurt you?"

Through her crying, she sniffed and said, "No, I'm not hurt. I'm sorry, Daddy. I didn't know if I should call you or not. It's going to ruin everything!"

Alex pushed his way through the crowd and said

quietly. "Petunia. Listen to me. I don't care about the party. I only care about you. I'm on my way. I'm looking for your mother. We'll be there in a couple of minutes. *Do not leave the room with that man!* Security is coming. Stay on the phone with me. Don't stop talking. Are you there?"

"Yes," she managed now between sobs.

He listened to Lily wail in the background as Harley and a security man caught up with him as he rushed toward the elevators. He covered the receiver and said, "Find Charlotte, bring her to the room. Get more security up there right now. Fast. Tell her David's in the room with Petunia."

Harley left as the elevator doors opened and he and security got on. Alex said, "Petunia, are you there? I'm getting in the elevator. Hang on. I'll be there in a just a minute. Is David still in the room with you?"

"Yes."

"Okay. Just keep talking to me. I'm coming as fast as I can. Is Lily okay? Is she crying? Is the babysitter still there?"

"Yes-s, the babysitter's here. She's trying to calm Lily down, but she doesn't know how." Alex thought he actually heard her teeth chattering.

"Alright, she'll be okay. We'll get her settled. Don't worry. Almost there," he said. They ran down the hallway, the security personnel barking orders over the radio.

Finally to the room, Alex barged through the door, and looked wildly around. Lily's screaming echoed from the other room as he saw Petunia holding onto her phone for dear life, squatting in a corner near a window. He ran to her and picked her up as the security personnel backed David up toward a wall, cornering him with an uncertainty about what to do. Dawna came out of the bedroom with a screaming Lily. Alex, still holding Petunia, gave her a violent stare and put Petunia down and grabbed his other daughter out of her arms. Using every last drop of his self-control, he said calmly, "Why don't you go wait over there with David and have a seat. We need to talk."

Dawna didn't argue and did as he instructed. At that point two other security agents, Harley, Charlotte, and Charles burst into the room. Petunia ran to her mom.

Charlotte grabbed her and held on. As their daughter began to sob again, Charlotte got onto her knees, trying to calm her.

"Baby, baby, baby, shhh, it's okay. We're here. It's okay, now. Everything is okay, sweetheart. You're not hurt, are you?" Charlotte pulled back and grabbed both sides of her head, looking at her face.

Petunia shook her head and mumbled, "No."

Charlotte embraced her. Alex could see Petunia shaking in her arms as Lily continued to wail in his.

"Okay, honey. Alright, it's going to be okay, come here, let's sit down over here," Charlotte said as she got up and maneuvered Petunia over to a sofa. She glanced between David and Dawna and then at Alex pacing in front of them.

"Alex, is she okay?"

"I think so. Do you think she's hungry?"

"Come over here and give her to me," she said as Alex

handed her the baby. He put a protective hand on Petunia as Charlotte rubbed Lily's back. "Maybe you should warm up a bottle. I don't want anyone else to do it." She shook her head. "Never mind, come with me. Let's all go together."

He put his arm around Petunia and they followed Charlotte and the baby out of the room.

Charles stood with Harley and the three security guards, glaring at David and Dawna sitting in chairs. It wasn't often that something rendered him speechless.

"Charles, it's been a long time," David said, nodding in his direction.

"David. You've got a lot of nerve." He turned to Dawna, his face heated with rage. "And what's your story? What the hell is going on here?"

"Just wanted to finally meet my daughter, man. Thought it was about time." David smiled.

"So you decided to break into her room and scare the shit out of her without Charlotte and Alex around to protect her? You're a goddamned fucking idiot, David. Always were. Your actions tonight prove it." Charles started for David, but Harley pulled him back.

David smirked. "Oh, I don't know. We'll see. I think I made an impression on Petunia. At least she finally knows who I am." He sat back and laid his arms casually on the sides of the chair.

"Yeah, we'll see. I'm going to check on her. Don't let

them leave," Charles barked to security, angrily pointing at David and Dawna.

In the kitchen, his niece seemed better now that she was away from David. He sank to a knee and swept a lingering tear from her cheek. "Petunia? Are you okay, sweetheart?"

"I'm okay. That man told me that he's my father." She looked up to where Charlotte was feeding Lily. "Is that true, Mom?"

Charles sat back on his heels and gazed up at his sister. Lily was blessedly calmer as she sucked on a bottle, but Charlotte looked like she too was going to cry. She nodded. "Yes. It's true, honey. He's your biological father. His name is David Torres. He didn't hurt you, did he?"

"No, he didn't hurt me. I was just so scared. I didn't know what to do. He told me I shouldn't call you because it's such an important night, but I was so scared. I'm sorry."

"Petunia," Alex said, hoisting her up and setting her on the small kitchen counter. "Listen to me. Listen to all of us. You did absolutely, one-hundred percent the right thing by calling us. Forget about the event. It's over, we're not going back there. We won't leave you."

Petunia held out her arms, and Alex hugged her. "We love you, honey. More than you'll ever know. Everything's going to be okay now. I don't want you to worry." He drew back from her and looked into her eyes, his hand gently cradling her chin. "You did the right thing, calling us. You were very brave. I'm sorry you had to go through this alone. You were very wise tonight."

"I'm proud of you too," said Charles, giving a small smile and putting an arm around her. He could feel her shaking. "Well done. Always call for the cavalry. I love you too, Petunia. We're going to take care of this, but I have a couple of questions." He stood before her and softly asked, "Can you answer a couple of questions for me quick?"

When she nodded, he continued. "Do you know how he got up here? Did he call or just knock on the door?"

She responded, "No, Dawna let him in. She told the security that he was her brother and that she forgot her medicine and he needed to bring it to her."

"I see. Okay. That's fine. Don't worry about this. Charlotte, Alex, what do you want to do?"

Charlotte and Alex exchanged uncertain looks. She said, "I think they need to leave, and the girls and I should go lie down for a while, just breathe a little in the bedroom by ourselves. Petunia, did you want to go lie down with me for a little while and we can get Lily back to sleep together? We'll get you into your jammas and just get under the covers. What do you think?"

"Yes, I want to do that. But what about that man? What's going to happen to him?" she shivered as Alex hoisted her off the counter and set her down, running his hands roughly up and down her arms to warm her up.

"We're going to get him out of here and have a talk with him," said Alex. "We need to find out why he thought it was a good idea to sneak into our hotel room and frighten you."

"But I shouldn't have been so frightened if he's my

dad." Her face was a mask of worry and confusion.

Charlotte handed Lily gently over to Alex and grabbed Petunia's shoulders. "You didn't know if he was your dad. He was a stranger. Of course that was scary. You had every right to feel scared. I would have been scared. We'll talk about it in the other room. You're shaking honey, maybe you'd like to have a nice warm bubble bath before you put on your jammas? Come on, let's get you in the tub and get you settled." She took Petunia's hand.

She stopped to ask. "Sh-shouldn't I say goodbye to him?"

The adults froze, a look of disgust passing between them.

"You don't have to," said Alex. "He's done quite enough damage here tonight."

The look on Petunia's face was clearly torn. Charlotte grimaced and said, "Okay, just say a quick goodbye, then you and I will go get ready for bed. Your Dad and Uncle Charles will see him out."

In the living room, David brightened to see Petunia, whose face was still blotchy from crying. He stood. "Petunia. I'm so sorry about the way this turned out. I only wanted to meet you. I hope we can see each other again soon. I hope you don't mind, but I put my phone number in your phone," he gestured to the phone lying on a table near him. "It's under David. Please know you can call me. Anytime." He smiled.

Charles went to the table and grabbed the phone.

"That's enough," Alex said as he attempted to herd Petunia out of the room.

She stood taller and nodded at David as she walked through the room. Charles was proud of her adult-like poise as she said, "Goodnight."

Charles followed his sister and her family into the bedroom and took Alex aside. "I need to know what you want to do. I don't want to do anything that you don't agree to, but we need to make some decisions. I know you need to get Petunia settled. In the meantime, did you want me to manage this, or did you want to come with me?"

Alex glanced down at Lily in his arms. "Why don't you bring them to your room and hold them there while I help Charlotte with the girls. I'll find a moment to have a quick word with her and then I'll be up."

"That sounds like a plan. Don't worry, Alex, we'll take care of this."

When he walked back in, the smug look on David's face infuriated Charles. He took Harley by the arm and led him away from their earshot. "I want you to go back downstairs. Everyone will be looking for us and wondering what's happened. I don't want to upset mom and dad. Tell them that I'm managing a security issue with a guest, and that Charlotte and Alex had to leave because the baby was sick. Tell them everything is fine, and I'll be down later. Keep the party going as scheduled and let my dad and Carey know they're in charge until I can get back downstairs. Tell Angelica that I'm sorry but that I'll see her later."

Harley left the room, and Charles turned to the head of

his security and said, "We're going to escort David and the babysitter up to my room for a small conference before we call the police. I'd like for all of us to go up there quietly. First, however, I'd like to snap a few photos of these two in my sister's suite."

David smiled and gestured around. "Go ahead, Charles. Happy to oblige. I'm pleased that I now have your undivided attention. So sorry to pull you away this evening. I hope you didn't have anything important happening." David smirked as Charles took the pictures. When he was done, David took Dawna's elbow and escorted her to the door. They all left together.

After a short, silent ride in the elevator, they arrived back at his suite. Charles opened the door and walked inside. He pointed to a sofa and glanced at David. "Take a seat."

As the two mongrels walked past him, he turned to security. "I want you two to stay at the door. They don't leave until I say so. Alex will be here shortly."

Charles watched as the security guards positioned themselves before he turned back to David. "We're all going to wait here until Alex can break away. He's Petunia's father and will want a say in this. If it were up to me, I'd call the cops and have you arrested."

"For what, Charles? Speaking with my daughter?" David, sitting comfortably in a chair, picked up his tie and smoothed it.

"Let's put you aside for a minute, asshole. What about this piece of shit," he said, pointing at Dawna. "You're the babysitter, and you lied to security to get him into the room and in front of my niece? What does that make you? A liar? An imposter? Certainly someone complicit. You set this up with my assistant, through Jacqueline. She told us you were reliable and licensed through an agency. Did the agency know you were using your position to secretly introduce a criminal to a child?"

Dawna said nothing but glanced quickly at David. Her jaw tensed, and she looked down.

Startled that she gave no response to the provocation, Charles looked to David who was smiling broadly. He registered that the two of them had been working on this plan for some time. "I see. Alright, then. I'm going to go outside to wait for Alex. You'll wait here," he nodded at security as he left the room to cool down.

———

As Alex had predicted, it took some time for everyone to recover. As Petunia got into the tub and Charlotte undressed, he finally got Lily back down to sleep. He walked into the bedroom and put an arm around Charlotte's waist and whispered, "Charles brought them up to his suite. He's waiting for me to come up and decide what to do."

"I can't leave them. Not tonight," Charlotte said, shaking her head, looking toward the bathroom door.

"Of course not. I agree. I thought I should have a talk with them. I'm not sure if we should call the police right now. What did you want me to do?"

"I don't know. I'm just so shocked by this. Did you see

Petunia's face? She's so confused and hurt. I can't believe he did this to her. I don't know, maybe we should have handled him better. We could have made this easier for her. I'm so angry that I don't know what to do."

"I know you're upset, but you don't have anything to feel guilty about, honey. Just hold on to that tonight while I go talk with him. I'll come straight back here when we're done, okay? You just stay with the girls and try not to worry. I'm going to have security posted outside of the door until I get back. No one's coming in here except me. Give Petunia a kiss from her dad and tell her I'll be back soon, okay?" He pulled Charlotte into his arms.

She nodded. "I'm so sorry, Alex. I'm so sorry this is happening to you, to all of us. Again."

"I love you, honey. There's nothing to be sorry about."

Alex left the suite after making the arrangements with security. Breathing deeply and trying to calm the adrenaline still coursing through his veins, he made his way up to Charles' suite and nodded at the two hulk-like Macchi & Macchi security men as they opened the door and let him enter.

Inside, the culprits sat in a corner and Charles was nowhere in sight. David pointed to the balcony, and Alex inwardly growled at him as he walked to the door and found his brother-in-law texting.

Alex walked outside. "Charles, I'm ready." He said, closing the door.

Charles looked up. "I just asked Jacqueline to come up here. I want the babysitter to break down and tell us about the conspiracy. I think Jacqueline may be able to get a response out of her. She's pulling a silent act right now."

"You don't think Jacqueline's involved in this do you?" Alex said, his mouth in a hard line.

Charles stood with his phone in hand. Alex could see his jaw muscles tightly clenched. "No. No. Impossible. I've known Jacqueline for years, and I trust her completely. I think she was a victim, and they got to us through her. I'm sure she'll be extremely upset when she sees what's happened tonight."

"Alright." Alex nodded. "We need to get to the bottom of this. Charlotte and I didn't have much of a chance to talk, but I think we all know David wants something. And I don't think it's Petunia."

Alex and Charles turned as Jacqueline Dunn entered the suite and was stopped in the foyer by security. They went inside and crossed to the enclosed front entry.

Jacqueline said, "Charles, Alex, what's going on? Did something happen?"

"We have a situation here. Let's see if you know the people in the next room." Alex gestured her inside.

Standing nearby, Alex watched as Jacqueline nearly screamed when she saw Dawna sitting in a chair in the drawing room.

"My God! What are you doing *here*? Are the kids okay?" she said, spinning to look at Charles. "What happened! What's going on?"

Dawna only gave Jacqueline a cursory glance, not cracking her silence at all.

"Dawna! Alex?" she spun. "What happened?"

Charles replied, "Jacqueline, do you know these people?"

She gestured to Dawna. "What? Yes, I know her. She's the babysitter I hired to take care of the girls tonight."

"What about him?" Alex said, pointing with his chin.

She looked again at the man seated next to Dawna. "I've seen him somewhere I think, but I don't know him." She turned again to Charles. "What the hell is happening?"

Charles motioned to Alex who nodded and said, "What do you know about her, Jacqueline? Tell us everything."

Jacqueline put her hand over her mouth, seeming panicked. She explained how they'd met and why she thought her safe to watch the girls. Now, stealing her eyes on Dawna, she gritted her teeth, realizing that her friend had obviously taken advantage of her.

"Alright," said Alex as he walked toward Jacqueline. "That's what we thought. Your friend used you to get to us. Or more precisely, she and this man, David Torres, used you to get to Petunia. He's Petunia's biological father. She conned security to let him into the suite after we left for the party, and they spent the next hour scaring the shit out of *my daughter*."

Jacqueline threw her head back. "Oh my God. Is she alright? They didn't hurt her, did they?"

Charles shook his head. "No, they didn't hurt her. Not physically, anyway."

"You piece of shit!" Jacqueline walked toward Dawna with her fists clenched. "How could you do that? You used me to get to a little girl? What kind of person does that? I trusted you, Dawna. God, Charles, Alex, I'm so sorry. This is all my fault!"

"Alright, Jacqueline," Charles gestured. "Come with me and I'll walk you out. We need to speak with them in private."

Charles left the room to have a few more words with Jacqueline as he escorted her out. Alex turned slowly and met David's cold eyes. An entire conversation passed in that look. Alex wanted to pound the crap out of his smug, satisfied face.

Returning, Charles said, "Alright. Let's all sit down." He encouraged Alex into a chair, positioning him next to himself and across a coffee table from David. "Let's hear what it is that David plainly wants to tell us," Charles said to Alex, then louder, added, "David, you went to some lengths to get our attention. You have it. What do you want?"

Smiling broadly, David locked his eyes again with Alex. He looked extremely satisfied. "So you're Alexander Macchi. We meet at last—father-to-father. Nice job landing a Carrows. Good for you. The only problem is that you have *my* daughter. You adopted her, right? I figured that would happen after you married Charlotte. And now you have another girl, Lily. That's very sweet—a happy little family with two little flower girls, and all that Carrows money. You got it all didn't you?" David extended his arms and glanced around the suite.

Alex gripped the chair to prevent himself from flying

across the table as Charles said, "What is it you want?"

"What don't you understand, Charles? I want my daughter. I want to be a part of her life. I'm her real father. And now, she knows it. She knows me. She knows what I look like and who I am. I'm the new daddy in town." He smiled.

Alex gritted his teeth and counseled himself to get through the interview without violence. He communicated a look to Charles who took the lead.

Charles leaned back into the sofa. "David, I know I don't need to remind you that you signed away all your parental rights. You also agreed to any future adoption proceedings and to never to see her again. Why are you here?"

David pushed himself forward. "See Charles, I don't think I agree with those terms any longer. I think it's time to renegotiate. I've changed my mind, and I want Petunia in my life."

Alex rolled his eyes as Charles continued.

"How do you think Petunia would feel about your past deeds and the fact that you were more than willing to give her up if we agreed not to prosecute you for the three and a half million dollars you stole from us?"

"Stole from you? Don't be astigmatic. I gave you my daughter. I was forced to walk away from her. Was three point five all she was worth to you?"

"You piece of shit," Alex said, standing up. "You came here to negotiate for her. You don't want anything to do with her, you only want more money. What about your family and our connections with the INS, David? Did you want them to find out about your criminal past? What about the shame you'll place on your parents when we prosecute you for stealing the Tsarina's Fancy? And what about the Met? They won't take it lying down that you stole the replica from them. They'll come after you, too. You're seriously mistaken if you think we'll let you get away with any of this."

David sat back and casually crossed his legs, looking—for all the world—untroubled. "Well, that's the thing. I think you will let me get away with it. All of it. We're in fucking Vegas, so I'm laying a wager on the table, but I know I have a winning hand. You'll give me what I want, because I know you're only bluffing."

"You think lawyers bluff? You think cops bluff? You think jail is better than whatever life you made for yourself?" Alex yelled, the volume of his voice increasing. He recognized he was losing control.

"The statute of limitations is over on the theft, Alex. You can't prosecute me for it. Neither can the Met. Well, you could try to prosecute me, but you wouldn't win." David rolled his head and smiled over at Dawna.

Charles jumped in. "That's bullshit, and you know it. We could make your life a living hell. You signed a legal agreement. Do you have $3.5 million to reimburse us?" he asked.

"No. I don't have it. But then, I don't need it. All I want now, is time with my daughter." David folded his hands in his lap.

"There's not a court in the land who would give you

any kind of custody when we lay out the facts that you're a thief and gave up your rights to her for your freedom," said Alex. "You can go to hell." He turned and walked across the suite.

"Charles, Alex seems a little emotional right now. Maybe we should continue this discussion in the morning. I think we should all take the evening and try to cool down. If I recall correctly, you have a party to attend." David stood up and held out his hand. Dawna accepted and followed suit as David continued, "But there are a couple of things you should consider before we meet again."

Alex seethed from across the room, afraid if he got any closer he might attack.

David held forth. "My parents successfully relocated to California and obtained their green cards. Illegal immigrants no more. Unfortunately, my mother didn't live long to enjoy that status. She died six months ago, and my father is in such a state that he no longer cares if he remains in the United States or if he lives in Mexico. My mother never got to meet her only granddaughter before she died and that is something I intend to correct for my father. My father is a practical man, and I'm sure if you lay everything out for him and do your worst, it won't ultimately matter. He's had to fight for survival his entire life, and frankly, I think he'd understand the deal I struck.

"So go ahead, call the DA. That door's shut. Call the INS. That door's shut. Call my parents. That door's shut, too. The only thing you have over me now is the money, and you have another thing coming if you think I won't tell

Petunia that you won't let me see her because I owe you *money*. That might just break her heart. She sure seemed like a sweet kid—until she started all that unnecessary wailing."

David put his hand in his suit coat. "So! Charles, Alex, here's my card. I'll expect a call from you tomorrow, so we can get this party started."

Alex watched sickened as David put his card on the table. He wondered how the hell Petunia could be so wonderful while he was so vile. He clenched his fist and glanced at Charles. It was time for this to end. "We have witnesses that'll testify to your actions tonight. In the meantime, go. We'll find you Dawna, even if you decide to wise up and disappear. And yes, David, you can count on us being in touch. Now get the hell out of here."

David smiled broadly as he escorted Dawna to the door and into the waiting arms of security. "Have fun at your party tonight," David called over his shoulder. "Congratulations by the way. It really is a great place."

Chapter 7

The next afternoon, after the family had been told about the darker side of the evening's events, they gathered in the Italian Suite, Charles temporary home. The last arrival, their family friend and attorney, Oliver Baach, who had attended the grand opening celebration of the casino with his wife.

Charles escorted Oliver to the group as they sat at a large rectangular table in the dining room of the suite. The black Italian table glowed from the gorgeous Murano glass chandelier with spiral yellow glass hanging suspended from a center chain. The black and cream quilted leather chairs held the party of seven as Charles gestured to his dad to begin the heavy discussion.

Henry, sitting at the head of table, shook his head. "I'm just sick about the way he got in front of Petunia. I don't know why I'm surprised, but I thought we had neutralized him. How is she today?" he asked Charlotte.

Inhaling deeply, she said, "She's okay. She slept with

us last night and actually fell asleep pretty quickly after her bath. I think it just took a toll on her. She had a lot of questions of course, and we've been answering them, more or less. We just can't decide if we should tell her the entire truth about what David did to us. Would it damage her more if she knew? I keep thinking that she's just too young to handle it and it's our job to protect her. I don't want her to feel any shame or feel like she wasn't wanted, and to know she was abandoned by her father. Twice. I mean, the first time he didn't know he was leaving her, but he was clearly willing to never be a part of her life once he found out she existed. We all know he used her as his get out of jail free card."

"Obviously she was upset last night," Alex said, sitting next to Charlotte. "She's asked about her father in the past, and until now, we've gotten away with being vague about him being out of the country and not really the 'Dad type.'"

"I thought we could avoid any serious discussions until she got older," said Charlotte, "but I think it's too late now. Then, of course, there's David himself, who told her last night that he loved her and missed her and had made a mistake by not being in her life. That has her really conflicted. I get the feeling that she doesn't want to hurt his feelings. I can't believe we have to deal with him again like this."

"Maybe we don't, Charlotte," said Henry, his fingers in a steeple in front of his mouth. "I don't really think he wants to be part of her life any more than we want him to. I think he just wants more money."

"I think you're right," Alex nodded. "I think that's exactly what he wants. So that leads us back to several points of discussion. If David only wants money and doesn't care about Petunia, then if we give him money, he should disappear again—hopefully. What can't happen is him getting access to her. I'm positive if does, he'll tell her any lie he can to confuse her, most likely blaming us for not allowing him to see her. Either way, he hurts Petunia again."

Charles, watching the faces of his family struggle with the problem, tossed out, "We don't know for certain that he's after money, but that would be my guess too. He orchestrated the event last night. He thinks he's got something over us. But most telling, if he really did care about Petunia, he would not have treated her the way he did and been so outrageously smug with Alex and I."

"He's blackmailing us. No doubt about it," said Henry. "Oliver, can they get away with what they did last night? What about our legal agreement with him?"

Oliver, always dressed like he just stepped out of court in a three-piece suit and pocket square, pursed his lips. "I believe dealing with David and dealing with the babysitter are two separate things. First, the nanny service needs to be notified that she used her position to sneak in a father who was in a custody dispute."

"Consider that part done. Jacqueline will handle that tomorrow," Charles said as he reached past Carey to pour himself a cup of tea from the arrangement on the table.

Oliver nodded. "To the next question, did they actually

break the law? I'm not sure. Clearly David breached our agreement, but by being admitted to Petunia's room by someone you put in place to provide for her safety, I'm just not sure. Possibly child endangerment. I'll have one of my associates look into that for us."

"My God," Julia said uncrossing her arms and laying them on the table, "They could have kidnapped her, and we wouldn't have even known about it."

"I don't think so, Mom," Charles said, doubtful. "They weren't going to be able to get her out of the Casino. She wouldn't have left with them. Not willingly."

"They could have drugged her and stuffed her in a suitcase," Carey offered.

"Jesus." Alex expelled his breath and hung his head.

Charles glared at Carey. "Not helpful. There are cameras everywhere. We'd have pictures of Dawna and David. The cameras are not just in the casino and garage, they're all over Vegas. I don't see where they could have gone without a manhunt that would have rivaled the one for Bin Laden. The FBI, an Amber alert, the police…everywhere would be on the lookout, and for what? So they could spend time with her? Get a ransom and go where? We'd find them. They couldn't hide for long. And frankly, I don't think he'd want to hurt Petunia, not if he can continue to use her like an ATM for the rest of his life."

"Well, thank God that didn't happen," Julia said, crossing her arms. "I can't believe we haven't gotten more serious about the security for the children. They are perfect targets for a kidnapping. We need to change our security situation immediately. I mean, what if this Dawna person had had a different partner in crime who didn't care about Petunia? What if they did try to kidnap her?" Julia put her hand to her throat.

"Mom, I agree," said Charlotte. "Last night shook us all up. We're going to be making some changes, believe me."

Henry pointed to each of them. "It's a new world. It begins today. I want everyone to have a security plan and security team around them from now on. Does everyone understand that?"

"Yes, sir. I agree, we'll take care of it," Alex put his fists on the table. "Back to David, however. He won't be able to access Petunia again and he knows it. The only way he could reach her now is if she reached out to him, or if we presented her to him. He told her he put his phone number in her phone. Charlotte and I took it out last night. Until this is settled, she doesn't need the responsibility of making the adult decisions. When she found out we deleted his number she was upset, already worried about him, for God's sake, but we told her that we needed to speak with him first. We reminded her about how he tricked his way in to see her, and that we only wanted to protect her. For now, I think she understands. She knows we're going to be speaking with him soon, so we're going to have to tell her something."

"Oliver," said Henry, "what about the theft. Is he right about the statute? The Metropolitan Museum has no rights to file against him either?"

"Ah." Oliver, at the other end of the table cleared his throat. "He may be wrong about some of that. The statutes relate to when a crime was discovered, in this case, the Tsarina's Fancy was discovered switched when Petunia was almost 18 months old. So yes, that statute, even though it was a felony, would have run out, especially since you did not report it. The agreement or the deal with David for forgiveness of the theft was struck about three and a half years ago, so possibly there is wiggle room there. We'll need to determine if Metropolitan Museum of Art is even aware of the replica ring's theft and if so, whether or not they filed a police report when it was discovered. Also, there is the value of the replica, I would assume it would also be classified as a felony based on its worth, but again, I don't know its value."

"I can check on the police reports in New York," said Alex. "That shouldn't be difficult to discover."

"Now," continued Oliver, "that is not to say that we couldn't attempt to collect the $3.5 million we conditionally forgave him. He agreed to reimburse Henry if he ever attempted association with Charlotte or Petunia. I believe that portion would be legally enforceable."

"But unsavory," Julia said with distaste.

"I think that's something else he's counting on," said Alex, nodding. "He doesn't think we'll drag this into the courts. He believes we won't do that, to protect Petunia. So, the question is, is he right?"

They all sat silent in consideration until Charlotte said, "That's what this all comes down to. If we tell David we'll sue him for the payment of the ring, and attempt to have him prosecuted for stealing it, then we'll also have to tell the Met that we had knowledge of their theft for the last seven and half years but didn't tell them about it. And we didn't return the copy."

Charlotte glanced briefly at Henry and continued. "Also, I'm sure David doesn't have the money to reimburse us, so what's the point in suing—to cause him aggravation? His leverage, his only leverage with us is Petunia and *her feelings*. If not for her, we would never have cared what happened to David in the first place and we would have called the police years ago."

"Well, we didn't call the police," said Henry, "because he was your boyfriend at the time he took it and we didn't want to have you embarrassed or our granddaughter shamed."

"Why can't we just have him killed," Julia asked the room.

"Mom!" said Charlotte as Carey next to her burst out in laughter.

Julia rolled her eyes at Charles who shook his head. "I'm just kidding. Stop looking at me like that everyone. Oliver, you can close your mouth, I was only joking." She mumbled, "sort of."

"I'll assume that's just emotional stress speaking, Julia," Oliver said, waving it away. "But I would advise you not to entertain that language outside of the family. God forbid if something actually happened to David."

"Okay," said Charles, "so back to actual solutions. We

need to decide if we are going to pay him to go away again since, to be honest, that's what we're all assuming he really wants. Money. Most likely, lots of money."

"Lots of money from *me*," said Henry. "I don't really care to give him any more than he's already taken. My God, look what he's already done to our family and gotten away with—all over emotional blackmail. Do we really think Petunia would be so completely distressed to learn about the real events prior to her birth? She's an awfully strong little girl. She made the right decision last night and called you. That says something. And she's doing better today, right?"

"She is, Dad," said Charlotte. "Today. But what about tomorrow? And the next day? I just don't want to see her in any pain, ever."

"Neither do we, dear," said Julia, "but I think your father is right, I don't think we can just give David a load of money again and hope that he stays away this time. I don't think giving him more resources is the solution."

"I think we need to know more about his financial status and his family situation," said Charles. "He said his mother died, but what about his father? Does he really live in the States? Does he even care about his son? I mean, David's such a shitty person, isn't it possible he's a shitty son too?"

"Last I knew," Charles continued, "he was working in a gallery in San Francisco. Not making a fortune but getting by. I assumed he wanted to establish residency for his family. They were originally from Inglewood. Yes?" He looked at Charlotte.

"Yes. They had friends in the area and wanted to move back there. David had to live in California to sponsor them."

"Okay," said Alex. "Let's assume what he told us was the truth, and that his mother is dead, and his dad is living in California, probably Inglewood. Let's assume that David doesn't have a great income and is looking for more. Let's assume he won't move to New York City or follow us home and that we can protect Petunia from him in the future. But if we don't give him money, he will be desperate. Or he must have some other threat he will hold over us."

Charles picked up the thread. "It's an emotional blackmail attempt. I think that's all he's got. If he said he would go to the press and announce his paternity and make up some lie about being kept from her, would we counter that in the press? How big would that blow up? How would we feel about that? I certainly don't like to think of Petunia being the center of a media event. That could leave a very big mark."

"If we give him money," Henry said, annoyed, "what's to say he'll take it and go away? How could we be sure he'll do that this time?"

"I think that's where we're at too, Dad," said Charlotte. "I think the emotional blackmail has to end now, and I think it's time we told Petunia the truth about him and what happened, but I worry it will break her heart. God, I'm going back and forth." Charlotte put her head in her hands.

"When do you think she will be ready to hear the truth, Charlotte?" Charles asked.

Charlotte brought her head up and looked at him.

"You were going to tell her sometime, weren't you?" said Henry.

She glanced at her father, her face hot with shame. "I don't know. I guess I hoped I'd never have to tell her, but that was probably short-sighted. I imagined as she got older she'd have more questions, but in some fantasy world, I hoped it would just go away."

"Hey sis," Charles said, softly. "I think she might be stronger than you realize. If we all support her and we're all open to her questions, and we love her just as much as ever, then her world won't radically change. Of course it's not a pretty picture. No one wants to hear that their parent is a thief and doesn't really care about them, but lots of people deal with this type of rejection and they get through it. I think it's time we told her the truth."

Charlotte's face contorted, her eyes filled with tears as she looked at her brother.

"Maybe we can go easy on the part about him not caring about her, Charlotte," Julia said with concern. "But I think Charles is right. She needs to be prepared and she needs to know the truth."

"I know you're right," Charlotte said wiping her tears. "I'm just so sad and scared for her."

"We'll do it together. All of us. She should know that there are no secrets amongst us and she can speak with any of us. I think we should speak with her tonight. While we're all together," said Julia.

Alex looked to Charlotte and reached out to hold her

hand. She closed her eyes and nodded. "Alright, we'll do it tonight. But that's only part of the battle with David. He can still make lots of trouble for her, and for us."

"So, let's meet with him and see what he has to say," said Charles. "We'll deal with him after that."

They agreed.

Chapter 8

Petunia held her mom's hand in the elevator as they rode up to her uncle's suite. They'd told her they wanted to have a family conference about her biological father, David. Angelica stayed back to babysit Lily and as she walked into the large, oval room, she saw the polite smiles on everyone's faces. She bit the inside of her cheek and walked to her grandmother who patted her sofa cushion. She took a seat on a small sofa next to her.

Grandma turned and took her hands as she spoke. "Petunia. We wanted to have a discussion with you in front of the whole family so that you know that there are no secrets, and you can come to us, any of us, whenever you need to. We will be there for you. We all love you very much." Grandma let go of her hands. She stroked her arm and gave her an encouraging smile. "Our concern this evening is your feelings. One of the things we love about you, my dear child, is your kind and gentle heart. But sometimes, bad things happen in the real world and we all have to face them. It's important to be strong, but we don't want you to be hurt, so this is very hard for us."

"Petunia," said Grandpa Henry in a commanding voice which made her sit straighter. "As you know, we had a family meeting today, about what happened last night when David surprised you. We had to decide what to tell you about him, and we all agreed that you were smart enough and brave enough to hear the truth. You come from a long line of extremely strong people, and I've seen that strength in you. We know you can handle what we have to say. You are a Carrows by birth, dear one, and I know you'll rise to the occasion."

Petunia smiled, proud that her Grandfather loved her so much and thought she was strong. But she sensed that something bad was coming. Everyone seemed to be a little bit nervous. She definitely felt that way too.

Grandpa turned and gestured to her mom and dad who sat on a sofa across from her.

"Last night," her mom began, "you met your father. Your biological father, David Torres Cordoza. You've always known that he was out there somewhere, but I guess I hoped you would be older before the time came...if you wanted to meet him."

Her mom clasped her hands and then straightened. "Okay, I'm stalling a little. He told you we dated, and that was true. We were in college together. We met in class, and during those years, I loved him very much. During that time of my life, as you know, I went by the name of Charlotte McGee. I did that mostly because I didn't want anyone to know that I came from a very wealthy family, because I found that some people would treat me differently when they found that out. That will be a challenge for you in your life as well, honey, but I hope you're stronger than I was and never feel the need to change your name." Her mom gave her a small smile.

Petunia smiled back. It made her a little bit sad when her mom was sad. She loved her more than any person on the earth. Petunia couldn't imagine what could have happened between David and her that made her so upset. No matter what though, she had to remember to be brave. She mimicked her mom and clasped her hands too.

"When David and I met, he only knew me as Charlotte McGee. After some time, I felt I could trust him, and I told him the truth about who I really was. It was a big step, a surprise, but as I learned later, David's problems began after that. He changed. He was more excited about my money than he was about me and he came up with a plan to get some money from us. His plan was to steal something and sell it, and then he would have his own money and he wouldn't need me. And that's exactly what he did."

Petunia was stunned, and something else. Embarrassed. That was the word. Her real father, that man in the suit with the dark hair who looked a little like her was a thief. She felt hot tears of shame come to her eyes as she listened further.

"There is a long story about what he stole from us, Petunia, but the bottom line is he took a valuable ring from your grandfather's safe while we were visiting Whispering

Cliffs and then when we returned to New York City, he left me. He mailed me a short letter telling me that he wanted to break up and that he was sorry. At the time, I was devastated. We didn't find out that he had stolen the ring until nearly two years later."

Petunia blinked, her chin quivering a bit, and tried to communicate love to her wonderful mom who got the unspoken message and nodded her thanks.

"Not long after he left me, I realized I was pregnant with you." Her mom stopped and finally gave her happy smile, but it didn't last long. "And while I was very sad that David had suddenly left me, I was very happy that I was going to have a baby. Your grandmother came to New York and helped me give birth. It was a wonderful time for us, Petunia, and we loved you from the moment you were born."

"Couldn't you have called him?" she asked.

Her mom shook her head. "I didn't know where he went. He left no information about how to find him. I had no way to tell him he had a daughter, but to be honest, I didn't really want to tell him.

"Then, about two years later, your grandfather found out that a valuable diamond in his collection had been swapped with a fake one. He also put together that David was the only one who could have done it. And because of that, your grandparents and I were very angry with David. So angry in fact, that we had a terrible fight, and our relationship suffered. It was your grandmother, Petunia, who decided that we needed to find David and hold him accountable for the theft, and to bring our family back together."

Petunia felt her Grandma's hand rub her back softly as she watched her mom reach over and take her dad's hand. She gave him a nice smile. "This is where Alex comes into the story. Your grandma hired Alex to find David. And he did. And while we worked together to find David, Alex and I fell in love. Alex discovered that David was living in Brazil, so that part of his story last night was true. He was living in Brazil, using the millions of dollars he stole from your grandfather to make a new life for himself. About three and a half years ago, he found out for the first time that he had a daughter and he contacted me. He didn't know that we knew he had stolen the diamond, but we did. He was a thief, and we were all very angry about that and the way he used us and treated me.

"Once he contacted me, I flew to Brazil and convinced him to return to the United States and meet with your grandfather, and the two of them, with the help of a lawyer, came to an agreement."

Her mom took a large breath. "The agreement was that your grandfather would not report him to the police, and he would not make him pay back the millions of dollars he stole from him, if David would just go away, and leave me, and you, alone. Forever. David agreed and signed legal papers giving up his parental rights in exchange for us letting him go."

Petunia had it all now. She could see the picture, and as she shyly scanned the serious faces of her dad and the rest of them, she knew what she was hearing was the truth. She saw the concern on their faces. She felt a heavy sadness in her heart.

Her mom shook her head and looked worried. "Petunia, you have to understand that we felt he wasn't a good person, and I didn't want him to be around you. I knew he wouldn't make a good dad. He's not like the dad you have here—in Alex."

Her dad took over. "We're so sorry, honey," he began looking sad too. He was always so sweet to her, his apologies almost made her feel worse. All of their pain, and hers too—she wanted it all to go away. Her dad's mouth turned down as he continued.

"We felt it was the best decision we could make to protect you. We didn't want to lie to you or keep secrets from you, we only ever wanted to protect your heart until you were old enough to hear the truth. But now, with his surprise visit, it is upon us. I hope you'll understand why we made the decisions we made."

It was a lot of information for her take in at one time and everyone was staring at her.

"Do you have any questions, honey?" her mom asked.

"He stole from you, Grandpa?" Petunia looked at him.

"Yes, he did. He took a very valuable, yellow canary diamond ring that used to belong to the Tsarina Alexandra Romanov from Russia. She was the queen, the Tsarina, of all the Russians once, and it was a special ring that her husband, the Tsar, Nicholas Romanov, gave to her as a wedding present. It was a beautiful ring with a wonderful heritage and I bought it for my Julia, many years ago as a present. She didn't wear it much because it was so big and valuable, but we kept it in my study, in my secret safe, and your father stole it from there."

"But how did he steal it?"

"He swapped it," said her mom. "He worked at the Metropolitan Museum of Art and had access to a replica. He knew through auction records that your grandfather had purchased the real ring, and he took the replica from the Museum where he worked. Then when we were visiting Whispering Cliffs, he asked to see the real one. Later, when no one was looking, he swapped the rings, and it wasn't discovered until the insurance auditors told your grandfather the ring was a fake."

Alex said, "He sold the ring not long after he took it and changed his name from David Torres, to David Cordoza, then he moved to São Paulo, Brazil."

"It was a Queen's ring?" Petunia eyes were big as she looked at her grandfather. She knew where her grandfather kept his safe. He'd shown her lots of stuff when she visited. She might be young, but she knew that what he had was valuable.

"Yes, but in Russia, they called them a Tsarina."

"Do you have a picture of it?" She couldn't visualize it and the ring meant so much to David, and so much to grandfather, and her entire family now, too.

"I'm sure we do," Henry nodded.

"Why do you want to see a picture of it, honey?" Charlotte asked.

"Because I think I'd like to draw it and give it to that man the next time I see him. That way, I can tell him I know all about him and what he did and how he hurt you."

Henry smiled. Julia smiled. Charles especially smiled. Petunia felt incredibly warm inside when they did that.

"Honey, you don't have to do that. In fact, we need to discuss your thoughts about seeing him again. Do you think you want to see him?"

Petunia could hear the quiver in her mom's voice. She could stand up to David and protect her. "Just give him the picture, Mom. After that, I don't think so. I have a family and he's not in it."

Chapter 9

David Torres Cordoza hung up the phone after his call from Alex. He rubbed his hands together pleased and turned in the bed to gaze at his naked partner. "It's all going well. They want to meet with me tomorrow. I'll lay out our demands, and I guarantee they'll give us whatever we want to make this all go away."

Dawna Hook was lying languidly on the bed staring at this man who had convinced her to participate in his plan to obtain millions of dollars from the Carrows family. She hadn't initially believed his fabulous story, but he eventually convinced her that he was the father of Petunia Carrows Macchi and that the Carrows family would pay him to stay away. It was risky for her to get involved, but there was a payday for her if David got the settlement. She ran her hands through her hair, moving it to the side. "When do you think we'll get the money, David?"

"I don't know that yet, darling," he said, lying next to her on their bed in her small condo and reaching a hand out to stroke her bare shoulder. "So far everything has gone perfectly, hasn't it? You did an amazing job, and I won't ever forget how much you helped me."

She stared at him. "No, you won't forget it, David. You told me you'd pay me $100,000 and I'm holding you to that."

David kissed her lightly then pulled back keeping his face near hers. He whispered, "I know that, dear. I'm not going to stiff you." He smiled and rose from the bed. He walked to a dresser, pulled out a cigarette, and lit it.

"I'm not like that, Dawna. You know me better than that, right? It's going to be great. We'll get the money, and then we'll decide what we want to do after that."

David grabbed his shorts off the floor and slid them on. He placed his cigarette in an ashtray on the dresser and moved a large pile of dirty clothes from the only chair in the room to the floor. Picking up the ashtray, he sat in the small armchair and smoked, appearing very satisfied as he blew the nasty smoke toward the ceiling. "My God. I can't wait to travel through Europe. I can't believe I've never had a chance to see what that world has to offer. Now, we'll be able to take our time and travel a little before we settle down. Definitely not South America, but somewhere out there, we'll find a home." He ashed and smiled. "It's finally time for me to totally dedicate myself to my art. To my painting."

Dawna watched as he kicked at the pile of clothes on the floor and bent to pick out his shirt. He draped it neatly over the side of the chair. "Well I haven't decided if I want to move out of the states, David, you know that. My family is here, and I really don't have all that much interest in living somewhere else."

"I know. I just thought perhaps by traveling with me, we could see what's out there, darling. We should begin in Italy and devote at least a month there, don't you think? There's so much to see, and so many places to visit."

Dawna Hook leaned over the bed and extracted a long t-shirt out of the dirty pile and slid it on. She considered David's comment but was not quite as keen as he was to do the mad art crawl all over the globe. She wasn't interested in art, and she didn't have a deep curiosity about other countries or historical places. She wasn't sure she could sustain a false sense of interest while watching David drool over every exhibit through the tonnage of churches and museums in every city in Italy, not to mention the rest of Europe.

"Let's just get the money in our hands before we book any travel arrangements." She slid off the bed and searched through a different pile of laundry on the floor for some clean underwear.

David flicked a hand. "I don't think you need to worry about it, Dawna. Really. They fucking despise me and want me to go away."

"I still can't believe that you rolled over for so little in the first place. I mean they have *billions*."

"I told you at the time...*not* going to jail seemed like a good offer. I needed time to get my parents settled and figure out my next move. And now that I've had that, I realize it's time for them to put up some big money, or I'm going to wreak havoc in their well-ordered lives. They'll pay me to go away. Wouldn't you? It's perfect timing because the kid is so young. They won't want to see her upset or have a big custody battle. You saw how emotional the little girl was last night. They'll want to protect her from big bad me. I probably won't be able to do this when she gets older, but right now, while she's young and vulnerable, it's perfect." David inhaled and smiled with his eyes.

She crossed her arms. "You haven't told me how much you're going to be asking them to give you. Don't you think it's time I knew?"

David rose and walked to her. He kissed her lightly, then said, "I don't think so, honey. It's still a negotiation, so let's just see what happens with my proposal."

She pushed him away and waved a hand to clear his smoke. "All right, but you owe me $100,000. And you'd better make sure that whatever deal you cut includes protection for me. I know you don't think there are any legal charges they can bring against me, but what about unlawful conduct toward a child or something else made up? I don't care that the nanny agency won't hire me again, but what about the Carrows? They were *really* pissed at me. You've gotta cover my back on this, David. You promised." She stared at him as he walked across the room and put out his cigarette. He put his hands in his pockets and stared back.

"I will, don't worry. More than anything in the world they just want me to disappear again. There's no way they'll say no when they see what I have coming. I'll meet with Alex and Charles tomorrow morning at a private cabana at the Bellagio—neutral turf. I'm a little surprised Charlotte isn't going to be there. Maybe she's afraid she'll fall in love with me again if she looks too deeply into my beautiful brown eyes."

Not that she needed any reminders, but Dawna was once more surprised at the largess of his ego. Most men had a healthy ego, but she had never met one the size of David's. She didn't argue with him because he'd never believe it.

Chapter 10

Alex waited with Charles at the Bellagio Hotel, a thirty-six-story luxury resort casino not far from Carrows. The Bellagio didn't normally allow non-paying guests to use their facilities, but they were more than willing to make an exception that morning for the short-term use by Charles Carrows.

David had insisted that they book a cabana and that he would meet them there at ten.

Alex paced the small space as Charles sat at the small round table next to lounge chairs sipping coffee. The white swag curtains were partially gathered back to expose the majestic pool, and the two of them were tense and apprehensive waiting for David to arrive.

"We didn't have to listen to him and book it here," Charles responded to Alex's complaint about following David's petty dictate about the meeting venue.

Alex stopped pacing and put up his hands in surrender. He sat down at the table with Charles. "It's done."

"I still don't understand why Charlotte didn't want to come and confront him," Charles said, shaking his head.

"She didn't want to leave the girls and we're assuming he'll have some evil demand that we'll bring back. She didn't trust herself not to create a scene."

"Well, we might present the same problem." Charles cracked his knuckles two ways and raised an eyebrow in Alex's direction. "I wanna kill that guy for what he did to Petunia and how he tried to wreck my grand opening. That was a crazy plan he made with that bitch nanny."

Alex stretched his legs out and sighed. A refreshing breeze floated inside on the December morning. They sat in contemplative silence, sipping their beverages until the curtains parted and David, bright-eyed like the emcee of a major production, walked in to greet them.

"Gentleman, good morning. Thanks for meeting with me. Hey Charles, do you have anything like this over at your place?" He motioned to pool. "Such a beautiful property."

"David, we're here. What do you want?" Alex crossed his arms, impatient with the process, disgusted by the man.

David sat and smiled, holding a small wrapped package in his lap. "Well, first let me say that it was an absolute pleasure to finally meet my daughter. She is a beautiful little girl. I'm pretty sure she looks a little like me with those big brown eyes, don't you think?" He paused, searching Charles' face, then turned to Alex and continued, "Such a sweet girl. And a budding artist too! I saw a little bit of one of her drawings and I gotta say, I was impressed. Interesting that she takes after me in that department as well, isn't it, Alex?"

Alex was agitated by the smug look on David's face, but he managed to remain silent through David's goading speech.

David looked around the cabana, his eyes lingering on the coffee service on the table. He took a cup, then stopped, and gestured, asking for permission with his eyes.

Alex and Charles said nothing.

David shrugged and poured himself a cup. "I'll really enjoy getting to know her better. I thought we could set up a visit with my father; he'll be delighted to meet his only grandchild." He looked up as if an idea had just dawned on him. "If you guys are going to be around for a while, I could get him to come to Vegas. Maybe tomorrow or the next day? We could have lunch with Petunia and get to know one another better."

"David, get to the point. What do you want?" Alex said, placing his hands slowly and deliberately into his lap.

"I told you what I want, Alex. I want to get to know my child! She's my flesh and blood. Everyone can see it; she looks so much like me. I want a *relationship* with her before it's too late. I've been kept in the closet of her life for too long, and she deserves to know more about her paternal lineage. She probably wonders about where she got her artistic abilities. God knows she didn't get them from Charlotte *McGee*. Where is she by the way? I'm a little surprised she doesn't care enough to be here." David smiled and pulled out a pack of cigarettes.

Alex and Charles remained silent. They both understood that the less that was said, the better, and they'd agreed to give David the lead. Alex's silence also radiated his distain perfectly, not to mention the technique of keeping quiet often produced interesting results.

David took a drag on the cigarette and ashed on the ground next to him. "So, tomorrow? Should I call up my dad, and we'll swing by the casino to pick her up?" He cocked his head.

"David, you're wasting our time. Tell us what you want, or we're leaving right now." Alex's voice was controlled—to both his satisfaction and surprise.

"Gee, Alex, I thought you'd be more agreeable. You know I have rights. They might not be big rights, but I still have them, and I intend to pursue them."

"How?"

David smoked and threw up an index finger. "I've been thinking a lot about that. There are the pesky legal problems. But with enough creativity, everything can be overcome. The first issue would be the outstanding matter of the ring. That little ring, the cause of so much happiness and so many problems. I'm suggesting that we revisit that document you coerced me to sign and wash that little item away. No harm, no foul. Nada. Just a small misunderstanding, forgiven by the Carrows. Then we'll really have a clean slate, won't we? Just you and me, two daddies, fighting over the custody of our precious little girl."

"Why would we do that?" Charles stared at him.

"I'll tell you why. Since the statute of limitations is over for the crime of theft, you really have no leverage except the payback of the money. And in case you're interested, as I'm sure you are, the Metropolitan Museum of Art discovered the replica missing and reported it gone over eight years ago. The statute of limitations on that too is over, although to be honest, they may be a little miffed at the *Carrows family* for withholding information about what happened to it. At least I'm assuming you didn't give them a call and tell them all about your personal security problems at your home? And, now that my father is firmly and legally imbedded in the U.S., we don't have the immigration issue to deal with either."

David tamped out his cigarette on a small coffee saucer and continued, "So really, all it comes down to is the money. The original $3.5 million that Henry put up for the ring so many years ago. Let's face it—$3.5 million—that's nothing. That's chump change for you, and while, at the time I thought it would be prudent for me to agree to your offer to go away for that amount, I no longer do. Let's not forget that you brought me to Whispering Cliffs at gunpoint."

Alex almost laughed as he remembered that sweet scene. Thank God he didn't have a gun on him now. Beyond that, Alex knew there was more to come, but he wasn't going to give David any satisfaction in the early rounds. He remained silent.

David shrugged and leaned over the table to sip his coffee. "So, to recap, we have the $3.5 million, which I assume we can easily wash away, and we have Petunia—my nine-year-old, impressionable, sensitive, biological daughter who needs to develop a relationship with her real father."

Alex stared into David's cold eyes. He shook his head. "You're sadly mistaken if you think I will ever let you see her again. You have no legal rights to her. None. You're forgetting...you signed all of them away."

David pointed a finger at both Alex and Charles. "Coerced. Coerced. Blackmailed. Forced. Given no option. Frightened, I might say. Mistaken! Not in my right mind. *Intimidated*, Alex. But not anymore. I think the courts will listen to me, and I intend to try."

Alex smirked. "You're deluded. The courts will not listen to you. They will not take kindly to you. They will not agree that you are a safe person or honestly sincere in the welfare of your child. You will never see her again."

Alex felt the steam rising within him and fought to suppress it as David and he resumed a hate-filled staring contest. David broke first and threw up his hands. "Oh, all right. I have another proposal. Another scenario I'll draw for you. Maybe this one will be more to your liking."

David put his hands theatrically in the air and said, "Picture this. A book is written, by a distraught father, estranged from his famous little girl. They were forced apart by his admittedly bad judgment, but he is *filled* with regret. Life is short, and after the death of his mother, the man, let's just say his name is...David, decides that he doesn't want to waste another minute. Even if he must spend some time in jail, more than anything in the world, he wants to be a better person and become a good father. One whose daughter will never have to wonder if he wanted her—which I hear can be very damaging. A father willing to fight for his daughter. Almost a hero! A hero who promised his dying mother that he would make this right. He would step up and be a man—a man big enough to admit his mistakes, big enough to deal with the consequences, and big enough to beg for his daughter's forgiveness."

David clapped his hands and moved his head back and forth between the stony, silent stares of Alex and Charles. He leaned slightly toward Charles, "Come now, aren't you slightly curious?" David placed the plain, wrapped parcel on the table.

"What I had in mind would be the sale and publication of this book, to the highest bidder. Just like the Vanderbilt story, the tale of little girl lost, a big custody battle, lots of scandal, tearful testimony in court, and extremely high interest in the media. It'll be big. I'm pretty sure the PR firm of the publisher will make it a bestseller. I'll probably have to promote it, do the talk show circuit. Blah, blah, blah, the whole nine yards. What a story. It'll be insane. I can't imagine who the chosen spokesperson for the Carrows will be. Will it be you, Alex, answering all the questions in the media? You, Charles, taking a hot-tempered swing at some photographer for your sister? Charlotte maybe? And poor Petunia, being photographed by the paparazzi? I can see it all now." David wiggled his fingers in a maniacal gesture by the sides of his head and smiled.

Alex and Charles glanced at one another as David put his thumb and index finger at the corners of his mouth. "But you know what, Alex, I have to wonder if that would be in our daughter's best interest. She's such a sweet kid. A bit sensitive and dramatic, though. Reminds me a little of Charlotte when she was younger. Interesting, isn't it? So maybe we can forego all of that nasty courtroom drama and media circus and reach some type of arrangement. I want to see my daughter. She is *my* daughter, and she deserves a relationship with me."

Charles finally broke his silence. "I believe you have a third option, David, and we're all waiting to hear it."

Sitting back in his chair, David spun the wrapped package on the table and looked around the white draped cabana blowing softly in the wind. "Such a wonderful place this is. So relaxing, such beauty. I've always been attracted to beautiful things. That was part of my problem. At one point in my life, Charlotte was one of them."

David pushed his chair back and stood. "I guess you're right about a possible third option, Charles. You'll give me ten million dollars cash, and I'll go away—this time for good. Otherwise," he put his index finger on the wrapped package and said, "this gets published, and scenario two goes into full play. You know where to reach me, kids. You have twenty-four hours."

As David walked out, Alex reached over and unwrapped the package. Inside was a fully written book, obviously self-published, entitled, *Petunia Carrows, My Daughter,*

Too. Petunia's face was on the cover.

Charles stared at it. "God forgive me, but I really want to kill him."

Chapter 11

Back in the Italian Suite at Carrows Casino, the family remained quiet as they watched Henry contemplate. After Alex presented David's case, they'd discussed and argued the merits of each option. Everyone agreed that David wouldn't get near Petunia again, that offer was completely off the table. Paying him off seemed easier to Alex and Charlotte, but Henry wasn't as sure. Finally, taking his patriarchal place, he said, "No. We're not paying him off again. Enough is enough. Let him try to come for us. We'll start the legal ball rolling and sue him for the money he owes us."

"She's going to have to worry about David the rest of her life," groaned Charlotte. "It's just too much to even think about."

"Well you picked him," Carey murmured under her breath.

"Carey!" Julia got up and paced. "We are not going there. We're not spending any time thinking about the regretful decisions we've *all* made in our past. We've come too far as family for any of that nonsense. What's done is done. If Charlotte hadn't met David, there would be no Petunia. Imagine our lives without her. She's the most precious thing in all the world, and we'll protect her, just like we'll do for your children, and Charles'. I won't hear another word like that again."

Carey donned an innocent look, rolled her eyes, and looked out the window.

Henry watched as Julia stopped pacing and stood before him. He realized tensions were running high but continued. "And as your mother pointed out yesterday, why would we give David more resources, so he can set himself up in an even better position to take further advantage of us? David was not intimidated by the fact that we have legal papers which state that he now owes us money."

"So let's work through the what-ifs." Charles pointed to the book on the coffee table in front of them. "I perused it," he shook his head. "It contains a whole lot of crap and not one mention of the ring. If it were published, what would happen? How would we feel about it?"

Henry said, "It's not ideal. It's not how I want my days spent dealing with bad press or tabloid journalism. I believe he may be right that there would be an interest in the story, at least from the bottom feeders. Even with the connections we have, I don't know that we could stop that. Assuming he managed to get it in the right hands, at the minimum, it would make us all slightly miserable."

Charles leaned back. "If there is press, we'll deal with it. It won't be the first time we've needed a PR team to help us. We'll do what we can to buy up the publishing rights if he goes forward with the book and we'll keep it from multiplying."

Julia finally resumed her seat next to Henry. "You're right, we'll manage it, and eventually it'll go away. We have right on our side here. This is a bad man, people will rally and support us for keeping Petunia away from him."

"But there is Petunia," said Charlotte. "How would this affect her when she found out about it? Because she would find out about it, in school, or through a friend. Girls love to gossip, especially at her age. I think this would hurt her."

Charles waved his hand. "If yesterday was indication about whether or not she was a fighter, I'd say she'd manage all right. She handled the David story quite well."

"Yes," Henry said, smiling with recollect.

They all felt empowered by Petunia's reaction, but Charlotte continued, "I was happy that she seemed to handle it well, too, but still, it's one thing to say that to us, when she was feeling protective, it's another when some kid at school says something unkind, or some photographer chases her down and yells something wicked at her to get a facial reaction."

"There's all sorts of things we'll never be able to protect her from Charlotte," Julia said. "Just being a Carrows is asking for trouble."

"She took the news like a champion," Henry smiled

as he rose from the table. "But we'll do everything we can to minimize the effect this has on her. She's already decided that she has no emotional interest in forming a relationship with him, so let's support her decision."

He stood in front of his family. "We already have legal documents that prove David is a thief and a liar. Now we'll make him a *poor* thief and liar, and he'll be left with no choice but to crawl away and leave us in peace."

Charles nodded his agreement. "So what do we tell David? That we're not going to pay him another cent and that we'll begin proceedings to sue him for the money he owes us? He will react to that."

Alex pushed his chair back and got up as well. "The decision's been made. I'll deliver the news to David tomorrow, then Charlotte, the girls, and I will catch our flight back home for the holidays. I'll have the extra security in place this week."

Henry walked to Alex and gave him a quick pat on the back. For all intents and purpose, the meeting was over. He put his hands on Charlotte's shoulders and kissed the top of her head. She looked up at him.

"It'll be fine," he whispered.

Chapter 12

David stopped to admire the plaid Brioni overshirt hanging on a rack in the men's section of Neiman Marcus. The tag read, $4,200. *No problem at all,* he smirked, thinking of the balloon payment his checking account would soon receive. He whistled as he left the department store and walked outside along the sidewalk toward his meeting with Alex at a nearby Starbucks. Thirsty, he decided he'd treat himself to a cool Frappuccino as a reward after their business was wrapped up. He stopped on his path to light a cigarette. Inhaling, he glanced at his watch—his priceless Patek Phillipe, which he refused to pawn, no matter how dire his circumstances had become. He was slightly late for their rendezvous. He smiled. He enjoyed the thought of that, too.

David walked into Starbucks and immediately spied Alex, sitting with Charles. He pulled up a chair and sat. "Hey guys. Glad you got back to me so soon. So, what's the big decision?" David scratched his temple and gave them a demure smile.

Alex said, "David. I'm going to try to appeal to what's left of your sense of decency one more time. Our *final* offer, and it's a very generous one, is this. Go away. Now. If you do not, and you publish the book or make any further attempt to be a nuisance or try to contact Petunia or ourselves in any way, we will begin the legal process to collect our money. It's over. Move on with your life. In the future, when Petunia is an adult and if she wishes to see you, we will support her decision and you may have a chance for a relationship with her then. But until that time, we have nothing further to talk about."

David's face flushed with shock; his heart skipped a beat. He couldn't believe it. His face contorted. "Are you kidding me? Really? That kid knows who I am now! She's going to want to see me before she's an *adult*. After she sees the pain I've suffered—the pain my *family* has suffered—and after she's read my book, I guarantee she'll want to see me." He shifted, attempting unsuccessfully to control his rage. "If she doesn't get a chance to read it, I'm sure someone will tell her about it, Alex. You can't shelter her from the world, asshole. She's my daughter— *my daughter*!" David slammed his hand onto the table.

Charles leaned over, putting his face close enough that David could smell his breath. "We all know that you're not interested in her as your daughter, so you can cut the crap. You're not interested in anyone other than yourself. Go. The. Fuck. Away."

David recoiled into his chair as Alex and Charles stood up. Alex reached into his jacket pocket and pulled out an envelope and placed it on the table. "We're leaving now, but before we go, there's one more thing. Petunia wanted me to give this to you."

Alex pushed his chair into the table aggressively. "Goodbye David. I hope you make the right decision for yourself, but mostly for Petunia. If you do care about her, somewhere inside, then do the right thing and leave her alone. Let her grow up peacefully. She has a good home and she'll be well taken care of. That should comfort you. Do the right thing this time—for her sake."

Stunned and enraged, David stared at their backs as they left. He couldn't believe their decision. His hands shook furiously as he reached for the blank envelope and ripped it open. Inside contained a drawing of a large yellow diamond ring, signed in the corner by the artist, Petunia Carrows Macchi.

Chapter 13

Julia squeezed her daughter and granddaughter in a hug. "We'll miss you, but I understand the Macchi's deserve to spend time with you this year. We'll be out after Christmas."

Charlotte, holding Lily on her hip, pulled back. "We'll miss you too."

They glanced at Petunia who was listening beside them. Standing near the three-story natural spruce tree in the lobby of Carrows, their luggage was being put into a car which would take them to the airport.

"You guys will be all alone this year, Mom. When Charles, Carey, and Angelica leave for London to check out the next property, why don't you and Dad join us. Marie would love to host you, and you like Alex's family." Charlotte gave her a hopeful smile.

"We don't want to interfere with Marie's plans." Julia leaned over and grasped the sides of sweet Lily's little face and gave her a soft kiss. Looking back at her daughter with wet lashes, she added, "Marie deserves to have a relaxing Christmas without worrying about entertaining us. We'll be there in January, and we should spend time firming up our family vacation plans. I've got some wonderful ideas about where we should travel over spring break."

"Charlotte," Henry said, giving her a hug and Lily a quick kiss. "I don't want you to worry about anything. Alex and I will be taking care of things. We'll all protect the girls. I promise."

"I know, Dad. I really appreciate all your support. Thanks for everything."

Henry leaned down to Petunia and gave her a hug. "Petunia. I couldn't be more proud of you. You're a wonderful granddaughter. You have a great Christmas with your Dad's family and we'll see you soon."

"Bye Grandpa. I'll miss you." She smiled and handed him a large envelope. "I wanted to give you something for Christmas before I left. You can open it later. I painted it from the Walter Crane picture in your office from the Faerie Queene. Mommy bought me a copy that I could look at while I painted."

Henry nodded his head at the gift and stood erect and proud. "That was very thoughtful. You have a wonderful trip home, and we'll see you soon." Julia stepped to his side as they watched their family walk out of the hotel for their waiting car.

She put her arm around Henry and looked down at the envelope as he opened it. The background of the drawing was of deep, dark greens of a forest. A knight loomed in front of a group of people holding a shield with a traditional crested design of four squares that contained a petunia, a lily, a sword, and a heart.

"She's very special," Julia said, giving his arm a squeeze.

Henry looked out the glass doors. They watched as the car pulled away from the curb. "I hope to God I made the right decision."

Chapter 14

Cheryl Davis sat in the chair at the salon considering her fingernails while the staff got to work on her pedicure. Long, pointy, silver metallic. Combine that with the white, off the shoulder sweater with long sleeves, her tight black leather pants, and her Pulp Fiction Mia Wallace wig, and she thought she'd be good to go. Joey was picking her up at seven. He'd love it.

She frowned, wondering what he had in mind for their first date. He'd been after her for almost two years now, but until this week, she hadn't made the decision to go for it. Joey, the Bacardi rep at the club, was a polished dude. Good looking, hard-working, ambitious, and not a total letch, she wondered if they had a shot. Not that she lingered on the possibility of happily-ever-after. With her background, in her profession, she'd found it almost impossible to find a real guy.

She picked up a magazine and flipped through the fashion, considering the styles and prices. Who the hell spent $800 on a dress? No one at the bar, that was for sure. She realized she could afford to spend a little more than she did on clothes, but she was committed to saving every penny she earned to buy out her partners and one day, solely own Lacey's, her very own strip club.

She flipped another page and stopped at a dress which looked remarkably like the one hanging in her closet. The one she wore on her date night with Charles Carrows. She wondered what her old pal was up to. A side of her mouth went up as she thought about how they had met.

Charles Carrows, boy billionaire, and some of his friends had wandered into Lacey's one odd afternoon. She'd been working her first shift of her long day tending the bar, not dancing. While his friends enjoyed the action on the dance floor, she and Charles had fallen into a conversation that struck her as oddly real surrounded as they were in the exotic atmosphere. Always guarded and playing the role of Cherrie Corona, her stripper name, she was caught off guard when Charles showed her an immediate, sincere respect. She knew the difference. Her bullshit meter was hardly ever wrong.

After that first conversation, he'd come into Lacey's periodically during the slower afternoons, making sure to visit when she was tending bar and not on stage, something he'd witnessed only once. The boy had not lingered on that visit. At that point, she realized that he was not coming around for the predictable reasons.

It was cool that she had a genuine friendship with him. She'd been completely startled when she'd learned that he was actually an heir to one of the richest families in the United States. Because he didn't treat her like a striper, she tried not to treat him as anything other than a human being too. He seemed grateful for it.

She also didn't let her imagination run so far away as to dream that they would have a long-term romantic situation. He'd never come on to her and stated that he'd enjoyed their friendship. She wondered about his lack of interest, but she came to know him and trust him to the point that when he asked, she'd agreed to do him a personal favor.

And my, oh my, Charles Carrows's favors were interesting. The first one required her to dress up and play the role as his girlfriend in front of another gentleman— hence the nice dress which hung her closet. She'd never understood the exact purpose of the dinner, but it intrigued her. Charles, ever the gentleman, had assured her that she had no obligation to help him and that if she was uncomfortable playing his girlfriend, there would be no hard feelings. He'd explained that from time to time, in his family, they would occasionally use people as props or players to advance their agendas. Those people, he'd assured her, would always be respected and well-compensated as long as they agreed to keep silent and play the game.

She'd seen no downside and Charles had never asked her to do anything remotely illegal. More than that, he was always extremely grateful and enormously generous in his compensation. They had a wonderfully trusting working relationship and a casual and easy going friendship, but there were parts of both their lives which they each kept private. And that was okay, with both of them.

"What are you up to these days?" she murmured under her breath thinking of Charles as she laid down the magazine and picked up another. She sure could use another influx of cash. The last time she'd worked for him as Paula Butler, he'd had a girl with him named Daizy Durand. She wondered what had happened to her as well.

She felt confident Charles would one day come calling again. She was looking forward to it. In the meantime, she had a hot date with Joey. Who knew?

Chapter 15

Dawna was furious with David that his wild idea didn't work out. After all her hard work, he was now asking her to get even more involved.

Standing in the kitchen of her condo, he'd just returned from his meeting with Alex and Charles and had given her the bad news. "Look, I'm sorry, I really am. No one is more surprised at this than me. I'm furious with them, but now I've got some decisions to make, and the only way to make money is if you help me. I've covered you so far, haven't I?"

She gritted her teeth as he zoomed in on her and grabbed her by the hips. "Dawna, I love you. Don't you care about what happens to me? We just need to implement my backup plan and see what happens."

She squinted at him. "I don't see me getting any $100,000 from this David. You promised me that money. How will I see anything from this now? If we go through with this, they'll sue you for back payment for the ring, and once you pay that three and half MILLION dollars back, what, you'll start paying *me*? Do you think I'm stupid? That'll take years! Even if we get lucky and the book sells."

David let her go and pounded away like a baby. "Shit, Dawna, alright! I'll give you some money up front, okay? I'll pay you, before I ever pay them, which I plan on *never* doing anyway."

Dawna wasn't so sure anymore that David knew what he was doing or if he really loved her, and she wasn't sure she loved him. She followed David from the kitchen into her small living room and watched him open a window. Was he trying for once to be considerate to her desire for him to at least blow his smoke outside? He said nothing as he held a cigarette and stared out into the street.

Dawna was fed up on his schemes. The scene at the hotel had scared the crap out of her too. She'd had a front row view of powerful and rich, and comparing those folks to David, who was wiping sweat from his forehead, she was worried that they'd bit off more than they could chew. "Maybe we should just forget about the whole thing. Just let it go, David. You can make a nice living, and I can too. We can still do some traveling and be happy. We just have to work, like regular people and save our money."

David turned on her, his face red. "Dawna! I don't want to be like regular people! I'm sick of having to grovel to all the rich people, and sick of the rich always getting whatever they fucking want. Including my daughter! Damn it! Don't you see that it's not fair? I want real money, and I want to travel, and I want to dedicate myself to my art! I've got talent, real talent. I've been told that for years, but I don't have the luxury of time to dedicate myself to it. I only just barely have enough canvases for a collection. I can make it as a real artist if I just get a chance. I'm sick of representing other artists, other art patrons, everyone else's dreams but my own. It's time I come out of the shadows and show the world what I can do. And this will be my platform—my big break. If I'm smart enough to use it. You just have to stick to the plan."

David lit the cigarette and blew smoke purposefully in her direction. "I'll pay you your money, Dawna. If you're not interested in helping me for me, you're at least still interested in the money, right? Well, then, we've got to stick with the new plan if you ever want to see it."

Dawna didn't know. The plan...the new plan...Plan B... would be really scary, and if she did it, there would be no going back. "Are you really sure I'm out of the woods about that nanny thing? You've checked into that right?"

He looked at her and played with his nails. "Yes. I went over it with the lawyer. He said he didn't think they could do anything to you. No one was hurt. Like you said, you won't ever be able to be a nanny again, but you don't care about that anyway."

She mulled, her hands on her slim hips. "You're asking me to do a lot here David. No kidding. The press, the police, I'll really be sticking my neck out. Again."

"All perfectly legal, and as a bonus, you'll be famous!" He walked toward her, smiling. "Who knows where that could lead for you? Look at all the stupid reality stars out there, making a killing and pulling down some serious money. It'll be good. You just have to roll with it, baby," he implored.

Dawna wanted the money—the fame, however, she could live without. Maybe she could minimize that part. David was the fame whore. Greedy for it, hungry for it, he believed it would make all the difference for him if he could become a *famous artist*. And who knew? Maybe he was right. There were an awful lot of people out there making money from their fame. You didn't even have to be famous for a good reason. You only had to look at some stupid reality star and remember that their millions began after they did a sex video. That was just David's point. Some were smart enough to cash in on it while they were hot, but those who didn't lost their opportunity. It was all a risk though.

David returned to the open window. "Look, Dawna, I've already spoken with my friend from São Paulo. He's got great connections with a big publishing house in New York. He told me he thought the idea was hot—really hot— and it would sell. All I need to do now is get him copy of the book and tell him to get us a deal, then we're ready to roll. I'm giving it to him tomorrow in LA. If you want to help me, tell me now. If not, then I need to meet with my dad and get him to help me. But, Dawna, if you don't help, I'm not paying you anything. I'm sorry, but you knew all along there was a possibility that we might need to go to Plan B. So what's it going to be? Are you in, or are you out?"

Dawna looked into the desperate but seriously

attractive eyes of her boyfriend and figured if anyone could make it, it might as well be David. After all, he wasn't lying about being the father of Petunia Carrows, and that had to be worth something. "All right, David. I'm in. Plan B. But it better work."

Chapter 16

Logan Nuedor met David Cordoza the next day in Los Angeles at his small office in Century City. Logan was a businessman who had worn a number of hats from venture capitalism, public relations, marketing, and publishing and knew David from their days in São Paulo, Brazil. He was happy to meet with David and remembered him as a handsome, charming man who had very passionate feelings about the art world. Logan also had an idea what the meeting was going to be about. He was excited by the prospect of an interesting new deal.

"David!" Logan stood as his friend smiled broadly and entered his office wearing an elegant suit and his typical easy going charm. They embraced. "It's so good to see you again. Meu Deus! The fun we had, my Paulistano friend! Do you miss Brazil as much as I do?"

David smiled as he took the proffered seat on a sofa across from Logan's armchair. "Brazil was certainly a good time. Yes, I miss it. I miss the nightlife. It had a wonderful, but completely different energy than Vegas, that's for sure. There's no culture in Las Vegas."

"What are you doing there then? Why not go back?" Logan rocked in his chair and smiled.

"I've been tied up with some personal issues in the states." David shrugged and tugged at the cuff of his shirt.

"You mentioned on the phone that you have a book that you think has some nice potential. The Carrows family thing?" Logan gestured to the book in David's hand.

"Yes. It's a long story, but I'm ready to go forward with the publication." David handed him the copy.

Logan read the title, "*Petunia Carrows, My Daughter, Too.* So, what you told me over the phone is true? You're the father of Petunia Carrows? From the Carrows family out at Whispering Cliffs?"

"I am. Her mother and I met in college. It's all in there. It's ready for publication as is, but it could probably use a once over by an editor if you'd like. I think there would be great interest in it. I really do. With the right backing and a public relations machine in place, it could be a bestseller."

Logan was impressed. He chewed on his bottom lip and did a fast flip through the pages. "Why don't you give me an overview of what's in here."

David unbuttoned his suit coat and sat back, extending one arm across the back of the sofa, and began.

"It opens with my childhood, being poor, raised in Inglewood by illegal immigrants with the constant fear of deportation, the hard work, the sacrifices my parents made for me, the fact that they had to return to Mexico for ten years to serve a time bar so they could apply for supported citizenship by me once I turned 21. Then, it segues into my life as an art student at NYU, where I meet Charlotte. At the time she was living under an alias, Charlotte McGee, and we fell in love. I didn't know she had any relation to the Carrows family for a long time. She was secretive, but she eventually told me about her real identity. About a year later, we broke up. It wasn't the identity thing or her being a Carrows; I was restless, young, impetuous, I wasn't ready to settle down, and I wanted a life of my own."

Logan stopped rocking, interested to see where this was going.

"I left Charlotte about a year after my graduation and found a new life in Sao Paulo, where of course, I met you. After some years there, I discovered, completely by accident, that Charlotte had had a child, Petunia Carrows. I did the calculations. Charlotte never informed me that I had a daughter. When I found out, I attempted to get back into Charlotte's life and negotiate some kind of relationship where I could be a father for Petunia. I wanted to meet my daughter, but the Carrows family stood in my way."

David pointed to the copy in Logan's hand, "The book will explain how confused I was."

Logan continued to listen, rapt. David's telling of the rest of the story was clearly emotional for him. He felt sorry for his friend and realized that publishing the fact that he'd taken a financial settlement in exchange for the rights to his daughter had been weighing on David's soul.

David got up, went to a window, and looked outside.

He ran a hand across his face and turned around. His face drawn, he continued, "Recently, last week, actually, I met my daughter for the first time. As you can imagine, it was very emotional for both of us, but the Carrows family stepped in again, and told me that they would not allow us to have any contact in the future. In essence, they are barring me from her. I told them if they did not allow me to see my daughter, then I would have no choice but to fight for her. Which brings us to today, and to my novel. I would like to see it published. This way, Petunia will know that I fought for her. That I wanted her. I think my story would be of interest to a great many people. Audiences, groups, parents, fathers who have had difficult custody battles, people interested in the secret world of the Carrows family and how they believe their money will protect them from doing what is right. It's been such an incredibly challenging time for me, Logan."

Logan stood. "I had no idea how much you've gone through. I always knew you were a strong man, but I see now that you earned it through a lifetime of struggle. I'm so sorry to hear about your mother, too."

"Do you think it will sell?" David looked at him under hooded brows.

"Yes, I know it will sell. Your paternity issues will be a big part of it, but like you said, there will be many people very curious about the Carrows family in general. They made you sign your rights away on your own daughter? I don't really understand how they got you to do that."

Logan cocked his head and sat back down as David walked toward the sofa.

"The Carrows family can be very intimidating, Logan. You have no idea. But I think everyone is entitled to some forgiveness as they grow up and to have the chance to make up for their mistakes, don't you? I don't have their resources, but if I speak my truth, it may make a difference. Maybe I'll be able to see her again, and if not, well, I will have fulfilled my mother's dying wish and at least tried. And Petunia, she will know that I cared."

"David, you realize that it also may antagonize them? They are a very powerful family."

"I'm willing to take that chance, but are you? I would like to get this published very quickly because I don't want to waste any more time."

"I'll get on it this afternoon. I don't see a problem at all in getting it published, and I think you're right, it should be a bestseller."

Over the next several weeks, David and Logan finalized the details with the publisher who was also extremely excited with the book's prospects. Much to David's chagrin, the publisher decided to remove Petunia's face from the cover, but rather, used pictures of her only on the inside pages from the few photos already published in the press.

They agreed to conduct a major print run followed by a publicity tour with David appearing on several of their media partnership television shows as well as co-owned print publications. The national media and publication house were impressed with David and his sad story and had great confidence that it would create a firestorm if it was managed properly.

David received a six-figure signing bonus which he promptly gave to Dawna, making her a more cooperative and happier participant in the next part of their plan. Soon after the book's publication, and after David's first taped television interview, he promptly disappeared.

Chapter 17

After the beginning of the new year, Charlotte, at her townhome in New York City sat at her long kitchen table trying to concentrate on some paperwork while Lily swung in her baby jumper attached to a doorframe and sucked on a plastic toy. The phone rang, Charles on the line calling from the Rosewood London where he, Angelica, and Carey had been staying. "It's starting," he said.

Charlotte put her head in her hands. "I know. I can't believe he went ahead with the publication. And I heard he did a television interview in LA."

"Yeah, mom told me. He was on the Early Show out there. I've got Jacqueline reading the copy of the book David gave to us in Vegas and comparing it to one which he published to see if there are any major differences. We're going to need to decide how to manage this."

"I went out and bought a copy of it last night. Thank God Petunia's face is no longer on the damn cover, but there are several large pictures of her on the inside. It makes me sick. I've been scanning the book, but I don't see any mention of the ring in it, so it's all a complete fabrication." Charlotte got up and went to the sink and grabbed some dishes, still on the counter from the family breakfast. "God, I hate him for doing this! I should have just paid him to go away. I feel so terrible that everyone, and Petunia, is going to be hurt by this."

"He's a piece of work. Dad is meeting with Oliver today to see what we can do to get the publishing rights or put pressure on the publisher. I'm also having a video conference today with Alana Whittaker, our head of PR, to see how we should handle the press."

Charlotte gave up on the dishes and sat on the floor near Lily who smiled and began to bounce enthusiastically. "Thank you for all the help, Charles. David burned his last bridge with us. But now that this thing is out there, I think we need to go public. Alex and I decided we need to counter his story with the truth and the fact that he's a thief then see if the publisher wants to deal with a lawsuit." She reached out and grabbed her baby's tiny hand.

"I hear what you're saying, but the more fuel we throw on the story, the more interest it will have. How about Dad and I take the meetings today and I'll get back to you. In the meantime, you need to prepare Petunia. There may be press after all of you. Have you and Alex given any thought to moving out of your place and into a more secure building?"

She sighed. "We've been talking about it for a while since we're getting tight on space with the girls. We no longer have a guest room. After we opened up the garden apartment to the rest of the house, that helped, but if we're going to need full-time security, I just don't know where we'll put everyone. We've been looking, it's just going to be hard to move. But Alex and I agreed that we need the extra security. Especially now, but maybe forever too."

"You upgraded your security around your place, though, didn't you?" asked Charles.

"Yes, it's tight. No one can pop in without us knowing about it."

"You need to get full-time security, Charlotte. At least a bodyguard for Petunia until this quiets down. God knows who's out there and could approach you guys."

Charlotte leaned back against the wall and closed her eyes. "Already got it. We've got a guy from Macchi & Macchi moving into the garden apartment tomorrow. His name is Renzo Castrogiovanni. He's been with Macchi & Macchi for the last fifteen years from back to when Anthony Senior ran the business. He's a single guy, divorced, so he has the flexibility to live with us for a while. Michael and Alex think he's a good fit for the job."

"Renzo. Got it. Well, if Alex thinks he's up to the task, I'd believe him. He knows what he's doing. I'm glad to hear he's moving in. You should give mom and dad a call and let them know too. Send everyone his cell number just in case."

Charlotte stared at her beautiful daughter, so happy, so unaware of the drama and danger circulating around her life. She softened her voice. "Charles, are you angry with me—like Carey is—over David? That this is all my fault for bringing this guy into our lives?"

"No, I'm not angry with you, kid, I love you. God knows I've never been perfect, right? None of us has. Don't worry about Carey. We'll get through this. Really, it'll be okay. When are you telling Petunia?"

"Today." She sighed.

"Yes, today. It's time to tell her. Tell her about David's extortion attempt and show her the book," said Charles.

"You know, it's interesting. Since we got home, she's been really focusing on her drawing. You know she's got talent, Charles. I cringe knowing she probably got it from David. She and David drew a picture together while he was with her. Did I tell you that? Do you think that's why she's spending so much time drawing?"

"Maybe. But she's always liked to draw and paint."

"She's so young, Charles. She's still only a baby. I wanted to protect her from the bad stuff in the world, and instead, I brought it home to her."

"This isn't your fault, Charlotte. Just keep reminding yourself that she is who she is, and she wouldn't be here if it wasn't for your relationship with David. Whatever he is, there must be something good about him because look at Petunia. So don't worry. I'll get back to you after the meetings."

That evening after an early dinner, Charlotte ensconced Petunia in Lily's room to watch over her sister. She and

Alex sat alone at the kitchen table and placed a call to Charles in London.

"It's been a long day," Charles began. "First off, Jacqueline finished reading both books and they're basically the same—just some editing changes, the book cover design, and interior pictures. There is no mention of the ring—it's just his version of the facts. They're twisted to make him seem like a simple guy who just made a bad mistake and is being taken advantage of by some terrible rich people.

"Second, Dad met with Oliver who is going to approach the publisher, Ares Publication, in Los Angeles tomorrow. He'll have a frank conversation and lay out the circumstances. Hopefully Oliver can convince them to have a change of heart about further publishing or selling us the publication rights. We'll see how that goes. I Skyped with Alana Whittaker and laid it all out. She needed the complete story so nothing will surprise her. Her opinion is that if we can't stop the publication of the book, then we should issue a press release stating the truth. We're not entirely sure yet when we want to go after David for the three point five, but we told Oliver to be ready at a moment's notice to launch a full assault on David's assets if, and when, we give him the green light. We need to play that card carefully."

"We've talked about this for a month now," said Alex who got up from the table and leaned against a counter. He folded his arms in front of him and continued. "We agreed that if David published his book of half-truths and lies, then we should get the real truth out there. Charlotte and I agree with Alana—we need to do a press release. But let's wait to see if Oliver can spin his magic with the publisher."

Charlotte looked hopefully at him. "Maybe the book won't even get traction. It's possible it might just die on the vine."

Alex shook his head. "Maybe, but we need to prepare. We'll work on the press release and speak with Alana directly."

"That sounds good. How did it go with Petunia? Did you show her the book?" Charles asked.

Charlotte picked up the phone from the table. "That's the next great thing we get to do when we hang up."

Charles, sounding tired said, "Well keep your chin up. I'll talk to you tomorrow."

Charlotte disconnected. Alex came to her and pulled her up from the table. He gave her a soft kiss on the cheek, and whispered, "Let's go."

Chapter 18

After Dawna Hook had dialed 911 with a shaky hand to report David missing, they told her she needed to go to the Las Vegas police station in person to file a missing person's report. Dawna wore the conservative, understated skirt and blouse David had picked out for her and delivered her lines with all the enthusiasm she could muster. "He's been missing for two whole days! He wouldn't just leave! Not in the middle of all this!"

She reached into a huge, boxy bag and frantically rummaged around until she pulled out a copy of David's book. She slammed it on the table. "He's put his heart into this book and he wouldn't just disappear when he has all these interviews lined up! Magazine interviews, television interviews, he has a whole media tour to do. Why would he walk out on all that? I'm so worried about him!"

The detective made notes, and said, "Does he have any enemies that you know of?"

Dawna, wide-eyed, looked at the book and back to the

detective. "Oh. My. God. What if the Carrows family did something to him to retaliate? Oh my God. What if they had him killed or something to keep him quiet!"

"The Carrows?" The puzzled detective reached out and picked up the book as Dawna rambled on. "His publisher has been calling my place looking for him, and they seem really upset, too. I've talked to his dad, and he hasn't seen him. I called the gallery he works at sometimes in San Francisco, and none of them have seen him either. I know he still has a place in San Francisco, but I don't have the keys. If I gave you the address you could check to see if he's there too, right?"

Dawna had practiced her delivery in front of a mirror, pulling random "question cards" from a pile and working on the appropriate, hopefully emotional, responses. She thought she did a swell job.

When she made it back to her condo, she called Logan, who called the publisher, who called their public relations office who felt it was a wonderful twist-a-poolza in the release of the new publication, *Petunia Carrows, My Daughter, Too*. Logan instructed Dawna to take any and all media requests for interviews. He offered her support, peppered with cautious optimism that David would be found, alive.

The Las Vegas police investigated David's disappearance, the LA police spoke with his publisher, the San Francisco police gained access to David's apartment and did not find him there. Being slightly baffled by the disappearance, the LA police decided to have a word with a member of the Carrows family to see what they knew about David.

Two Los Angeles police detectives showed up unannounced at the gates of Whispering Cliffs. After entry into the grounds, they got no farther than the front steps. Henry met them outside and told them emphatically that neither he nor anyone in his family knew David's whereabouts. After the police delicately questioned him about David's relationship with the Carrows family and the publication of the book, Henry directed them to their attorney, Oliver Baach. They left as they came, baffled, but now suspicious.

———

Charles Carrows took a call from his mother. Julia launched without preamble, "I've sent you a link to a story which aired on the local Las Vegas news station. It's being picked up here in Los Angeles too." She finished with a note of exasperation.

"About what?" Charles asked from London.

"Just watch it. I'm disgusted. As is your father. Call me back when you're finished."

Charles stared at the dead connection on his phone a bit wide-eyed at his mother's uncharacteristic hang up.

He pulled up his mail and hit the link. A news report filled the screen.

A banner scrolled across the bottom, announcing a KCNV News Breaking Story. A captioned aerial photograph of Whispering Cliffs hung on the screen as the news anchor spoke.

"And now to an increasingly bizarre story related to the billionaire Carrows family of California. Our affiliate in Las Vegas brings us this."

The screen cut to a female newscaster holding a microphone next to Dawna Hooks, who was wearing a t-shirt with the words, "Where's David?" above a custom, screen printed image of one of David's oil-on-canvas portraits of Petunia.

"Hello, I'm here with Dawna Hooks, girlfriend of David Cordoza, the missing California artist and father of Petunia Carrows. Dawna, tell us what you know about David's disappearance. When was the last time you saw him?"

Dawna bit her bottom lip. "It's been nearly a week now. David just wouldn't disappear like this, I'm mean, not willingly. I just hope the police are taking his disappearance as seriously as you are." Dawna bowed her head and ran a hand under her nose.

"David Cordoza is the father of Petunia Carrows, is that correct?"

Dawna sniffed and nodded. She held up a copy of the book. "Yes. He's in a custody dispute right now for his daughter and he published this book about his only daughter Petunia to let her know about the struggles he was having being granted access to see her."

"What do you know about the relationship between the Carrows family and David Cordoza?"

"Well, everything! David is an amazingly gifted, talented artist and about nine years ago he traveled to Brazil to pursue his art. But while he was there, completely unbeknownst to him, his college girlfriend at the time, Charlotte Carrows, had their love child. She never even told him about it! But now that he knows, he's fighting to even see Petunia. He's struggling, see, with the family, and oh my God, it absolutely couldn't be a coincidence that as soon as he published this book—he disappeared! That's like foul play or something, right?"

Dawna held the book up to the camera with tears in her eyes and continued. "Go to David's website, *David Cordoza, Artisan.* There's information about a reward for tips leading to his whereabouts. I beg you to help me find him!"

Dawna shook her head and emphatically continued, "He's so talented! His series of portraits he painted of his only child is a *stunning* tribute. His artwork is available on postcards and t-shirts.... Please help me get the word out. Not only to find him, but to help the cause of so many fathers in custody disputes who are being simply overwhelmed by the mother's rights. Add that to the billions of dollars the Carrows family has to hide behind, it's just no wonder David had to go to these lengths for help—but now he's missing! It can't be a coincidence, Tiffany, it just can't!"

Conscientious news reporter, Tiffany Gleason shook her head and turned to the camera. "So where is David Cordoza? The police are investigating. We have it from confirmed sources that the Carrows family has been brought directly into the investigation and are now being questioned by the LAPD."

The screen cut back to the studio where the anchor spoke over famous photographs of the family and images of David's oil-painted 'Petunia-Series'. "Thank you, Tiffany. It certainly is a mystery. We'll keep you posted of any new developments."

The link stopped. Charles stared at the screen, his mouth hanging open. He picked up his phone to call his mom and dad. This madness had to stop.

Sometime later, David sat next to Dawna in her living room, cordially explaining his disappearance to a plain clothed detective from the Las Vegas police department.

"So you were in Rosarito, Mexico. This entire time." The detective moved his tongue inside his mouth to his cheek and squinted with disbelief.

David wrung his hands. "I had no idea, Detective, that my short retreat would create such distress." He reached over and picked up Dawna's hand. "I'll admit, not telling Dawna was thoughtless. I guess I underestimated her concern."

"Uh huh. And your father? You didn't think to notify him?"

"I'm afraid we don't have the type of relationship where we check in on one another regularly."

"Right." The detective made more notes. "So if I were to call, this friend..." the detective flipped back a page, "...a

Mr. Tadeas Palma in São Paulo, he'd verify that you called him, to ask for the use of his beach house in Rosarito, and he gave it to you."

David gently stroked the back of Dawna's hand. "It was entirely spontaneous on my part. I was so badly shaken after that first television interview, and I've been under such stress with the custody dispute and the concern over my relationship with my young daughter, I needed some time alone to reflect. I was simply overwhelmed."

The detective glanced at his partner who said, "How did you provide for yourself?"

David scratched his head and smiled. "I had quite a bit of cash, but my expenses were limited. Gas, food—really, I lived very simply while I worked to overcome what I believed was the onset of a mild depression. I'm an artist you see. Contemplative, sometimes intense, and my work requires a certain amount of isolation." He turned to Dawna and gave her a small shrug. "I'm so sorry I created this stress for you, darling. I never meant to cause you this type of pain. I guess we have a lot to talk about." He gave her a short nod and then sheepishly hung his head.

The detective barked. "You turned off your phone. You never reached out to anyone during your entire stay in Mexico?"

David shook his head. "I'm afraid not. It wasn't until I got across the border that I even bothered to turn it on, and then, of course, it had no charge. It was only a six-hour drive home. I didn't realize what had happened until I arrived today."

"And you heard nothing about the investigation into your disappearance through any media channel?"

"No. The small beach house had no television, no internet. Well, in fairness, there was a small set, but it had limited transmission. My friend had a radio which I listened to occasionally, music channels, that sort of thing."

The interview wound to a close. The police seemed skeptical, but they eventually retreated. David apologized all the way to the door.

He closed it and pressing his back to it, smiled. He ape-walked over to Dawna and picked up her hands, gleeful, and whispered, "Darling, you were wonderful." He gave her a short hug and pulled back. "Time for you to contact your newfound relationships in the press and let them in on the good news. I'm back! Alive and well!"

"And very tan," Dawna scowled, pulling away. "That was scary as hell. I don't like dealing with the cops."

"They seemed satisfied. Tadeas will vouch for me. We had no plot, he knows nothing."

David walked over and sat in front of her computer laptop. "Come on, now. I can't wait to see how many hits the website got while I was gone. Sales, queries, video of your clips. I've got to get Logan on the phone and tell him I'm back. We'll get miles of press over this."

David threw his arms in the air and grinned. "I'm goddamn brilliant!"

Chapter 19

Cheryl Davis walked down a hallway in the back of Lacey's and yelled over her shoulder. "Leave the inventory sheets on my desk." She put her head down and concentrated on her phone to retrieve a message.

She never enjoyed issuing tedious instructions to one of her virtually absentee partners. She stopped in the hall, startled, as she ran head-long into Joey.

"Oh, sorry." She flattened herself to the wall to let him pass.

"Cheryl." He put a hand out and grabbed her arm. "Stop. Can't we talk?"

She pulled her arm back casually and shrugged. "Nothing to talk about."

"You won't give me another chance?"

She thought back on their disastrous first and only date. "One and done. Sorry, babe."

She saw a fleeting moment of frustration pass his face as she turned and continued walking toward the bar. What the hell. This was why she shouldn't ever mingle business with pleasure.

She went behind the long marble bar, the place not yet open, and began inventory on the booze delivery from Joey. Disastrous may be over-stating the event, after all, no one had died. But her gut still clenched when she thought about it.

Joey had worn jeans and a sports coat that night. He'd looked really good. His company Mercedes was all a-gleaming too, but he'd surprised her as they headed out from her West Hollywood apartment when he announced they were going to stop by a friend's house in Toluca Lake for a party.

"What kind of party?"

"My friends are having a few people over. He and his wife. I just thought we'd stop in, socialize, have a drink or two before we head out for dinner."

He'd given her thigh a squeeze and turned up the charm. Whatever. She was game.

The house was nice with a Spanish influence, surrounded by palm trees. A cute street with neat homes, they'd parked a few doors down. Joey had grabbed an ever-present bottle of Bacardi out of the trunk and they'd gone up to the home. Her black stilettos clicked on the entry tile as they heard laughter coming from the kitchen.

Joey called out and she was surprised as a guy she recognized from the club walked toward them.

"Hey, hey, Joey!" the guy named Tripp embraced his friend.

"Hey," Joey handed over the booze and she cringed as

he used her real name in the introduction, something she never shared with her customers. Especially the assholes. "This is Cheryl Davis. My good friend, Tripp Spencer."

Cheryl stood tall and extended her hand. She recoiled at its sticky wetness.

"Hey, Cheryl. Thanks for coming," Tripp smiled broadly and slapped Joey's back. "Let me introduce you guys to the gang."

Cheryl walked into the upscale kitchen and what was obviously a convention of waspy young women. At least two of them were pregnant, munching on a spread of appetizers on the center island. Tripp grabbed Joey and left the room as the women spoke with her briefly about how she knew Joey. The hostess, particularly, seemed blinky and insincere as she spoke about Joey's single status.

"He's such a catch. Where did you meet him?" She gushed.

All eyes in the room on her, she said, "At the club, where I work."

Blinky's mouth turned into a small o. "Where is that?"

"West Hollywood. He's the Bacardi rep. But I s'pose you know that." Cheryl smiled and wanted to change the subject.

Blinky said, "Is tonight your first date? I heard you're going to club."

She'd heard? Joey had told everyone their plans except for her?

"What club is that? Joey hasn't mentioned it."

Blinky laughed. "He's a scamp. He's taking you to the Lakeside Golf Clubhouse. It's where we met." She gestured around the group, most of them in some form of pastel with pearls. "We're all members."

Cheryl gave her a simpering smile. He was taking her to a country club? In her black Mia Wallace wig? Yeah it was a damn good wig, but still, she thought he'd said they were going to have fun, not purse their lips to the cheeks of the gentry.

Cheryl put her thumb in the direction where Joey went. She could hear the men's laughter from the kitchen. "I should go see him."

"What's the name of your club? Where do you work?" Blinky cocked her head.

Shit. Her raunchy, nasty husband sure knew. "Lacey's. Ask Tripp. He's a regular." Cheryl left the room before they could ask anything more.

She walked through the great room and outside into an outdoor deck under a pavilion. The tropical ceiling fan turned, the men gathered and turned almost as one as she made her entrance. She stared past them to the artificial turf in the backyard and a tacky cherub waterfall situated among the landscaping.

Beer in hand, Joey came to her side. "Ready to go?" she whispered.

His eyes grew wide. "Really? We just got here."

Nasty Tripp smiled at her from across the room, his tongue minutely darted in and out.

She gave him a wink and grabbed Joey's arm. "Yup.

I'm walking. Uber can be here in minutes. You coming?"

She walked through the house and out the front door. Joey followed. Dinner at the country club went no better. No one died, but then again, maybe inside, she had, just a little bit.

Chapter 20

Charlotte walked along the midtown Manhattan street, her head down in contemplation. She felt overwhelmed by the heavy decisions that lay in front of her. As much as her supportive family wanted to counsel and help, ultimately, she felt that the buck stopped with her. Whatever long term path they chose to deal with David, she had the power to say no. A yes vote was even more daunting.

She pulled her coat tightly around her as she moved amongst the crowd, most of them with heads down resisting the slightly blustery wind that blew through the streets. Tuning out the sounds from a nearby construction site, she'd needed a walk, but she was irritated by the thought that she might be scolded for being alone. The Carrowses were changing their modus operendi, body guards were being hired for her and her family. While she was comforted by the thought of her children being protected, the loss of her personal privacy was upsetting.

That morning, on a whim, she'd asked her car service to drop her several blocks from the offices of Macchi & Macchi. She was meeting Alex for a conference at his office where they could be assured complete privacy while they spoke with Charles.

She stopped in front of the building and looked up. What had started as a small security company headquartered in a renovated Brooklyn delicatessen, Macchi Security had grown. Begun as a family owned business, Anthony Senior, the Macchi founder and patriarch, changed the name, after his son, Michael, joined him. After Anthony passed and Alex came on board, Macchi & Macchi moved their headquarters to this larger space in Manhattan.

Charlotte walked into the lobby, refreshed from the brisk walk. She rode the elevator to the sixth floor and walked to Suite 600. She opened the door to a modest, enclosed front entry with a small, unmanned reception area with cameras. The inner sanctum was tightly secured, and employees were alerted when a visitor arrived. The door opened, and Alex's smiling face greeted her.

"Hey, come in." He held the door open for her. She smiled and put a hand on his back as she followed him inside. A large friendly open plan encompassed the converted commercial loft space. The central area held several seating areas, a kitchen, and dining table. High ceilings and windows surrounded the bright room, but the offices and conference rooms were behind closed doors.

It was early afternoon. London, being five hours ahead, they wanted to speak with Charles while he was fresh.

The late-night conversations they'd had together after Alex returned home from work in the evening weren't as productive as they would be during the day. They would need the assured privacy and all their faculties for the heavy conversation today.

Most of the employees were either in the field or in their office, but Charlotte waved to a familiar face on a sofa as she followed Alex as he stopped to key in a code next to a closed door. Each hidden space served a purpose, but clients were generally wooed in this particular conference room with an impressive array of presentation electronics and advanced technology. Modern, it also boasted a few nods of traditional furnishings as well as comfortable leather chairs and a Persian rug. Alex flipped on soft lights, illuminated behind partitions near the floorboards and the ceiling. As the door closed, the hushed privacy, with the reinforced and sound proof walls, enhanced the somber mood.

Charlotte removed her jacket and threw it on an empty chair as Alex said, "I'll put him on the big screen." She watched while he worked with the technology and took a seat at the table. A large video screen appeared on a wall and not long after, her brother's face came up large on the screen.

Charles was sitting in his hotel suite, alone. Pleasantries aside, they got down to business.

"It's a goddamned shit show and should be obvious to anyone with a pulse that he was attempting to get some free press coverage for the book," said Charles.

"Have you been to his website, Charles? Have mom and dad?" Charlotte asked.

"Yes, we've all looked at it. The fact that he's using Petunia's face in his artwork is unbelievable. He didn't pull all that work together over the last couple of months either. He must have been painting her for quite some time before he made his move to see her at the casino."

"His character, or lack of character is getting worse. I have no idea who he is and what he's capable of doing next." Charlotte shook her head.

Charles raised his brow and threw up a hand. "David is a dangerous guy. We all agree. The problem is we don't know what this could escalate to if we make him broke. The publisher of the book, Ares Publications has not accepted our offer to purchase the rights. But the book aside, it's David that's the problem. There is obviously nothing he won't do to get what he wants. He's out there right now, scheming, plotting—he wants to hurt us. We need to stop him before he goes any further."

Charlotte glanced at Alex who nodded and said. "I agree. Henry called last night, he basically said, whatever it takes."

Charles said, "So a permanent solution."

Alex nodded. "Yes."

Charlotte closed her eyes and didn't speak. Finally, Charles prompted her. "Charlotte?"

She swallowed hard and murmured, "Yes."

Alex took in a large breath and said, "Then it's back to the press release. Now that David is no longer a missing person, we need to go back to our original version. We put it out there tomorrow. Agreed?"

"Agreed," said Charlotte and Charles in unison.

Alex continued, "Then the next step is a plan to lure David into a trap and close the lid."

Charles said, "Exactly. Angelica and I played out a scenario last night." Charles smirked. "Remind me not to ever get on her bad side. The timeline's pretty loose. We can't accomplish it overnight, and we'll need to recruit some talent, but I think it has potential. If we're successful, it should put David out of our lives for the next ten to twenty years."

Charlotte furrowed her brow and looked at the delighted smile plastered across her brother's face on the big screen. "Twenty years?"

"Charlotte. Some animals—think wild predators, require an indecent training period along with punishment to tame. David does not learn well. He raised the bar and tried to break out, now we'll lower it. Or slam it closed as the case may be." Charles rubbed his hands together. "Angelica and I have a flight to the States tomorrow. Specifically, to New Orleans. Let me tell you the plan."

For Immediate Release

Contact: Alana Whittaker
Address: 4950 Los Robles, Los Angeles, CA 90274
Phone: (323) 521-9900
Email: alana.whittaker@hoststrategiccommunications.com

Headline: A statement from the Carrows family

It is with great sadness that the Carrows family is forced into a public battle with the biological father of Petunia Carrows Macchi. Due to the age of the child, it would normally be unconscionable to share the private details of a nine-year old child with the press and public, but the Carrows family has been compelled to set the record straight regarding the allegations against them, lies, and omissions of facts that have been made by David Torres Cordoza.

The Carrows family has great regret in acknowledging and airing the crimes of the biological father of their beloved child and grandchild but felt that due to the increasing publicity, the continual extortion attempts from Mr. Torres Cordoza, and the disgraceful use of his child to further his career and his wallet, that the truth, although shameful, was their only recourse.

The family is asking for privacy as they deal with the emotional impact this has created for their only real person of concern, their much loved and innocent daughter and granddaughter, Petunia.

The relationship and timeline of events between Charlotte Carrows and David Torres Cordoza are outlined below.

The press release went on to outline a full timeline of the events.

Charles was right about it not being so easy. Although the press release was generally accepted to be the truth, it only increased the popularity of the story and further sale of the book. A Tsar's stolen ring, a Romanov story, the fabulously wealthy and glamorous Carrows, the escape to Brazil, the blackmail, was all too intriguing.

In addition, the publisher of the book, Ares Publications, took it to another level. David would author, and they would quickly publish a second book, countering the Carrows' press release...*The Ring of Betrayal.* It too would become a bestseller.

Chapter 21

Charles and Angelica stepped onto the tarmac of the charter jet terminal at the Louis Armstrong International Airport in New Orleans and crossed the runway to meet the waiting limousine sent to collect them from the Ritz Carlton Hotel.

They'd had a nice, albeit long, ten-hour flight across the Atlantic. Arriving in New Orleans at eleven a.m. local time, it was only five p.m. in London. With the nap they took on the plane, both felt refreshed and ready for the potentially long day and evening ahead.

Charles snuggled next to Angelica in the back of the limo, his hands roaming. The partition up, they kissed deeply and then he whispered, "Maybe we can reschedule Marcel. How about we take the day off and roll around between the sheets of the big, soft bed waiting for us instead."

Angelica smiled and pushed him back. "Come on. You said we don't have much time, we have to get back.

Twenty-four hours, a quick turnaround, remember?"

Charles nestled his face in her neck, kissing it tenderly. "We could stretch that. Forty-eight, fifty-six..." he said between kisses.

She put her arms around his neck and turned her face toward his. They kissed, until Charles pulled away and sat back, lying his head back on the soft leather and sighed. "Alright then, a new and improved plan. We'll extend the trip, but you're right, Marcel is expecting us today. I told him I'd text him when we landed. You and I get to spend the day wooing one of the coolest guys I know."

Angelica lay her head on his shoulder and said, "That's okay. I'm looking forward to meeting this man you speak so highly of. And I've only been to New Orleans once when I was much younger. I can't wait to see more of the city."

A side of Charles' mouth turned up. "I'm sure Marcel will show us a good time. You'll like him."

Charles thought back on his friend, Marcel Broussard. Nearly the same age as he, their backgrounds couldn't be more different. Marcel's uncle was a master gardener and the primary caretaker of Whispering Cliffs. Marcel was his de facto ward.

Born in New Orleans to mixed-race parents, Marcel never knew his father. His mother, at the time of his birth, was not equipped for the job of motherhood. And thus, Marcel was given to his uncle to be raised in Los Angeles. By the time Marcel was fifteen, he was a familiar soul on the property. Henry, Julia and the children, especially Charles, had formed a lasting friendship with him.

Charles and Angelica looked out the window at the passing scenery, the freeways packed, the energy of New Orleans palpable. "My dad got him his first job at an art gallery in San Francisco." Charles looked at Angelica. "He loved it there, but his real dream was to someday have his own, back in what he always considered his home town. He has some extended family in New Orleans, I think he's very happy living back here."

"And now that dream is realized, he owns a studio, Broussard's, in the French Quarter," said Angelica. "Did you or your family have anything to do with that?"

Charles picked up her hand and kissed it. "Yes, indeed we did, my love. My good friend, Marcel, has been one of our special helpers for many, many years. He may enjoy the game even more than I do."

Angelica smiled. "Charles. What exactly has he done for you?"

He kissed her. "Maybe I'll tell you about it this weekend while we indulge in room service."

––––––––––––––

Charles stood on the terrace of his suite and gazed out over the French Quarter and the Mississippi River. Lake Pontchartrain was out there, feeding itself from the Atlantic. The April day was temperate, not yet impossibly hot and humid. The Ritz Carlton, perched right on the edge of the French Quarter, was charming and Charles appreciated its world class sophistication.

He moved inside the suite into the living room, leaving

the doors to the large terrace open, the breeze coming inside and warming it. As a new hotel owner himself, he scanned the elegant interior with a critical eye, marveling at the exquisite taste of the room design on which the Ritz had built their reputation.

He looked at his phone as a text came in. "He's on his way up," he called loudly as he walked past the billiards table and dining room and into the master bedroom. Both he and Angelica had taken time to freshen up and change. She appeared now from the bathroom, tying a side bow on a simple wide-legged jumpsuit.

"How do I look?" she said as she finished and slid her hand into her top to adjust her ample breasts under the v-cut bodice.

Charles smiled. He didn't know where to look first. Her beauty nearly always took his breath away. Her long dark hair curled naturally in the humidity and he loved it when she wore it down.

She put her hands in the side pockets of the black pant suit, smiled, and stuck out a leg. "The wedge on these espadrilles isn't obnoxious. I thought they'd do for walking around the city and dinner. We're not doing anything too fancy tonight, are we?"

He sat on the side of the bed and put his hand on one of the posts of the king-sized canopied bed. "No. You look perfect. Come here."

"No. I'm not going anywhere near you." She laughed as she bent to pick up a bag and hurried past him out of the room. "Come on, Charles. He's on his way up."

Charles followed happily, looking forward to seeing his old friend, as well as spending time with his beautiful girl. He truly loved his life, and he could no longer imagine it without Angelica.

She was walking through the terrace doors as the bell rang. Charles turned to open the door and was stunned, as usual, when he laid eyes on his friend. Marcel filled the entry, not only with his enormous height and girth, but with his energy. Holding a small dog in one arm, he threw his free one around Charles as he yelled his name.

"Marcel," Charles said as he pulled back and looked at the dog. "Who is this?"

Marcel had a loud, masculine, baritone voice, but an extremely soft underbelly. He scratched the top of the mongrel's fluffy head and cooed. "This is my baby, Steve."

"Steve?" Charles laughed as he gestured them inside and shut the door.

"My little half breed…just like me." He smiled and stopped, taking a moment to lift one of Steve's tiny paws and wave it at Charles. "Part Chihuahua and part something else. I found him on Bourbon Street, of all places, hiding in a corner, collarless, and scared to death. He's a little shy, but once he gets to know you, he's friendly."

Marcel stopped as Angelica walked into the room from outside. "Hello! Angelica, nice to meet you," Marcel said as he walked toward her with his free arm extended.

"Nice to meet you too," Angelica smiled as they embraced. "What a cute little dog! May I hold him?"

"Yeeessssss." He said as he gently shifted the dog into her arms.

Angelica snuggled him close and kissed the top of his head. "He's so sweet!"

Marcel stepped back and placed an arm around Charles. "There now Charles, how's ya mama an' them?" He reached out a hand and squeezed the sides of Charles' face.

Charles slapped his hand away and laughed. "Just great. Come on," he gestured to the door. "Let's go outside. It's gorgeous out there."

"Yah, it certainly is," Marcel said, gesturing Angelica to go before him.

They assembled on the large terrace, the white granite columnated balcony lined with large planters filled with greenery and flowers. A potted tree stood shading one of the comfortable outdoor seating areas. Charles gestured to the water and coffee alongside a plate of fruit and cheese he'd had delivered to the room.

Marcel walked over to the balcony and looked down and out toward the Quarter. "Marvelous view. It's splendid up here. Angelica, Charles told me all about you, but he didn't mention if you'd been here before?"

Angelica sat near the coffee table, still holding the dog. "Once before, but I didn't really see the city. Not as an adult anyway."

"Ah, well, then we'll make a day of it." He sat in a large club chair and put out his arms toward Steve. "Come to mommy my little baby boy."

Angelica handed Steve back to Marcel and leaned

forward to pour some coffee. "Marcel, would you like a cup?"

"Ah, no. Thank you. Maybe something a little stronger? Charles, you're in New Orleans. Where's the booze. The wine?"

Charles put his hands up, poured a glass of water, and handed it to his friend. "I'm afraid this will have to do for now. Give us an hour to re-hydrate after our flight and catch our breath."

Marcel graciously accepted the water and took a large drink. "Water. Straight. Very exotic of you."

The old friends caught up on their lives, and Marcel learned more about Angelica. After they'd socialized for a bit Marcel pulled a leash out of his pocket and hooked it to Steve's collar. "I'm afraid he'll slip though the bars of the terrace. He's such a naughty boy. Charles, did you want to get some business out of the way, so we can get off this wretched, secluded balcony and see the sites, or did you want to wait until later?"

Charles grabbed a slice of apple and sat back. "No, let's talk now. We've got a job for you."

Marcel leaned over and grabbed a piece of cheese and gave it to Steve. "Yes? What kind of job?"

Charles said, "Let me explain something first. Angelica will be a part of this conversation. There is nothing you can say around me, that you can't say in front of her."

Marcel raised an eyebrow. "I see. And this *Carrows* business, is it something she has experienced before, or has only heard about?"

Angelica reached down and picked up Steve who had his tiny front paws on her chair staring at the piece of cheese she held in her hand. "May I?" she asked Marcel.

Marcel nodded his permission as she said, "I have first hand experience about the way the Carrows take care of their problems, Marcel. It's how Charles and I met. Well, actually, I met him first at a poker table. He lost a boatload of money after I bluffed him, but he was a gracious loser."

Marcel laughed. "Charles? A gracious loser? I suppose, but maybe only for someone as beautiful as you."

Charles leaned his elbows on his knees, his tone more serious and said, "I'm going to give you a long version of the back story first. It will explain why we've come to the decisions we have."

Charles recapped the David Torres Cordoza saga for Marcel, Angelica jumping in occasionally to speak about Charlotte and Petunia and the emotional toll this was taking on them. As he finished, Marcel said, "You have the moral high ground here, and as usual, you can count on my support. What is it you'd like for me to do with our nidorous mark?"

Charles crossed his legs. "You need to boost his ego. You need to become an avid fan, supporter, and mentor. I'd like you to woo him to your gallery where he will have his very first professional exhibition of his art."

Marcel made a face. "This art—I have a reputation to uphold Charles. It will be of Petunia's face?"

Charles pinched his lips together. "I'm afraid so. Most of what we've seen on his website has her image in place, one way or another. There are other pieces, but she is a main focus." Charles pulled up his phone and brought up the website. He handed it to Marcel who took some time and scrolled through the images.

"If I'm honest, I'd say he has some talent, Charles." He handed the phone back. "Sorry."

Charles nodded. "It's not relevant. What we want is for David to feel loved, secure, and in demand. We'll obviously secretly fund the damn show for you, and there will be a generous budget for advertising. We want it well attended. We want his already enormous ego to grow exponentially, and once his head is in the stratosphere, you will offer to manage him. For a fee, of course, but a doable one. Once you've established that relationship, a commission will be queried to you, at Broussard's, for David to paint a portrait. Our hope would be that David will jump at the offer. You will encourage him to do so."

Marcel nodded. "A portrait. Of whom?"

Charles picked up a grape and popped it into his mouth. "We haven't got that end completely worked out yet, but we will soon. Hopefully in the next few weeks."

"And after he paints this portrait, for this unknown person, what happens then?"

Charles smiled. "There will be another talented individual in place to bring it to the next level."

"The next level being?" Marcel asked.

"I've always thought deniability was an important word, don't you, Marcel?"

Marcel smirked. "Yes, it is. But before I agree to my

bit, remind me what's in this for me. Other than of course, my willingness to go to the ends of the world for you, and you for me."

Charles rubbed his hands together and grinned. "I'm sure you'll come up with something fair."

Marcel stood up. "As a matter of fact, I have some spectacular work that is waiting at Broussard's for the perfect buyer. My clients and I would be so appreciative if you and Angelica would spend some time with me this afternoon showing you our inventory. I'm certain that you'll find a few of the pieces priceless. Perhaps even for your hotels?"

Charles and Angelica stood as Steve left Angelica's lap and jumped to the ground. He promptly positioned himself back in front of her and barked at her to pick him up. She lifted him into her arms and kissed him, cooing. "How about Steve? I don't suppose you'd be willing to let go of him?"

"Ah, no, *cher*. Regretfully there is only one Steve. One of a kind. Just like you, my beautiful girl." Marcel lifted an eyebrow at Charles and nodded. "Priceless."

Charles smiled. He wholeheartedly agreed.

Chapter 22

Primarily due to Julia's concern about the risk of malaria and Henry's lack of spleen, the family rejected an African safari for their family vacation. Instead, they took an entirely different route and booked a trip to Zermatt, Switzerland. The thought of traveling abroad and escaping the media attention in the States would be a welcome break for all of them.

The gang from New York was bigger for the getaway. Charlotte, Alex, Petunia, Lily, Renzo Castogiovanni, and Alex's youngest brother, Nick Macchi accompanied Henry and Julia on their private plane. They flew direct from New York to Sion, Switzerland—the nearest airport to the skiing village, Zermatt.

At the Sion airport, Henry and Julia transferred to a helicopter that delivered them to a private luxury five-star chalet roughly twenty minutes later, while the rest of the party boarded a train for the two-hour ride across the Swiss countryside and into the Swiss Alps to meet waiting horse-drawn sleighs at the station. Staff took care of all the luggage, offered them hot chocolate, and tucked the traveling party into the warm furs of the sleigh. Like a dream, the horses jingled as the sleighs drew up a hill to one of the most beautiful chalets in the country, with views overlooking the village of 5,800 at the foot of the iconic Matterhorn Mountain. Ingeniously tucked into the mountainside, the modern architecture was designed to amplify the opportunities for windows, allowing the guests to enjoy the vistas from many rooms.

Charles, Angelica, Carey, and Harley had arrived the day before and welcomed the last of their arriving family to the vacation retreat. The staff of the chalet was on duty twenty-four hours a day and gave the family the grand tour, making them comfortable for a relaxing evening after a long day of travel.

"We have a special surprise for Mademoiselle Lily," the French butler, Jean Luc, said that evening after dinner. Previously informed about Lily turning one year old their day of arrival, he dimmed the lights and the staff serenaded Lily while presenting her with her first birthday cake. It was a wonderful beginning to a week that would be filled with hiking, skating, sledding, dining, shopping, and of course, skiing. Spa services and sumptuous meals were only a moment away, and the family thoroughly enjoyed the closeness and privacy afforded them in their exquisite private chalet nestled in the mountains.

One evening, Charles and Angelica, Carey and Harley,

and Charlotte and Alex had a quiet dinner apart from the rest of the family in the village.

"It's time to head back." Charlotte stretched slightly after a short dinner. "I'm so tired after all that ice skating." She yawned. "God, the bruises! I can't wait to get back and into the hot tub. Are you all ready to go?"

"I think I'd like to stay and have dessert," Charles said, questioning Angelica with a look and raised brow.

"Sure," Angelica smiled. "That sounds great."

"Well I'm beat, too," Carey said as she stood and threw her napkin on the table. "Let's leave them and head back. We'll see you guys later." She and the rest of the group didn't linger.

Charles grimaced as his sisters made faces at him when Angelica wasn't looking on their way out the door. With a slight, internal exasperation, he took a breath to regain his composure. Rubbing the back of his neck he said, "How about we finish up here and head down the street to that Italian bistro we saw yesterday. They had a balcony out back and a fire— we could try something over there?"

Angelica smiled and nodded. "I love exploring all the places they have tucked in little nooks and around every corner."

They paid the bill and gathered their coats and headed out smiling arm-in-arm into the brisk air and the charming village streets. Zermatt being car-free, they watched as several horse-drawn carriages went past.

"I'm having such a wonderful time," Angelica said, squeezing his arm. "I can't believe how beautiful it is here.

There are so many places we could have gone, and even though this is a world different than Africa, I can't imagine being anywhere else."

"I'm glad we're here too. And you're enjoying my family too." Charles gave her a glance. "I'm not making that up, am I? Are you okay spending this much time with all of us packed into the chalet?"

"No! I love it. I love spending time with all of them. I hardly ever see Charlotte and her family, and your mom and dad are so nice. They've all been wonderful. I feel very protective of them now."

Charles took her hand as they walked. "They can be a bit much. I know there's been a lot of public drama lately, and chances are, if you're going to be around our family, the tradeoff is having to deal with some of the unpleasant sides—the photographers, press, rumors, and haters. Not to mention the campaigns." He rolled his eyes in her direction. "It can be overwhelming sometimes."

Angelica looked at Charles and frowned, shaking her head. "It's not. I mean the hurtful stuff is awful, and I hate to see any of you being used, but I understand. I was a little surprised by the press at the airport when we got here. I didn't think there would be photographers at the Sion airport."

"They're opportunists. They hover around the private planes." Charles stopped at the entrance of the small bistro tucked into a corner street. Bella Sotta le Stelle, was guarded by a large man.

"Here we are. Buonasera," Charles said nodding to the man.

"Buonasera," the man said as he smiled and opened the door.

They entered and were the only customers in a room filled with candlelight. Angelica whispered, "Charles, my God, look at this place, it's all lit up but we're the only ones here? Are they about to close?"

"No, it's okay, they're open. Let's go through." Charles smiled as he took her hand and led her through the room and out the back to a patio filled with more candlelight and warmed by a fire overlooking the mountains.

Amazed, she looked around at the empty, beautiful patio as they sat at a table. A waiter came to take their order. "Let's order that dessert," said Charles. "Would you like some wine or brandy with it?"

"I'll try some brandy if that's what you're having."

Charles nodded and spoke with the waiter. "We'll have a couple of glasses of the Frapin Cuvée 1888, and the crème brulée."

They nestled into their coats and took in the breathtaking beauty of the night sky, the Swiss mountainside, and the soft, warm inviting lights twinkling from the village. The waiter returned with the rare cognac and a plate of cheese.

Charles lifted his glass to Angelica. As they sipped, they were immediately warmed by the sweet spices. "I can't believe we're the only ones here," Angelica marveled.

Charles cleared his throat and rubbed a sweaty palm on his pants. "Yes. They were very gracious to allow us to have a private evening here. I arranged it because there's something special that I'd like to speak with you about."

Angelica tilted her head and blinked. Charles leaned across the table and took her hands. "Angelica, you've become the most important person in my life and the more I get to know you..." He shook his head and began again. "Every day I fall more in love with you. I didn't even know that I could love someone this much."

He got up and bumped into his chair almost toppling it before he dropped to one knee. Angelica's hand flew to her mouth, and tears filled her eyes. He smiled nervously at her while fumbling around in his jacket. "I know I'm older than you, and I know I come from a complicated family, but I'm hoping, if you feel the same way about me....?" He trailed off, flustered, as he finally looked down and using both hands, tugged, releasing a velvet box.

Angelica began to bounce and smile as tears escaped her eyes and streamed down her face. "Charles."

He put his head down briefly then gazed back up into her adoring eyes, thankfully filled with encouragement. "Angelica Renner, I have spoken with your father, and he has given me permission to ask for your hand. Will you marry me?" He opened the box.

Nestled in a bed of satin sat an oval-cut three carat blue diamond, surrounded by brilliant-cut diamonds of pink tine, between pear-shaped diamond shoulders. Stunning and one of a kind, Charles had purchased it at an auction in Hong Kong for roughly two million dollars. He'd arranged for an emissary of the auction house to deliver it to him in person earlier that day in the village. He was so relieved once he had it in his hand, but once he did, he'd carried around with him all day anxiously waiting for this private moment.

Angelica jumped out of her seat and threw herself down into his waiting arms on the cold stone patio of the bistro. Holding one another on their knees, she kissed him and said, "Charles, I love you so much. Yes, I'll marry you. Oh my God, of course I'll marry you!"

They rocked in one another's arms, then separated, sitting back on their heels as Charles, happier than he had ever been in his life, looked into the brown eyes of his beloved girl and slid the ring onto her finger.

"Such a relief. I wasn't sure what you were going to say," he teased.

"My God, it's got to be the most beautiful ring in the world. I've never seen anything like it," she said, staring at her hand.

Charles cupped his hands on her face and said, "I've never seen anything as beautiful in my life either, Angelica, and I'm not talking about the ring."

They kissed, jubilant, until they stopped to rest their foreheads together and gaze into one another's eyes. Their breath fogging, and co-mingling in the cold, he kissed her cold nose and smiled. Believing with all of his heart that their commitment to one another was mutually real and deep, he grabbed her to him and held her tightly.

"I'll love you forever, Charles Carrows," she whispered. He could feel her hot tears against his face. He glanced over to the windows of the restaurant and spied a small group of waitstaff watching. Angelica wasn't the only one crying.

Chapter 23

The next morning before breakfast, Julia felt like a small child waiting for a Christmas celebration to begin. Everyone but Angelica and Petunia had known that Charles was going to propose the evening before, but the family wanted to give them privacy when they returned to the chalet. They intentionally stayed out of sight when the couple arrived home, but now, she was more than ready to pounce.

Julia took a sip of coffee and glanced at Henry who was playing with Lily's toes, as Charlotte held her in her lap near him. Both children were early risers, and Petunia had gone into the kitchen to regale Jean Luc about her adventures on the ski slopes and check on breakfast. With Petunia and Lily rising early, Charlotte and Julia along with the Alex and Henry now waited.

Julia anxiously glanced down the hall, hoping to spy Charles and Angelica emerge from their room. "You don't think there's any chance she would say no, do you?" she asked, tapping her cup.

Charlotte laughed as she held baby Lily up in the air and said, "No. Not a chance, Mom. She's in love with him just as much as he is with her. They're a perfect match, really. I was just dying last night to get the dinner over with and get out of there. Carey and I kept looking at the time and rolling our eyes at Charles, and it was making him crazy. God it was great. He was so nervous."

"Well, I hope you're right. She fits in perfectly with the rest of us. I don't know that I've met many people who are so genuinely themselves and not swept away with the money and lifestyle we lead. It could turn someone into something they didn't know they could become. I've seen it with some of my friend's children after they get married. But then look at you and Alex! You couldn't be less affected by the whole thing, could you? And of course, let's never forget that I knew you were right for Charlotte from the moment we met."

Alex laughed. "Of course. Our entire project was only a ruse to get your lovely daughter and me together. I thank you again, Julia," he said, taking Lily from Charlotte.

Carey and Harley entered the room and Julia made a shooing motion. "Carey, go wake them up. Where's Nick and Renzo? They should be here for this too."

"Mom, I just texted them," said Charlotte. "They're coming. God, poor Angelica, she's going to be mobbed when she gets out here."

"Just as long as she said yes. How do we even know for certain?" Julia said taking another sip of her coffee.

"Mommy," Carey said, flopping down on a nearby sofa.

"She said yes. Don't worry about it. She loves him! They're crazy in love with each other, you can see it."

Just then, Charles and Angelica—still wearing comfy clothes and smiles—came into the dining room, and Charles said, "You're right, Carey, we are crazy in love with each other. Would you agree with that Angelica Renner?"

All eyes were on Angelica as she began to joyfully jump up and down and then ran into Julia's arms. "Oh my God, Julia, I'm so happy!" She let go of Julia and launched herself on Henry. "Mr. Carrows!"

Everyone began clapping as an excited Petunia ran into the room and they shared the announcement. One by one they shook hands, hugged congratulations, and stared with wonder at Angelica's engagement ring. Julia had given Jean Luc instructions to bring champagne immediately at her signal, and it was now being served to everyone, including Petunia who had a glass filled with a small amount.

Henry took his glass, and after everyone was served, pronounced a toast. "Charles, Angelica, we couldn't be happier for the two of you. Your love for one another is a precious thing, and Angelica, we are all delighted that you will become a permanent part of our family. Charles, today, I couldn't be more proud of you for having chosen such a wonderful young woman. I know you will have many happy years together, and we should thank the Gods today that you found one another. We love you both."

The Carrows family had grown by one, and they celebrated.

Over the next several days in Zermatt, the family unwound from the strain they had been under back in the real world, and from the pressure of the scandal David had caused. Now that they'd spent some time reconnecting and recharging, they were finally ready to discuss the plan to once again extradite David from their lives. It was difficult to be reminded of such a heavy topic when they were surrounded with such beauty and happiness, but it needed to be done, and they were ready to do it.

The after breakfast planning party of Henry and Julia, Charles and Angelica, Charlotte and Alex, and Carey assembled in the large, open space of the living room where the windows looked out at the preposterous grandiosity of the Matterhorn. Julia had requested the house to be empty of staff so they could have the privacy they needed for a family discussion. Petunia and Lily also left with Harley, Renzo, and Nick to go into town to shop.

Charles sat on a sofa next to Angelica. He crossed his legs and sat back, ready to address the group. "Let's get everyone up to speed. Mom, Dad, Carey, this first part is for you. We all agreed; it's time for a long term solution. With that in mind, Angelica and I came up with a plan, and we ran it past Charlotte and Alex."

He stopped to look in his sister's direction. "They agreed, and we've set it in motion. As you know, a couple of weeks ago Angelica and I went to New Orleans to meet with Marcel."

"Oh, Marcel," Julia threw up her hands. "Angelica, what did you think of him?"

Angelica smiled and reached over and put a hand on Charles' arm. "A gregarious bear of man. We had so much fun together. He has the cutest little dog named Steve, I wish we could have taken him home. His gallery is beautiful, although we visited after closing hours, so no one saw us in there. His home, that he purchased after Katrina, he's working so hard on it, it's going to be gorgeous, too. 'N'awlins' was amazing. We saw a wild parade and crawfish boil, but there was no way I was going to eat crawfish. People were ripping apart these horrible insects and sucking on the heads, it was gross. We didn't have time to do a riverboat cruise, but they play this game called bourre, like poker, it's crazy competitive. I've got to learn it. So much history. I wanted to do a voodoo and vampire tour, but Marcel said it was corny." She rolled her eyes and swayed. "The food was hea-ven-ly. Oh my God. The beignets. We didn't meet Marcel's boyfriend, but he said he wasn't really that serious, but maybe another time. We talked about him attending the London opening, but of course, our relationship has to be kept quiet. It's so sad, really. You know he smells so good too. His shampoo—"

Charles placed a hand on her knee. "I'm sorry to interrupt, but we should get back to the topic at hand."

"Charles," Julia scolded, "she's just being enthusiastic. I'm glad you had a nice time. Marcel is very special to us too."

Charles patted Angelica's knee, "I'm just worried about

the time. Petunia and everyone will be back soon."

Henry cleared his throat. "Has Petunia seen the second book?" He looked at Charlotte, curled in an armchair.

She tugged at the white turtleneck under her chin. "She has. Some kid brought it to school. The teacher took it away, but of course, everyone knew what it was about, and she was embarrassed. David's probably made it impossible now for her to even have a chance at a normal childhood."

Henry shook his head and turned to Charles. "What's Marcel's part in this?"

Charles went into detail about Marcel laying the groundwork for David to eventually accept a commissioned work. "He's already contacted David. He's working his end and knows exactly what to do. He'll get David to New Orleans for a show by next month."

Charles got up and walked over to a window to keep the group's attention. "The next part is twofold. We need to recruit talent. I've got an idea for the closer."

"Cheryl Davis," Angelica interrupted. "Remember her? She and I worked together on the Quentin thing."

Heads nodded as Charles continued. "She'll play a vital role which I'll get to in a moment. But we'll also need a stronghold, and a party who would be interested in commissioning a portrait. Mom, Dad, this is where you come in."

"After our vacation here has ended, Angelica and I were planning to go directly to London to check on the progress of Carrows London and to meet with a realtor to do a bit of house shopping. Alex, Charlotte, the kids, and Renzo were going to join us, and Nick was going to get started as the point person for the London office, representing Maachi & Maachi for the security aspects of the casino.

"I know you were planning to spend some time with Charlotte and the girls in London, but instead, we need to secure the cooperation of your old friends, the Linningtons. You need to go to Yorkshire and visit with the earl and countess of Hambley."

"Jane and Barford?" Julia said.

Charles nodded. "Yes. In getting ready to launch the London casino, Dad and I have spent some time thinking about our connections in Europe. In regard to the David campaign, Alex, Charlotte, and I reviewed it, and they stood out as an option–assuming they are recruitable."

Charles took a seat on the edge of Charlotte's large chair. "Alex and I did some detective work and discovered that the earl and countess of Hambley have been auctioning their art and heirlooms in order to maintain their country estate in Yorkshire. The point is, Dad, I believe they would be happy if you and Mom rang them up and asked for a visit. Then, when you're with them, you can see if they would be interested in a mutually beneficial partnership."

Henry put out his bottom lip and rolled his head from side to side. "Your mother and Jane Linnington, the countess, go way back," Henry said thinking aloud. "She's originally an American and was a friend of your mother's when she lived in Europe."

Julia, distracted, played with her earrings. "Yes, Jane

and I were flat mates in London while I was there with my dance company. She was wonderfully welcoming to me while she was studying abroad. I've kept up with Jane and her husband, the Earl, but mostly through correspondence. We haven't seen each other in years. Do you remember when they visited us at Whispering Cliffs, Charlotte? She and the Earl, Barford is his name, have a couple of children, a boy, Barford III, but he goes by Brandon, and a girl about your age, Ashley. Such nice people."

Alex leaned his elbows on his knees and clasped his hands. "Charles asked me to use my contacts with Sotheby's and they verified that the earl has been slowly liquidating the family assets with them. It's a terrible—but unfortunately, very common scenario that's happening to all the old family estates. Most of them are barely hanging on or having to sell their homes to people outside of the family. Apparently, there has been a Linnington in Hambley Hall since the 1700's, and I'm sure they would like to keep it that way. As Charles said, they might be interested if we make it worth their while."

"I'm not sure exactly what we'll be asking them to do, but I think the Linningtons would be interested," said Henry. He looked over at Julia who gave a short nod of agreement.

"Do you believe they can be trusted?" asked Charles.

Henry nodded. "Completely."

Charles asked, "And do you believe that they would be willing to help us?"

Julia responded, "Jane Linnington is one of the most

generous, sweet-hearted women I have ever met. Yes, I believe she would help us."

Alex said, "Alright then, can you see if they are available? And if they are, you need to tell them you'd like to visit with them on a private matter and be sure to tell them you'll be traveling incognito. They cannot let anyone know your real names while you're there."

Henry nodded. "Alright. Julia, darling, why don't you give Jane a call and ask them if they're up for a visit. Let them know we'll be in London next week. Where are we staying?" Henry looked at Charles.

"The Savoy," said Charles, getting up and resuming his place standing at the window. "Speaking of, Alex. I booked connecting rooms for Nick and Renzo like you asked. The two of them need to spend more time together."

Alex sat back and relaxed. "Nick and I have been scouting London on-line for a place for him to live and for the new Macchi & Macchi offices. We've got a lead on a space in an apartment building with offices on the first floor. It would be perfect for him and the company."

"How long are you going to be in London to get things running?" asked Charles.

"About two weeks. We've set up some interviews for staff, and already have some business referrals for some other clients."

Henry smiled. "Nick's a nice young man, fresh out of law school. Another Macchi going into the family business. We've really enjoyed spending more time with him. When will he hear about the results from the bar exam?"

"He's hoping to hear any day now," said Alex, smiling at Charlotte. "He won't be a practicing attorney for a while, but it will be nice if he can put the bar behind him and call himself a lawyer. Hopefully he'll enjoy living in London and won't be too homesick."

"It's a big step moving abroad," Julia said, moving to a nearby desk and retrieving her phone. "Charles, you and Angelica will be living there for some time, so at least he'll have you. Does he have any other friends in Europe?"

"He knows a couple of guys from the semester he went to school over here, but that's about it. Of course, he'll be hiring staff, so he'll have associates, and obviously the work will keep him very busy."

Julia smiled as she returned to her seat. "I see, well, perhaps the countess and I can do something about that too."

"Mom," Carey rolled her eyes. "Isn't it enough for you that Charles got engaged only last night? Really, how many weddings do we need in one year?"

"Speaking of, Carey," Julia looked at her wide-eyed. "I don't see you and Harley rushing out and making any plans. My goodness, the two of you have been hanging out for years now. I'm a little surprised you're still only dating since you seem to like each other so much."

Carey grabbed a pillow and buried her head, muffling a scream. "Mom. Give it a rest! We're not in any hurry. We just like what we have right now. Stop with all the pressure."

"No pressure from Harley, you mean," Julia nodded

deeply. "I, on the other hand, think it's time for the two of you to make some decisions. I mean, my goodness, do you even date other people? What are you waiting for?"

Carey sucked in oxygen through her nose and turned to her brother, "Charles, am I going to be needed for this campaign or not? *Harley and I* need to make some plans about where we go when we leave here."

"If the Linningtons are around and can meet with Mom and Dad, I think you can go back to Vegas, but stay loose. I'm going to need you over here to help me sell Carrows London. Did you want Angelica and I to look for a place for you to stay, or do you want to do that yourself?"

"I'm sure I can trust you guys to find me a temporary home until the Casino is finished. I'm not fussy, or particular, or anything." Carey yawned.

"Sure you're not," Charlotte said out of corner of her mouth.

"Hey, if you want my help, you should try to be nicer to me, Sister." Carey threw a pillow in her direction.

"I am nice to you. Mom, aren't I nice to her? God, I'm always polite with you!"

"Girls," said Julia. "Honestly, it never ends. Just stop it now. Charles, if this meeting is over, I'm leaving to call the countess and arrange for our visit. I expect we'll need to spend a few days with them?" She searched his eyes for confirmation. "Yes. And I'll be sure to tell them to keep our visit very quiet and that they shouldn't go to any fuss for our sake. Should I tell them it will just be myself and Henry?"

"Yes, just the two of you, and your checkbook," said

Charles as he walked back to sit next to Angelica.

"*My* checkbook," said Charlotte. "It'll be my pleasure to write a check to get David out of the way."

"No," said Henry. "I'm going to take care of all of it. If and when, someday, Petunia comes to you and asks if you paid anyone in a campaign against him, I want you to be able to look her in the eyes and say no. I don't want this to come between the two of you. If she ever asks, you can say that her grandfather may have had something to do with it. Are we clear?"

Charles gave his sister a supportive glance as he saw tears come to her eyes as she accepted the gift. He was proud of them both.

"You see, children," Julia said, placing a hand on Henry's and smiling. "Your father may have been slightly hard on you when you were growing up, but he will always protect you, and his grandchildren."

Charles tilted his head. "My reference to a checkbook might be too literal. There can't be any direct financial connection between the Linningtons and ourselves. We'll need to discuss that." He turned to Angelica and picked up her hand. He saw a small smile come to her lips.

"You know, guys," said Angelica. "There is an old saying which goes, "Children wish fathers looked but with their eyes; fathers that children with their judgment looked; and either may be wrong.""

Carey shook her head and said, "Geez, Angelica. I'm assuming that's more Shakespeare? What's up with that?"

Angelica shrugged and blushed. She glanced at Charles

slightly nervous and said, "We studied a lot of the classics in my school and they just stuck."

"They more than just stuck," Charles smiled. "She has an eidetic memory. It's one of the reasons she's so good at poker."

"Hmm, that's interesting," said Henry. "We might be able to use that."

Charles leaned over and kissed her cheek. "She's wonderful, isn't she?"

Angelica glowed under his adoration and whispered, "I love you, too." She squeezed his hand and said, "Now, if business is concluded, I think we should all go outside and enjoy the rest of this amazingly beautiful day."

"My, my," Henry said, rising. "Charles, I have a feeling that you'll be well taken care of over the next fifty years." He extended an arm in her direction. "Now, Angelica darling, let's take a walk while we discuss your feelings about children."

Julia beamed. "You two have a nice time. Angelica, you can fill in Henry, and Charles, you follow me. I'm curious how you envision the Linningtons' role. This Cheryl Davis, she's originally a stripper out of Los Angeles, isn't she? Yet you believe she will blend with the Linningtons and help us rid ourselves of David. I'm very interested in learning more about her. Poor Barford and Jane, I'm assuming this plan will mean that David will be traveling to England. Tsk. Tsk," she said as she left the room.

Charles got up to follow Julia and noticed Alex go to Charlotte and comfort her. His sister was too tender-hearted, and he knew that the plan was difficult for her. He respected that, but he also knew that David had it coming. It was the right thing to do. His feeling was supported later that afternoon when Petunia and her three escorts came home from the village announcing that several people had taken their photograph walking down the street. Petunia's face and story had followed them abroad. Their only hope was that it was American tourists who had recognized her and not yet the Europeans.

Some days later, however, a picture appeared in *Hello!* Magazine and it was confirmed, like a virus, that the Carrows name and the custody story had spread.

The caption read, "Poor little heiress to the Carrows dynasty, Petunia Carrows Macchi and her baby sister, Lily, surrounded by a team of protection while strolling through the elite skiing village in Zermatt." It was a striking picture of her innocent face startled by the cameras surrounded by Nick, with his sad Italian eyes holding Lily, Renzo looming huge and menacing, and the extraordinary looks of the pony-tailed Harley.

"I guess it was inevitable," said Charlotte with a heavy heart.

"But we can use it," said Charles.

Chapter 24

Ten members of the Carrows party flew in a private jet to London's Heathrow airport and were once again disconcerted to encounter photographers. Keeping their composure, they were nonetheless grateful for the help of Nick and Renzo as they pushed them through a gathering crowd. The family felt considerable relief once they arrived at the sumptuous Savoy Hotel. The top-hatted bellman escorted the party through the revolving doors and safely into the comfort which they sought. First night arrangements were made for Petunia and Lily to stay with Henry and Julia, under Renzo's security watch. The other five were headed out on the town to visit some of their London competition.

Charles' original inspiration for a chain of private luxury casinos and hotels was largely based on a visit to London nearly a decade before and having the rare privilege of visiting some the member's only clubs. When Charles returned to the United States, he applied for membership. The rigor and vetting process was extreme, and it had been rumored that the membership committee considered an application only if they would personally enjoy a drink with the applicant. Charles Carrows' membership was accepted.

While Carrows London did not yet have such an excess of obduracy regarding its own membership, Charles would consider all applications and financing partnerships carefully. Now that the clubs in Atlantic City and Las Vegas were wildly successful, it was time to begin to cull the herd, and nowhere would there be a better tone to set for that than in London. Membership would definitely be more exclusive.

Over a year ago, Charles had carefully selected and purchased a large, rather old, run down hotel in a good part of the city. He began demolition and the reconstruction of his dream club, which would hopefully one day host the elite of fashion, politics, art, and celebrity for evenings of fine dining, dancing, and gambling. Fashioned similarly to his other two casinos, the top six of the nine floors would be hotel suites, and the building would soon resemble an exquisite manor home more than a traditional hotel. The design and structure would carry the same ambiance of the other two properties, and guests would be greeted under an immense signature crystal chandelier. A marble staircase would ascend to the upper floors supported by elaborate wrought-iron balustrades.

The basement level of Carrows London would be the home to a nightlife club luxe with brushed gold walls and bars underlit by a variety of color options to enhance rotating themes. Charles was spending a fortune on the property's interior design and was angering not a few of the local clubs and restaurant owners in London's Mayfair district as he began to woo the best managerial talent and chefs from every corner of the city.

Alex and his team at Macchi & Macchi had been heavily involved in the design of the security systems from day one of the architectural planning. It was coming together beautifully, but it was time for Charles, and now his fiancé, Angelica, to move to London to oversee the final stages, gather more investors and members, and to bring his dream full circle.

Twenty-three-year-old Nick Macchi, the baby of the Macchi family, had finally learned that day that he had passed the bar exam in New York. It was an exciting time for him made more astonishingly outrageous by vacationing with one of the richest families in America. It had been a heady experience, and one that a young man from Brooklyn could only dream about. When Alex married Charlotte Carrows, Nick knew that she came from serious money, but it was one thing to know that, and quite another to live it.

From what he had seen in New York, Charlotte and Alex lived fairly normal lives. Alex and their brother Michael had worked hard to build on the reputation of their father's company. The relationship with the Carrows family had cemented Macchi & Macchi on the map. In addition to other clients, being the sole firm in charge of security for the Atlantic City, Vegas, and now London Carrows casinos and hotels was a full-time job for a small army of employees. That Alex wanted Nick to come on board full-time as head of the division out of London was a tremendous responsibility and showed great faith in his abilities not only as a lawyer and member of their firm, but as a brother and a trusted part of their dream.

Nick had been aware of the press and scandal surrounding his little niece and his brother's family, but until he had spent the last two weeks walking in their footsteps, he didn't really understand what their lives were all about. He knew now, that there was very little difference between the Carrows family and the Macchi family of Brooklyn. Underneath all the different scenery, and extreme advantages, they were just a family who loved each other. Nick could relate to that, and he'd do whatever it took to make sure he did an exemplary job for the casino entrusted into his care and to the Carrows family who'd welcomed him with open arms.

After they settled into their rooms at the Savoy, Alex had called him to his suite. Upon entering, he was surprised to find Charlotte, Angelica, and a small team of people gathered around racks of clothing.

"Nick!" Angelica yelled warmly as he entered the room. "Guess what. Charlotte arranged for us to be put together by these lovely stylists. And guess what else, dear boy, she gave them your measurements and we have a few suits for you to try on for tonight!"

Nick was surprised but had been getting used to the experience of being catered to since he had been hanging out with the Carrowses. Secretly in awe of these women, he didn't know if he was in love with them or if he was feeling the effects of just one long dream-like fantasy.

Recovering, he stopped and shot his brother a look as Alex made a circle motion with his index finger and pointed him toward the women. "Yeah? That was nice of you, but you know, I packed a suit. I'm sure it's fine for a night of bar hopping in London."

Charlotte shook her head at Alex and walked over to Nick. She put a protective arm around his shoulder and walked him over to a leaning floor mirror. "Nick, what do you see when you look in that mirror," she asked.

Uncomfortable, Nick put his hands in his pockets and shrugged. "Brooklyn?"

"Nick!" said Charlotte. "You're young, handsome, and you have those beautiful Macchi eyes. This is my treat. Please, let me dress you." She kissed him on the cheek as she gestured for the tailor.

"Mr. Macchi," said the older, fashionable tailor from the hotel. "If I may begin with the Armani, Sir?" The tailor held a dark jacket out for him, and Nick cooperated, extending his arm. "I believe we have a comprehensive selection of suits and accessories that you'll find quite appropriate for this evening, Mr. Macchi. Our tailors will make any last-minute adjustments."

The tailor ran his hand down the back of the jacket as the three of them looked at Nick in the mirror. "This is just too much, Charlotte. Really, I don't need for you to buy me any new clothes."

"Nick," said Angelica, coming over to his other side and appraising with a wide smile. "Don't spoil the fun. We just want you to feel as special as the rest of us tonight. New clothes are so wonderful, and you look great in that jacket. Let's try the Burberry," she gestured toward another gentleman who brought it forward while the tailor helped him discard the Armani.

Nick donned the slim-fit herringbone double-breasted jacket. Angelica said, "Ah, look at that. You're gorgeous. Remember, you're going to be representing the casino all over town, and I'm afraid you're going to have to put up with me shopping for you and Charles for some time to come. The only thing I'm concerned about is your head. You're not going to flip for the first cheeky girl who tells you she loves you right? I mean, you are a total catch, so you have to be careful."

Charlotte put her hand toward his throat holding a couple of ties. "There now, look at that. Look at what it does for you."

Angelica, from the other side, said, "You're just so cute Nick. Oh my goodness, I can't believe how motherly I suddenly feel about you! You've got to be careful out there in this big bad world. People will try to take advantage of you, you know that don't you?" she said suddenly serious.

Nick looked at his reflection and at the two women standing on either side and knew there was nothing in the world he wouldn't do for them.

"Ladies," he patted the air. "I'm gonna be alright. I have some excellent role models, don't I?" He turned and gave a sardonic look at Alex who sat in a nearby chair. He returned to Charlotte. "Thanks for what you're doing." Then to Angelica. "Both of you. I appreciate it."

They all smiled in the mirror as the tailor poked his head in their line of sight. "Will the women be leaving for the trouser selection, sir?"

Alex looked at the group and raised an eyebrow. "I certainly hope so."

————

Later, that evening, Nick, Alex, and Charles, were waiting in the American Bar at the Savoy for Charlotte and Angelica to join them.

"I'm glad Charlotte has someone else to play dress up with," Alex said, chewing on an olive from his martini. "Now that Angelica has an unlimited budget to spend on clothing, the two of them will accomplish some serious shopping. But more importantly, I won't have to tag along."

Charles smiled. "I'm sure it'll be well worth it, Alex. There's nothing I enjoy more than a grand entrance, and we'll be the lucky beneficiaries who get to bring them home. I'm glad they have something in common. Nick, we're going to have to make some proper introductions for you now that you're in London. I know Mom really wants to jump in there to lend a hand, and I have some friends who wouldn't mind meeting an eligible, single lawyer from the States."

"I don't know," he shrugged as he looked at his empty glass. "When are they going to get here? Should we order another one?"

"Last time I saw them," said Charles, "they were oh-my-godding in the bathroom. Some girl was going in and out and they were trying on clothes. How did you enjoy your fashion moment with them today, Nick?"

Nick blinked and glanced down at his exquisite Tom Ford blue linen jacket. "Don't get me wrong, I love my new clothes, and I'm not really sure who to thank for that," he looked to both his brother and Charles, "but I felt a little like a dress up doll in the room with all those people." He shot his cuff and played with a gold cufflink. He had no idea how much any of this had cost them, probably a fortune. Nick looked up and caught the knowing smile passed between his brother and Charles. They most likely enjoyed the thought of him being mauled by the girls and their fashion staff.

Charles raised his glass to him. "It will be well worth it, you'll see. It's going to be a big night out and whether you realize it or not, our image is part of our success. Our new public relations staff here have alerted some of the papers in town and I'm sure there will be a few selected photographers around tonight. The only difference is that this time, we called them. So no drunken fights with the photogs if they spew any nasty comments our way. It's all part of the game for them so just look good, keep your cool, and smile."

Nick was slightly unsettled that the evening was more of a staged performance than a fun night out on the town but understood that the publicity was necessary for the casino. "You'll have to let me know what to do as we go along. I'm not used to any of this stuff. I thought we tried to keep a low profile."

"We do," said Charles. "Mostly. But there are times, and hopefully the ones we control, where it's important to be seen displaying the Carrows image. My hotels and casinos will depend on it. I'm trying to create a legacy in them that will last past my lifetime and for the next generation of Carrowses. And Macchis. Ahhhh, here come our beautiful ambassadors now." Charles gestured toward the arriving women.

Charlotte was wearing a black Akris leather combo dress with a sleek leather sleeveless bodice with a round neck and a contrasting asymmetrical fabric skirt with short black boots. She wore her hair down with a glamorous Cleopatra gold collar necklace with fun gold earrings and chunky gold bracelets.

Angelica was completely opposite in a feminine silhouette—a Naeem Khan sleeveless white feather dress. She also wore her dark hair long but with a loose half bun in the back. Bouncing off the colors of her glorious blue and pink diamond engagement ring, she wore lovely Bvlgari Italaliane drops of 72 aquamarines and pink diamonds.

Charlotte extended her arms. "Well, how do we look? We're opposites— light and dark."

"You look amazing," Charles said as he walked past his sister and embraced Angelica.

"I'm over here," Charlotte waved a hand as Alex gave her a kiss on the cheek and whispered in her ear.

Charles glanced back at Charlotte. "Hey, you look great too. I expected nothing less." Charles turned back to Angelica and smiled.

"Okay," said Charlotte laughing. "Let's get out of here and have some fun tonight. We need to celebrate Nick's passing the bar!"

They started with dinner at The Ivy, then had drinks at George, and finished the night enjoying the music at Clementine's. As predicted, they were photographed arriving and leaving each of the clubs and entering and exiting their limousine. It was a heady experience.

Finally on the way back to the hotel, Charles turned to Nick. "We did a good job tonight. The Carrows image is secure as a family of not only wealth, but style. Did you have a nice time?"

Nick had never, ever been to clubs as beautiful, sophisticated, and awe-inspiring. He hadn't even known they existed. He'd been to a few nice places of course, especially since hanging with the Carrowses, but these were special, and he tried explaining that to Charles.

"I completely agree," said Charles. "They're the archetype for our brand. It's the Carrows' turn to host the glamorous crowds of Europe now. We'll steal their customers away from them and give them a run for their money."

Nick smiled as he looked out the window and at the illuminated clock tower of Big Ben. London was his new home. It was hard to believe.

———

The family gathered the next morning for breakfast in Henry and Julia's Edwardian suite. Spanning the entire fifth floor and overlooking the River Thames, the suite was comfortable and filled with bright colors, the dining room cozy as a butler and maid saw to their needs. Julia politely dismissed them after they had finished and asked for privacy.

"There now," she said as she dug a small teaspoon of hard-cooked egg out of a porcelain cup. "Our hosts are expecting us to arrive sometime today. I know we have a car service to drive us there, but your father and I had a thought. We were wondering whether Nick would like to join us for a short tour of the country before he starts his business week with you, Alex. Nick, what do you think?" Julia smiled at him sweetly.

Petunia squinted at Julia. "We're splitting up? I thought we were all going to be together in London this week?"

Julia's eyes darted to Charlotte and then quickly back to Petunia. "Oh. I'm sorry, sweetheart. We'll be back, but we have a friend who's unwell, in the south country...near Southampton. Hopefully we won't linger too long."

She smiled at her granddaughter. "Be sure to wait to see the crown jewels with me. It's been far too long."

Charlotte looked over to Petunia. "Sweetheart, you're excused. Why don't you go brush your teeth and get ready for our day while we finish talking?"

Petunia hopped down and ran out of the room.

Charlotte said, "Good cover, Mom. Remember, no one discusses Yorkshire, or the Linningtons, or Hambley Hall anywhere within earshot of Petunia."

"Of course," Julia nodded and took a sip of juice. "Nick, I'm sorry, how about it? Would you be interested in joining us?

Nick seemed confused and turned to gauge his brother's reaction to this information and change of plans. Alex nodded his permission. "Of course, if you'd like me to come with you I'd be happy to go. It's about a three-hour drive to Yorkshire, right?"

"Probably closer to four hours with traffic," said Henry. "It's important for you to get out of the city and see some of the countryside. Also, meeting the Linningtons couldn't hurt. Their son, Brandon, the next Earl, works in town. He might be a good person for you to know. We should cancel the car service and let Nick drive. Nothing like London traffic and driving on the wrong side of the road to get your feet wet."

Julia looked at Nick's horrified expression and reached toward him, patting the table. "Nick, I don't want you to worry now. Honestly, I'm not trying to fix you up with anyone at this moment, I just thought it might be a nice idea, and we might need your help sorting things out on our arrival. A short visit to a stately country home, albeit extremely grand, would give you a different taste for what life has to offer in England."

Charlotte cut a small banana and put it on a plate in front of Lily who sat in a high chair next to her. "I kind of wish we could all go. The country out there is so beautiful, and we could have toured some of the castles in the area. Petunia would have just loved it."

"We'll leave right after breakfast if that works for you, Nick. I already told Jane that there would be three of us," Julia said, winking at Alex.

"Julia," Alex gave her a percipient smile. "Thank you for thinking of my little brother, but please do me a favor and don't have him married off to an heir of Hambley Hall before he begins his work here."

"Oh, Alex, please, I'm good, but I'm not that good." Julia waved her hand in the air.

They all enjoyed the levity and Nick's slightly uncomfortable expression.

Charles said, "Our calendars are full here this week with sightseeing, realtors, and wining and dining."

"Don't forget shopping," Angelica said as scooped some berries onto her plate. "Charlotte and I plan to hit a few boutiques and score some dresses for all these dinners filled with schmoozing."

Charles took her hand and kissed it and said, "Shopping may be priority one. Also, we need to do something about that ring. We can't have you walking around unescorted with that on your finger, you'll be a target for some crazy person to rob you or worse."

Charlotte said, "That's another thing. I don't want everyone talking about crazy people robbing us and so forth when Petunia's around."

Charles nodded, "No, sorry, you're right. But she knows about our security issues. She knows she has Renzo with her when she's in public."

"I know," said Charlotte. "I just don't think we need to hammer home the danger-factor in front of her."

Angelica squinted at her hand and her rare blue diamond. "I don't understand what you mean about my ring?"

He responded, "I've made arrangements today to meet with a jeweler who will take it and have a copy made in Zurich. For safety's sake, you should only wear the real one on special occasions."

"What are you talking about, Charles?" Angelica shook her head. "Fake or real, someone out to hurt me won't know what I'm wearing."

Henry nodded. "She has a point. We've done that in the past with some of your mother's jewelry, but times have changed. I'm glad Renzo has come aboard for Petunia. Alex, how is the security detail for the rest of the family shaping up?"

"I have interviews lined up today." He responded.

Angelica put a hand out to Charles and gave him a small smile. They all sat for a moment absorbing what would be their new reality. It was a new way of thinking about their lives, not through the lens of paranoia, but with caution. Julia glanced at the concerned expressions of her children and was relieved that both Charlotte and now her dear sweet Charles had such strong partners to lean on.

Charles resumed the conversation. "Okay, no Zurich jewelers, but let's be careful out there. Mom, Dad, you know exactly what to say to the Linningtons, right? Remember, you're there to close this deal so we can get the job done."

"No worries," Henry said, taking a bite of a piece of turkey bacon, and frowning. "I can't recall the last time I had trouble convincing someone to see things from my perspective." He tossed the bacon on his plate and reached for a croissant.

"I got a call from Marcel this morning at 5 a.m. Confused about the time difference, my ass. He knew he was waking me up," Charles smirked.

"I just love him," Angelica cooed.

Charles sat back. "He got a yes from David on painting something for Broussards."

"What did Marcel ask David to paint for him?" asked Angelica.

"More of the Petunia series I'm sorry to say, but once it's complete, Marcel will sell it back to us. We want David to keep thinking that his series is a successful, in demand commodity. A sick and twisted commodity, but one that we'll use against him."

"Let's get a move on then, Julia, Nick," Henry said, pushing back from the table. "We have a lot of work to get done this week."

Slightly deflated from their earlier merriment, the Carrowses left the table determined to get the David matter settled.

Chapter 25

Henry instructed the concierge to arrange for a very nice Range Rover with an automatic transmission for the Yorkshire traveling party. Once outside of London, Henry as navigator, watched with amusement as Nick's white-knuckled grip on the wheel relaxed. They were rewarded for their efforts as they began to thoroughly enjoy the scenic green countryside of Britain.

The conversation flowed, much of it from Julia in the back as she happily espoused her grandiose plans for Charles and Angelica's upcoming wedding. The topic of food from around the globe and what they might expect from their time in England was also hotly discussed.

"Don't ever expect a glass of ice, at least outside of the Savoy. Ice in a glass to the Brits is a cube or two. Bizarre really, I've never understood it," said Henry.

Julia patted Henry on the shoulder from the back seat. "I'm sure the Linningtons will stock up on the ice for our visit. Jane also knows about your spleen and that your diet should always contain something green, and of course the leaner the meat the better. I expect we'll be eating a lot of fish, because she seemed a little flummoxed by what to serve."

They drove past a number of farms, some old and dilapidated—relics of their former past, and other's more modern and updated. They gazed at ruins of an old church, its graveyard ancient yet proud, and Henry wondered what history transpired in the vast acreage around it.

As they got nearer to their destination, Julia discussed the logistics of their subterfuge. "I told Jane that we needed to keep the visit very hush hush and that we were bringing a young man in the guise of our driver and valet, but that he was really a friend of the family. I'm afraid she didn't know what to think about that either. I know this may be confusing to you, Nick, about our reasons for keeping you somewhat in the dark, but I hope you understand that we're just looking out for you."

Nick glanced back at Julia and shrugged. "Alex talked to me. I trust you."

Henry nodded, proud of Nick, and the Macchi family. It was gratifying to know that they could be counted on. "Thank you for that, son. We'll be having a private conversation with Barford and Jane this evening. You could go to the local pub if you'd like. Just remember, our name is never to be mentioned to anyone. Make up whatever name you'd like if someone should ask."

"No, if it's alright, I'll just stay and not go anywhere. I wouldn't want to do anything that might cause you a problem, sir. I'll take a walk around the grounds or go to bed early."

Henry smiled at Nick and continued to gaze at the countryside until he recognized that they had nearly arrived.

"Oh, look at the view! Nick, stop the car," said Henry as he gazed at the stunning green valley and the magical estate of Hambley Hall. Situated perfectly in a lush valley with a small lake surrounding two sides of the home, from their vantage point it looked like an immense grand chateau.

In addition to the natural lake, there were cleared parklands and woods as well as clever architectural lines of formal gardens. They could see a tennis court near the main house and several outbuildings dotting the property. A modest number of sheep grazed nearby on a small golf course.

"Absolutely charming," said Julia. "Really breathtaking from up here, isn't it? We came here only one other time and that was for Barford and Jane's wedding. Henry, wasn't that a wonderful day?"

"It was. Very English. The local vicar in the parlour and a nice breakfast celebration afterwards. We all played a round of golf later that day if I recall. No shooting, but they do hunt quite a bit around here. Carry on, Nick, let's go meet the family."

"What do I call them?" Nick said as they wound down into the valley.

"We'll introduce you to them by their formal titles

but after that you may call them Lord Hambley and Lady Hambley until they give you leave to call them Barford and Jane."

Driving down a tree-lined avenue, they pulled up to the front of the home. Henry admired the well-preserved, centuries old Georgian manor. The three-story house had large flanking pavilions connected to each side, with a modillion cornice between the second and third stories. The limestone hues of warm cream and yellow were much darker and dirtier in places, showing their age, but with grace, as were the sculptured figures and urns lining the parapet.

Henry got out of the car and he, Julia, and Nick were warmly greeted by the earl and countess of Hambley. Introductions were made as well to Sorsby, the butler, who they were told had joined the household after Barford had inherited the title of Earl some fifty years before. The only other live in member of the household was the cook, Emma. Nick offered to carry the luggage and Sorsby said he would guide him, after which they were to take tea in the library.

The day passed pleasantly as they caught up on one another's lives. The years had been kind to all of them, and as often happens with good friends, they quickly picked up their friendship right where they left off. After a very nice dinner the first evening, Henry asked Barford if the four of them could have a private conversation. Nick excused himself, and the remaining foursome adjourned to the drawing room.

"I remember this room," Julia said to Jane as they entered. "It has such a vibrant, yet cozy feel."

Henry looked around the large rectangular room recognizing a few pieces from his previous visit. The room felt welcoming filled with tasteful decorative touches and generations of furniture. The walls were papered with a repeating bold pattern in green. The mouldings were elaborately carved and painted to match the heavy, pleated swag draperies of green satin. A lingering combination of floral scents and ash from the fireplace gave the room a very lived in feel. Henry looked over some family photos on the mantle as the earl came up to him and handed him a glass of brandy. Henry thanked him and seated himself on one of the many cream brocade sofas. He raised his glass and said, "We thank you for having us, and yes, as you suspect, we do have a terrific favor to ask of you and Jane."

The earl, a glass of brandy in hand had positioned himself next to the sooty fireplace surmounted by a large gilded mirror. He said, "Ah, well. It's time then, eh? You're going to let us in on something that you need help sorting, is that it Henry? Why the visit and why it needs to be hush, hush. Not that we aren't delighted to see you again, old boy."

Henry nodded. "Yes, it's time. But please understand two things. If you aren't able to help us, there will be no hard feelings on our part. And second, regardless whether you help us, I would ask that you never tell anyone about what it is we are asking you to do. Before I continue, I'd like an assurance from you that you're comfortable keeping our confidence."

Barford looked bright-eyed and surprised, but glanced at Jane who said, "Of course, yes, you have our word."

Henry nodded and considered his brandy before he took a small sip. "You probably know that we have recently been the victim of a scandal in the press, at least in America. And I'm afraid it's followed us abroad."

The earl brought his hand to his mouth and cleared his throat.

Henry raised his brows, "*Hello!* magazine? It's a rather ugly situation with the biological father of our first grandchild, Petunia. Are you aware of what's going on?"

"Yes," Jane said leaning forward to Julia. "We're so sorry you're going through this. We've heard about it, of course, but we didn't want to bring it up, because it must be terribly painful. If that's what this is about, please know we'll do anything we can to help you."

"Thank you for that, Jane," said Henry. "And yes, that's primarily the reason we're here. The coincidence that Charles is opening a casino in London at the same time that this scandal is reaching a peak led us to a possible solution to the problem. We need help from someone outside of the U.S., someone Petunia's father doesn't know is connected to us, someone who cares about us enough to help, and someone we can be count on to keep silent. We thought of you."

Jane glanced at Barford and said, "Well, yes, we'd be

happy to help, but I can't imagine what is you want us to do."

"That's the tricky part," Julia said folding her hands in her lap. "We have a plan, but it's a bit unorthodox. We're asking you to help us send Mr. David Cordoza to prison, here in England. We need to stop him from emotionally torturing our granddaughter and our family, and if we can put him away for many, many years, we'll give Petunia some time to recover from the betrayal and hopefully find some peace with her situation."

Looking to the startled faces of his hosts, Henry said, "Have you read David's first book of fiction?"

"No," Jane shook her head. "Based on the allegations we heard he was making, we assumed it would be a load of rubbish."

Henry swirled his brandy and continued. "Well it was, completely. The second one is even more vile. I assume, however, that you have a broad outline of the circumstances? Perhaps our public statement to the press?"

Jane smoothed a hand down her skirt and crossed her ankles. "Yes, we read it. It's a disgrace that this boy stole from you while he was dating Charlotte. I understand completely why you didn't want to prosecute him for it at the time, but now that he's twisting the story you must be truly outraged."

"Don't know that I would have had the same temperament as you had, Henry, if Ashley had brought some ponce home and he nicked up something so valuable," Barford said, his lips pursed. He took a seat in an armchair across from Henry.

"Believe me," said Henry, "I wanted to see him punished too, but at first we didn't even know where to find him."

Henry and Julia went into detail with the Linningtons, sharing the events first hand of what happened in the past and over the past several months.

"The man is a monster." Julia slapped her leg at the conclusion of the recitation and got up and paced. "A liar, a thief, an extortionist, and frankly dangerous. The emotional toll this has taken on all of us...I cannot tell you about our sleepless nights."

"What a despicable man," Jane said, staring at her friend. "How old is Petunia now?"

Julia stopped in front of Jane and put a hand to her throat. "She's only nine. It has crushed her to know that her biological father put a price tag on her head. She's embarrassed by the entire thing. Ten million dollars! Imagine! Now the media has latched onto the story and it's getting bigger every day. Photographers trying to get her picture—it's a nightmare."

"Isn't there some legal way you can stop him from publishing?" Barford asked.

Henry shook his head. "So far we've been unsuccessful on that front, but we'll continue to pursue it. In the meantime, we've come to the conclusion that no matter what we do, this man is going to continue to make trouble for the family, and Petunia will continue to be hurt. Putting the legal piece to the side, we've decided to take matters into our own hands and do something about it. But we'll need some help."

Jane's brows knit. "So you want to send him to prison? Over here? For what exactly? How are we to be involved in this?"

Henry sat back and looked at Julia who regained her seat on the sofa next to Jane and said, "We want him to rob you."

"Good God. Rob us," Barford said, shocked. "Of what?"

Henry put his brandy aside again and raised his brows. He said softly, "Your Lord and Ladyship, we don't want to be indelicate here, but it has come to our attention that you have been auctioning off some of your family's valuables at Sotheby's. It doesn't surprise us that you might be having difficulties covering the overhead on Hambley Hall, and the taxes, and upkeep. I can't imagine what an enormous financial burden it is to keep the Hall and land together for the family. I'm sure having to make the sacrifice and selling your heirlooms must be very painful for you. That is the crossroads where I think we can help each other."

Barford had been seated in an armchair next to Henry. His face flushed as he cleared his throat and got up with his glass. He went to a large, ornately carved oak bar on a side of the room. "I see," he said as he poured more brandy from a crystal decanter. "Well, I'm a bit put off here, but I suppose it's no secret that we've had to sell a few items to keep ahead. The blightly taxes alone are enough to put anyone out of their game. When I go, the estate and death taxes on Brandon are going to be enormous, and we're trying to get ahead of that for him, so he can keep Hambley Hall in the family. Rather awkward here, though, I'm afraid."

"Barford." Henry threw up his hands. "You should be proud of what you've accomplished holding on to the estate. You're one of a handful of old families in England who can claim that they still own their family homes. Truly, it's a small miracle that must have come from good planning and hard work and a tremendous amount of sacrifice to keep it intact for Brandon and Ashley."

Barford shook his head as he stared into his glass. "Yes, well, we've had to make some difficult decisions over the years. I'm not too much of a toff to admit it. Wet rot alone, not to mention the farming, have nearly gutted us several times. But we're still here, and we'll keep it together for the next earl if it's the last thing we do."

Henry picked up his glass and got up and walked toward the bar. "I'm sure you will, Barford, and I'd like to help you do that. We're in a position to help you, if you'd help us with David. I'm confident we would be able to work out something mutually beneficial."

"I still don't understand what it is that you want us to do," Jane said, leaning forward and turning to stare at Henry. "You want David to rob us? Of what, and how?"

"What would be more natural for David to steal than jewels?" Henry ran his hand holding his brandy glass across the room. "And I happen to know that you have some extremely valuable pieces which would be perfect for the job."

"You're talking about the parure, aren't you?" Jane said, glancing back at Julia.

"Yes, I am," said Henry. "Also, I've recently learned that you have sought the help of Sotheby's to value it and keep an eye out for the right time to sell."

"Sotheby's has been speaking with you about it?" Barford said loudly as he came around the bar.

"Not directly, but we have a source who has been willing to share their latest inventory and potential sale items for clients who are interested."

"I see," said Jane as she relaxed back into the sofa. "So you would like David to steal our family jewels and then be caught and put into prison. How did you say you would get him to do this?"

"We have some thoughts about that, Jane," said Julia. "It's rather complicated. But first, may I ask, do you still have the parure and is it true you've been exploring your options to sell it?"

"This is rather uncomfortable, speaking of all this so openly." Barford said as he walked to the fireplace. "Those jewels have been in the Linnington family since the 18th century and it is not without considerable angst that we have been discussing the sale of them so Brandon would be able to retain the estate after I die."

"Yes, but do you still have them?" Julia looked at him.

"We do. Intact, I'm rather proud to say." Barford put his chin up.

"Are they here?" asked Julia. "May we see them?"

"Yes," Jane said rising. "Let's go take a look, and then maybe you can give us a few more details about how you want them to be nicked." She smiled at her husband's shocked expression and left the room.

The earl and countess escorted Henry and Julia to a large vault in an ancient wine cellar. The earl opened a cleverly concealed false brick wall which contained a large, modern safe.

"Stand down there, Henry, while I get this thing open," Barford said turning his back on the group. The safe opened and Barford pulled out two ancient velvet boxes.

Taking the boxes and laying them onto a center island in the middle of the room, Barford opened the first box and said, "May I present the Linnington Jewels."

A parure is a French term referring to a matched set of pieces of jewelry that are intended to be worn together. In the Linningtons' case, the first box contained a necklace, pendant, and earrings.

Barford waved a presentation hand over the jewels. Clearing his throat, he put his hands behind him and proudly began a recitation. "As you know, King George II gave the first Earl of Hambley his title after the Battle of Culloden in 1745 when the first Linnington held true to the crown and pushed back the young pretender, the Bonnie Prince Charlie. The king gave him these lands and the village of Hambley and the title of Earl. The first Earl did a fine job constructing the bones of the hall. Sixteen years later when George III became king, the titled gentry were all expected to do honour to the king and queen at their coronation by putting on a display of wealth at Westminister Abbey."

"Kind of an early one-upmanship," Barford chuckled as he ran a finger over the jewels. He puffed up and continued. "The second Earl had these pieces commissioned for the coronation and every Earl and Countess of Hambley since then has been seen wearing them, representing the Linningtons at every coronation. As you can see, they are a splendid example of Georgian jewellery with rose cut diamonds, rubies, and pearls with the most handsome piece being the riviere necklace. The largest stone is the centre diamond which, although cut somewhat roughly, is still quite stunning. The pendant could be hung from a chain or I believe it was once used to decorate a chatelaine by an earlier countess. The earrings are intriguing as well."

Opening the second box, he continued, "This contains the Earl's brooch which is a matching piece to the parure and has a centre diamond with the ruby and pearls in a rather delicate gold starburst. The Earl's brooch was last worn by my father at the coronation of Queen Elizabeth. My mother, the countess, of course, wore the full parure. There were portraits done of them wearing them for the coronation upstairs that we can look at. The collection is truly priceless to us, but then again, I suppose everyone has his price," he said, sadly.

Henry put his hand on Barford's back. "They are exquisite, Barford, and perfect for what we were planning. Shall we go back upstairs and speak about what we're proposing and our scheme of how to use the Linnington

Jewels, the perfect parure from the second earl of Hambley, to destroy David Torres Cordoza?"

Chapter 26

Henry Carrows called Charles with an update. "Let everyone know I have good news. The Linningtons have agreed wholeheartedly to the plan. He and I will send the parure to Zurich this afternoon to have replicas made of the set. They are quite extraordinary, made in the 1700's for the second earl. It's a fine piece of history that they're very proud of. It'll be interesting to see what the Zurich boys think about the stones after they get a deeper look at them. Barford is slightly nervous about letting them out of his sight, but I've assured him that the courier service from the jeweler is above reproach and can be trusted."

Charles said, "I'm assuming the Earl's parure will take a little extra time since they cut the stones differently in the 1700's?"

"I sent him a picture and he said he would have a better idea after he can examine them. He thought it might take a month or two," said Henry.

"That's okay. In the meantime, it'll give Marcel an

opportunity to sell David on a show at his gallery and keep him busy producing his highly sought-after art."

"I wonder if he'll actually sell anything. Part of me understands why we need to keep his head in the clouds, but the other part of me would love nothing better than to see that rat face an empty gallery."

"We build him up, Dad, and I'm giving Marcel money to advertise it and gain momentum. I know it seems counterintuitive to the cause of breaking him down, but the more David thinks he's a big shot, the more he thinks of himself as a successful, *selling* artist, the better for us to make him believe the Linningtons would want him to do a portrait for them. In the meantime, I've got to get back to the States and recruit our closer—Cheryl Davis. She's the last piece of the plan. I'm going to invite her to visit us at Whispering Cliffs."

"When are you going home?" Henry asked.

"When are you leaving? Maybe we could fly back with you and mom."

"That would be a good idea. Your mom, Nick, and I will be back in London this evening, and we'll be ready to get back to the States in about a week. Will that work for you?"

"That'll be fine. We're meeting with the realtor again today and we're narrowing in on a couple of places over here that would be a good investment."

"I'll let your mother know that you and Angelica will be traveling home with us. That will definitely be a highlight for her. Wedding planning with the bride-to-be."

"Maybe we should have that discussion ourselves before I let mom loose on her."

"You know she has her heart set on a wedding at Whispering Cliffs, Charles."

"I know. We'll see."

Chapter 27

Cheryl Davis had worked hard over the years, and now at thirty-one years of age, only filled in as a dancer or bartender at Lacey's when they were short staffed. She no longer enjoyed being on stage, but her years of hard work had allowed her to put enough money away to ensure that her mother's home was paid for. She also gave her mom a monthly allowance that kept her comfortable and secure. Cheryl was now her sole supporter. It was a complicated relationship and she knew the story of her mother's past. Her mother had not had it easy.

Ann Davis, Cheryl's mom, was a single mother who had had little family support and even worse support from Cheryl's non-existent dad. Ann was raised in a hotter than hell suburb of Houston, Texas in a small tract home surrounded by cracked concrete, a small weedy yard, and a chain-link fence sadly situated next door to a used car lot. An only child, Ann thought her ticket out of the depressing neighborhood would be through the use of her face and body, which she had been told were her only assets. Believing this and having very little self confidence in any other abilities, sixteen-year-old Ann eventually used her looks to land herself a job as a receptionist for her next door neighbor, Larry—of Larry's Used Cars.

Walking to work each day after school, Ann was enormously appreciated by the entire sales staff of men, most of whom knew better than to make a move on the underage girl. That caution didn't apply to Larry Mack, the owner. Used to getting his way by any method possible, he wooed young and naïve Ann into believing they were in love. Larry Mack wasn't married, Ann had made sure of that, but she also knew her parents wouldn't allow her to date a guy who was nearly twenty years older than herself, so they did the most reasonable thing two lovers could do and snuck around. Larry Mack, born salesman and closer of the deal, finally did just that late one evening in his office with then seventeen-year-old Ann Davis. Nine months later, Cheryl was born.

No one was happy the day Cheryl Davis was born. Ann's parents were disgusted by the situation and horrified that their only daughter's future had been ruined. Larry Mack was horrified that he was saddled with a kid, which would be a major interference in his wild nights at the strip bars, and poor Ann was sick to death that she suddenly had a kid and not a clue how to raise it. Eventually, the family friction proved to be too much, and Ann and little Cheryl moved away to live with a friend in Brownsville.

Ann's friend was actually a new boyfriend by the name

of John Pearce who saw Ann's primary value in her God-given, rockin body. He knew if he could set Ann up in a really nice job, and if she was smart enough to use her assets, they would manage just fine. He moved them to a small apartment in Brownsville just across the border from Mexico where he had an active part in a small marijuana transportation ring. They arranged day care for little Cheryl, and Ann went to work in another used car dealership where she was encouraged by John Pearce to put her body on obvious display as a way to get ahead.

John eventually proved to be a just another burden and bad mistake for Ann as he was regularly either in trouble with the law or with his gang who frequently hung out with them in their cramped apartment. Tensions grew, and by the time Ann realized that her situation was not an improvement from her parent's home and the allusive, grumbling Larry Mack, she was in too deep.

One night during a terrible tequila-fueled fight with John, he completely lost his mind and attacked her with a knife. Stabbing her in the shoulder and then watching the blood pour out of a deep slash in her face, John sobered up enough to flee the apartment, leaving poor Ann alone with young Cheryl, who called for help. Ann never saw John Pearce after that day, but he was never farther away than the mirror. Her beautiful face was forever changed by the vicious work he did to her combined with the gross negligence her cuts were given by the apathetic doctor who stitched her up in the emergency room.

After the attack, Ann Davis struggled through her

years in Brownsville depressed. Cheryl believed her mom was only vaguely aware that bit by bit she began to fail in her parental duties. She began to depend on Cheryl to put bread on the table.

By the time Cheryl was sixteen, she was the sole earner of the household. She dropped out of high school and began making a great deal of money on stage as a stripper named Cherrie Corona. Cheryl had inherited her mother's once pretty face and body and was sadly aware that it caused her mother unintentional pain whenever she looked at her. But she loved her mother and realized that she had no one in the world to help her if Cheryl didn't.

Even though she was forced to support them, it was Cheryl's dream to make her mom happy. Her goal was to make enough money to pay for the surgeries Ann required to make her face beautiful again. It was a goal which pushed her forward, but Cheryl eventually realized that her mother didn't want to undergo the pain and expense of surgery. Ann Davis had become content to live in the small house that Cheryl had purchased for them, spending her days quietly in her garden, cooking, and cleaning.

While Cheryl and her mother both silently accepted the fact that Cheryl was the financial support for her mother's increasingly reclusive life, Cheryl had no intention of spending the rest of hers stripping in the limited Brownsville area bars. She knew that if she wanted to capitalize on her looks, she would need to move to a bigger market with a more upscale crowd. A driven, good looking, seasoned dancer who had the stamina and professionalism to keep her head on straight and not be lured into a darker side of the business or fall victim to the tragic consequences of drug and alcohol abuse, could make some serious money.

She built some security for herself in California, but the years in the strip club business had made her extremely cautious in her private life. She wasn't exactly sure if people thought of her as hard hearted, but she was definitely guarded, and had few close friends who knew anything about her work, her home, her mother, and her dreams. Successful romantic relationships with men had not been possible. She just carried too much baggage for them.

She'd been working twelve-hour days for as long as she could remember and was beginning to feel slightly fatigued from the day to day bar and strip club business, the sad stories of the girls, the sad stories of the customers, the fantasy of the environment, and the seediness that always worked its way in. But she was a protective owner, good to the girls, fair to the employees, and was proud that she'd built Lacey's reputation for being one of the better clubs to work for in Los Angeles.

That afternoon, Cheryl sat in her office in the back of Lacey's, listening indulgently as one of her girls apologized for breaking the rules.

"I promise it won't happen again, Cheryl. Listen to me, I promise, okay?"

The girl's leg jumped with nervous energy, she scratched at her arm and twitched almost imperceptibly, but Cheryl caught it. She was using and bringing it into the club.

Cheryl shook her head. "No. I can't have drugs on the premises. You knew that. We could lose everything if we were raided, and I'm not going to risk it."

Cheryl saw the real pain in the girl's eyes and softened her tone. "Look. You can have your job back, but only if you pass a pee test. As long as you're using, you're not going to be able to stop yourself. You need to get help and clean up. I really hope you call one of those numbers I gave you. You're a good kid, but that shit is going to kill you. No kidding, I've seen it."

Unfortunately, the girl wasn't in the head space to listen. She slammed her bag against a wall and stormed out.

Cheryl sighed and rubbed her head as she pulled up the weekly schedule. "Damn it," she complained to no one as she deleted the girl's name from the line-up. It was always something. Every weekly schedule was a miracle of achievement after listening to the drama-filled requests. She should be used to it by now.

She got up and re-filled her cup of water from the spring water cooler she'd brought in. A personal expense since her partners were unwilling to shell out for it, once the girls tried it, they didn't want to go back to the bar's tap water. They went through nearly ten gallons a day now and her partner's lectures peppered with the "I-told-you-so's" and "If-You-Give-a-Mouse-a-Cookie" crap meant that Cheryl paid for it out of her pocket. But it was water, damn it. They were thirsty. She couldn't take it back.

She sat in her chair and looked at her desk as her cell phone rang. Ah, now here was something to smile about. It was her friend, Charles.

She tapped her phone to accept the call. "Hey there, baby. What's up? How's the hardest working billionaire on the street?" Cheryl leaned back and smiled.

"Cheryl, my love, how are you? How's the hardest working bar owner in Los Angeles? Are you ready to make the big move and buy out your partners? I'm always here to help."

"Right. We don't play that way, darlin. It's one of the things that keeps it real between us. We don't take advantage of each other. Unless of course you are finally interested in my remarkable C-cup assets?"

Charles laughed and said, "No. As appealing as they may be, you know we don't have that type of relationship. I'm also very much taken, so you can keep the girls holstered."

"Ahh, does this mean that you and the lovely *Daizy Durand* are still together?"

"As a matter of fact, yes. We just got engaged."

Cheryl sat up. "Charles, that's wonderful! Congratulations to you both. You make a really great couple. I'm happy for you."

"Thank you, Cheryl. That means a lot to me—to us. Also, at long last, let me reveal her true identity. Her name is Angelica Renner. We're in town and we're wondering if you would have some time to help us celebrate. Are you available for dinner this weekend, at my folks' place?"

"Are you asking me to come to dinner at the famous Whisperings Cliffs?" Cheryl cocked her head.

"Yes. As a matter of fact, why don't you come for the weekend? Pack a bag. Super casual, we'll just lay by the pool, have a few drinks, talk about old times."

"Charles. I would love nothing more than to spend some time with the two of you, but really, you obviously have something up. Do I detect a wee job in my future?"

"Alright, yes. That's part of it, but really, Angelica and I would sincerely love to see you and spend some time together. She speaks of you often, you know."

"I think about her too. Quite a kid. She did a great job for you with that thing in Santa Monica. Do you like her better as a blond or a brunette?"

"Brunette. Definitely. Although the blond was good too," Charles said with a small laugh.

"Alright then, when do you need me over to the big house?"

"The sooner the better. We just got back from London. How about Saturday. For lunch. By the pool. You can meet my parents too. They've heard a lot about you. All good stuff. "

"Shit, Charles. This is weird. The family, your famous mom and dad, your new fiancé, and me, Cherrie Corona, at Whispering Cliffs for a cozy weekend. I have a feeling whatever you're up to may be bigger than usual."

"One of the things I loved about you from the first was

your ability to read people, Cheryl. You're very wise. May we expect you?"

"You may. I'll see you poolside on Saturday. Be sure to leave my name with the guards and hold back the Dobermans at the gate."

"Sure. We'll see you then, Cheryl."

Cheryl ended the call and stared at her phone. *Wow. I've been invited to the infamous Whispering Cliffs. I wonder what they're up to now?* She smiled in anticipation.

———

Cheryl Davis gaped as she turned into the oak lined drive past the gatehouse and spied the house for the first time in real life. "What the hell are you doin here, girl," she said out loud as she drove through the ficus-lined courtyard and up to the Renaissance-style palace, bordering the Pacific Ocean. She drove up to the circular turnaround and stared at the massive front elevation surrounding her and the enormous grand staircase leading to the front door. Getting out of her car, she saw the doors open, and Angelica Renner, her long lost partner in crime, also known as Daizy Durand, flew down the steps and into her arms.

"Paula! Oh my God, it's so good to see you! You look so great," Angelica bounced as they hugged.

Cheryl pulled away and smiled at the wild, enthusiastic beauty in front of her who she hadn't seen in about a year. "Sweetie, it's actually not Paula you know; that was the name Charles and I chose for the Santa Monica thing.

Did he not tell you my real name?" She looked over at a smiling Charles standing behind them.

Angelica smiled. "He did. I know it's really Cheryl Davis, but I only knew you as Paula."

Charles came over, gave her a hug, and grabbed her bag. They walked up the grand staircase and into the cool interior and the stunning atrium of the home.

"Holy shit!" Cheryl said as she looked up and around. "Are you kidding me with this?"

Angelica laughed as she grabbed her arm and dragged her further in. "It's totally overwhelming, I know. The first time I was in here, I almost died I thought it was so beautiful. Just wait; it only gets better and better."

"Well, hey, now you're going to be living here too, right?" Cheryl said, her head back, looking around the grand salon. "Congratulations on the engagement! Oh, I'll bet he got you got a nice ring, let me see." She grabbed Angelica's hand. "What the...is that a blue diamond? My God, what are those, pink ones? It's beautiful."

"They're all diamonds. Thank you, it is pretty wonderful." She dropped her hand. "I'm so excited we have all weekend to catch up. We have so much to talk about."

"I'm sure we do. Charles wouldn't be dragging my ass all the way out here and introducing me to the pater and mater if something big wasn't up."

Charles grinned at her attempt at humor.

"Just trying to fancy up the lingo," Cheryl shrugged.

He walked toward a stairway and started up. "Let's get

you settled into your room and then we'll bring you out to the main pool to meet my parents. It's going to be a long weekend."

"Yes, but we intend to have loads of fun too," Angelica said taking Cheryl's arm in hers as they walked up the carpeted marble steps together. "The truth is, Cheryl, the Carrows have another problem. But let me sum it up this way. Double, double, toil and trouble, we've gotten ourselves into a muddle."

"Even I know that one's not right," Charles smiled, looking back.

"Good Lord," Cheryl sighed. "And now you two clowns are dragging me into it."

Angelica squeezed her arm. "Yes, because we know you're the best."

———————

Cheryl was properly welcomed by Henry and Julia poolside. They got acquainted as they were served a delicious warm Greek salad with freshly baked salted bread by the housekeeper and cook, Rosita.

She had never occupied a space or been treated with such tender care as that afternoon sitting by the magnificently tiled pool, surrounded by gardens and breezes circulating through the Spanish inspired arches. Off to the side was the biggest most dramatic fireplace she had ever seen bordered by brightly colored chandeliers.

"It must be beautiful out here at night," said Cheryl as

she and Charles and Angelica lounged after lunch by the pool.

"It is. The good news is that we can hang out here this evening if you want to. I know the owner," said Charles.

"Or in any of the other perfectly wonderful rooms," said Angelica. "Did you want to take a walk down the beach? We thought dinner should just be the three of us tonight. We can have it anywhere in the house you'd like. Rosita will be happy to set up a picnic for us if we ask her."

Cheryl pulled down her sunglasses and looked at Angelica. "Guys, I don't care where we eat. Anywhere we go in this place would be perfect. You don't have to go to any trouble you know."

"I know," said Angelica, "but you're the first person I've ever entertained here now that I'm almost officially part of the family. It's fun to play house when you have a palace to play in and a staff to cater to you."

"Rosita and John are really more like family," explained Charles. "They've been here for the last twenty years and helped raise us. They live in one of the cottages on the grounds to the east beyond those walls. Nicely situated off the kitchen. They keep the place running smoothly with the help of day staff and gardeners and other assorted handymen. Something, somewhere is always either being fixed, or replaced, or cleaned. Not that I'm complaining."

"God Charles, you grew up here, didn't you," Cheryl took off her glasses and sat up, taking it in. "I can't imagine what that would feel like. I mean it had to shape you, just like my childhood home in the desolate baking brickness of southern Texas did for me. It made me the girl I am!" Cheryl smiled.

"It's so cool that we're both from Texas," said Angelica.

"Maybe that's why we got along so well. Do you miss it? Do you get home often?"

"I do miss it," Angelica said reaching over for a glass of iced tea. "My family's there, my mom and dad and sisters, but it's more than that. It's Texas, you know, it's home."

"Well I don't miss it at all, honey," Cheryl said, reclining back in her chair. "Not where I came from. I miss my mom sometimes, I guess, but we were never that close. I was always working, and then I moved to L.A. to make it big in the business," Cheryl gave a derisive laugh. "Just like you, Charles! If I'd only put more hours on the stage, one day this too could have all been mine." She made a sweeping gesture of the grounds and out toward the Pacific.

"Hey, I couldn't help where I was born any more than you could. It's all about what you do with it. I know it probably seems ridiculous for me to compare my circumstances with yours, and I'm not. I'm just saying that what a person is, who they want to be and how they behave, is sometimes a choice. I could easily become a complete asshole but thank goodness that didn't happen." Charles smirked.

The girls laughed, and Angelica said, "And thank goodness you had the great sense to see *our* extraordinary value."

"My exact value," Cheryl said, "you've yet to quote me.

What grand purpose am I going to serve for you this time guys?"

Angelica patted the air in front of Cheryl. "Now, now, I thought maybe you'd just like to relax this afternoon, and we could speak about it over dinner."

Cheryl shrugged. "Sure. That's fine. I'll just enjoy the ride. How about I take you up on that walk on the beach?"

"Great plan," Angelica said jumping up and adjusting her swimsuit. "Let's go commune with Neptune and talk about what you want to have for dinner. You can have *anything* you want really but let me tell you what I'd thought we'd have."

Cheryl was in no hurry. She intended to enjoy the special day.

———

That evening after the three of them changed for dinner, they met up in the outdoor sala next to the pool. The outdoor living room had walls of hand-cut stone and sliding window walls on either side open to the garden. Actual candlelight flickered from the candles in the chandelier that extended from heavy wood beams. Thick rugs and a fireplace crackling with wood brought the best of the indoor and outdoor elements together in a garden of privacy.

They enjoyed a delicious dinner of braised short ribs and corn muffins and managed to go through a couple bottles of red wine before Cheryl had had enough of the intrigue. She was bursting with curiosity to know what they wanted from her.

"Okay…" Cheryl, slightly drunk, drummed the table. "It's time for you guys to get it out there. We all know that there's something you need for me to do and frankly, the longer I stay here, and the longer we don't talk about it, the more jittery I'm getting. Tell me what's going on."

Charles and Angelica gave Cheryl the story. They left nothing out, all the way up to where matters stood now.

"So you have a plan to take this scumbag out, and you need my help. Is that it?" Cheryl asked, her feet propped up on an empty chair next to hers.

"Yes," said Charles. "We need someone he doesn't know to set him up for a fall. A very big fall—to send him to prison. In England."

"England?" Cheryl dropped her feet and sat up. "Why the hell does he need to go to prison in England?"

"Fate mostly," Charles shrugged with his hands. "I'm sure you know that we're opening our third Casino in London?"

"Charles and I are house shopping," Angelica jumped in. "We plan to move over there in the next week or so to get Carrows London off the ground. It's still under construction and there are a *million* details that need to be watched over including hiring staff. Carey will be coming over soon too, or maybe going back and forth, and Charlotte's husband, Alex, and his brother Nick will be handling security for the casino through their firm Macchi

& Macchi out of New York. Nick, Alex's youngest brother, is living over there now."

Cheryl shook her head to clear it.

Charles picked up. "We knew that the David thing was coming to a head and when we thought about ways to get him out of the picture, we thought it would be perfect if he got into trouble out of the country. That way it would be more difficult for him to involve us and once he's convicted, he'll be far, far out of reach. Once we made the decision to stop David, we went over the list of close friends, or people we could count on for help in Europe. We found them. In Britain. We've spoken with them, and they've agreed to help. They have the stronghold—or the place, and the rest of the setup. Now we need to get David over there and send in his assassin. That would be you."

"By assassin," interjected Angelica, "he doesn't mean actual killer of course."

"Of course," Cheryl said dryly. "What type of crime do you see him committing? How are you going to get him to do it, and where do I come in?"

Charles raised his brows. "We don't actually expect David to commit any crime, so we plan to frame him for one. Serendipitously, he'll be caught, robbing a family of their jewels."

"And how do we frame him for doing this?" Cheryl said squinting her eyes.

Charles leaned over the table. "With the cooperation of the English family, you will plant them on David, they'll be reported stolen, the police will look to David and find them in his possession, he will be arrested, convicted and sent to prison for a very long time."

Cheryl felt her heart sink. Charles had crossed a line and this time was asking her to do something illegal. Big time, illegal. She leaned her elbows on the table. "So let me get this straight. You want me to go to Britain, finagle some jewels, plant them on an innocent man so he can get sent to prison, lie to the police, all without getting caught and sending myself to prison. That's quite a lot to ask, don't you think?"

Angelica had a pained look on her face as she said to Cheryl, "First of all, he is hardly innocent, he stole a three and a half million-dollar ring from Henry and tried to blackmail his way out of his daughter's life for another ten. Now he's using Petunia's nine-year old *face* and making her a public spectacle. He deserves whatever is coming his way. Secondly, you don't have to do this. We told you that up front, but either way we're asking you to never speak about this with anyone else, ever."

Cheryl was a little hot as she listened to Angelica. She nodded emphatically. "No, I get it. You have my word. I'm not going to tell anyone about this scheme. That part's a no-brainer. And I get that this David guy is a scum bag, and I totally get why you want to get him out of your lives. I've seen the book. I haven't read it, but I've heard about it." She paused. "But really...wow. You want me to commit some crimes, and not even here, but in England for God's sake where they have who-the-hell-knows what kind of laws. If something goes wrong, I could be in deep trouble, Charles. You must know that."

Charles nodded. "I do know that. But if you listen to the rest of the plan, and how we propose to protect you, and that you won't really be managing this alone, I believe you'll feel better about it."

The room was quiet enough to hear night noises, chirping crickets and birds serenaded them from outside. Charles and Angelica silently waited for her answer. Cheryl sat back and stared at the two of them, their faces earnest and her eyes fell on Angelica's exotic engagement ring. In a low voice, she said, "Gee, Charles, let me ask you something. Is this the kind of thing you'd ask your fiancé, Daizy, I mean, Angelica, to do, or just someone like me?"

"Oh, Cheryl, please don't get mad," said Angelica.

Charles put up his hand to stop her and said, "I've never lied to you, Cheryl. Do you believe that? Alright then, let's start with that. I think of you as a very talented, underappreciated human being who I immensely enjoy being around. Our conversations and the occasions we had to work together were not only extremely satisfying, but they're also enjoyable because I like you.

"I, me and my family, have a number of resources, around the world actually, that we tap for our various projects. A lot of what we do, what we have done, and what we'll continue to do, could be considered outside the law, or at the very least, using questionable methods and ethics. But I'm not ashamed of them and I never will be, because almost always, it will be against someone or something who deserves what's coming."

Charles sat back in his chair. "I don't give my trust lightly. Nor does my family. If I go to my father, my sister, and tell them we have a plan that can bring peace into our lives and mete out justice for the creep who hurt us, and I tell them I know who we can ask to help us, they trust me because I trust you. You've earned that trust. That's huge for me. It's as close as I can get to combining my respect and admiration for your skills. And no, I would not ask Angelica to do this because she is now known and will forever be known in the press and public as my wife. She'll no longer be able to participate in any role that needs anonymity. If I'm honest in answering your question, you're right, there is risk, and I'm afraid I wouldn't want Angelica to take that either. I'm sorry if that upsets you, but it's the truth. I wouldn't be asking you if we couldn't protect you. If something unforeseen happens, well, then you will have the best legal defense money can buy."

"We're not asking you to steal anything, Cheryl. Just take the jewels from the family who will be working *with you* to distract David, plant them, and walk away. There are a million details to work out, but that is the big idea." Angelica said.

Cheryl considered what they were saying. Pushing back the layers, what they were offering her was a job. A big scary job, the biggest one yet, but this was a whole new level. She looked at Charles in the eye. He'd always been square with her. He'd never crossed a line and had always been true to his word. She thought she could trust him, but a part of her was sad that he was willing to ask her to do something so dangerous. She realized she was something close to a commodity for them, and she was surprised she felt so emotionally let down. Cheryl bowed her head and said, "And what's in it for me?"

Charles smiled, "Well that's the easy part. Whatever you want, really, within reason. I have some thoughts on the subject you might find interesting, but I can guarantee you that we will make it worth your while."

"Do you have a current passport?" Angelica asked.

Cheryl gave her a lopsided smile. "Well, that's to the point."

Angelica reached a hand toward her. "Do you remember when we were hunkered down at the table playing strip poker in my tiny apartment in Santa Monica?" Angelica tapped the table with her finger. "This was the war room that night. Where we're sitting right now. The Carrows family was watching us from this table, and apparently some of them were a nervous wreck," Angelica smiled at Charles. "But the point is, they take care of their people, Cheryl, and you know that."

"I didn't see your boobs on display that night, kid," Cheryl said with an edge. But as she looked at Angelica, she softened her tone. "But then again, you should always go with the best in the house." Cheryl grumbled. "The A team—or the C team, in this case."

"God, they were awesome," Angelica said, shaking her head. "Charles, did you get a good look at them?"

Charles put an elbow on the table and put his head

in his hand. He shook his head. "I'll make no comment on that. This is a chick thing or something, and it isn't a competition.""

"Maybe not a competition, but a pretty big operation," said Cheryl. She pulled herself up straight and reached for the decanter of wine. "Why don't you tell me the rest of the details, and let's see what I think about it after that."

Chapter 28

Near dawn the next day, alone in the king-size bed, cocooned amongst creamy sheets, and protected by the of lushness of Whispering Cliffs, Cheryl Davis, lay awake and stared at the ceiling. The three of them had worked all night, developing a strategy, pulling a plan together, taking it step by step, and poking holes in it. It was frightening and exciting at the same time.

Cheryl had always received a nice chunk of cash from Charles after their local assignations, but she was aware that after the Santa Monica job last year, Angelica had received a wee bit more than her. Granted she'd played a larger role, but Cheryl had supplied the talent and made the show possible. She wasn't angry. She had just wanted to make sure that this time, she would be justly compensated for sticking her neck, and possibly other body parts, out on the line.

She realized now that Charles had had every intention of securing her participation by offering her a deal that would be almost impossible to decline. He'd completely surprised her when he opened his negotiations by offering her a job. In Vegas, or Atlantic City if she chose, but what he really wanted was for her to accept an offer to work for them full-time in the London casino, as the manager of their bar, Angelos. In addition to the job, he was offering her $500,000 cash, and an apartment either in London, or the city of her choice.

That crazy offer had suddenly made her feel less like a commodity, and more like a partner. She didn't know she'd been holding out hope for this next level of intimacy. Charles had always said he respected her, but he used her for jobs. Paid gigs—but nonetheless, paid.

But as the night progressed, the seduction of what he was really offering Cheryl began to sink in. It was an opportunity to begin her life again, as a wealthy, successful, and respected woman.

If Cheryl allowed herself to cry, now would be the time. She hadn't allowed herself that, nor embraced the fantasy in the moment it appeared, but she remembered when that light went off with particular clarity. She didn't really know until then that it was something she desperately desired. She had always been a realist, and it surprised her.

Cheryl got out of bed and went to the balcony doors. She pulled back the curtains and looked out at the moon and down to the ocean below. She breathed deeply and thought about what it would feel like to be a completely different person in a completely different country. That and the fact that she'd been offered a job she was itching to do. She knew how to run a successful bar with almost no resources. The thought of having the Carrows bankrolling a first-class club combined with her years of experience and street smarts? It was exhilarating to think about.

She let the curtains fall back into place as she realized it was too early to get up. She crawled back in bed and closed her eyes, but they popped open as she dreamed about what a transformation might feel like.

People had always only seen her as hard-working stripper, Cherrie Corona, and bar owner, Cheryl Davis. After she arrived in London she would be living under a new name, sporting a glamorous wardrobe, and have an opportunity to try on an entirely different person. She had never been overly respected outside of Lacey's, and she wondered what it would feel like to be admired by others in the world beyond the small universe she had created for herself in LA. To be seen by others not as the marginally socially acceptable Cheryl Davis, but as a rich and respected person in the opulent world of the Carrows.

There were way too many reasons not to jump at this. It was a heady, once in a lifetime opportunity and she intended to make the most of it.

Chapter 29

David Cordoza thought things were going really, really well. Not exactly perfect, but if he was honest with himself, he realized he was lucky.

An angry cop could have wrecked his plans, or the media sensationalism might've fallen flat. Dawna's big mouth could've expelled some gaffe while her head was lost in the clouds. It could have all gone very differently. But he was encouraged with his success. Standing in a San Francisco U-Haul store, he thought about his circumstances as he waited to fill out his registration to rent a small truck for his cross-country trip.

The first book had surpassed his wildest expectations, and even after the Carrows family had contradicted him in their press release, the clever move on Logan Neudor's part to slap together a second book in response, had been genius. David's name was all over the media, and apparently the old adage that there was no such thing as bad press was true. Even the haters and the angry reporters that chased him for interviews built his notoriety.

There had been some difficult moments. Dumping Dawna. After she took her big payday and her role in the operation was mostly complete, she didn't even pretend to be supportive of his art career. In between press events and book signings, he wanted to devote himself full time to working on his art. In order to accomplish that, he had moved back to his small apartment in San Francisco to paint.

While working feverishly in San Francisco, David had expected that Dawna would continue to support him by taking care of the administrative headaches, vetting the calls, coordinating his schedule, and fulfilling the shipment of sales off his website out of her Vegas apartment. But apparently, she was too selfish to care. She told him that she wanted her time to be her own, and that she'd had enough drama and wanted to cut ties with him. He wasn't emotionally impacted by Dawna's decision to leave the relationship, he could always find a woman, but he was upset that she wasn't around to shoulder some of the work.

"Sir," the U-Haul representative said. "Sorry for the wait. Let's get you started."

David answered the questions and filled out the tedious forms. He paid for the one way trip to New Orleans, uncertain if he would need the truck for the return after his first gallery opening. Eventually driving away in the U-Haul, David felt frustrated that his valuable time was being disrupted with these menial and time-consuming tasks.

There weren't enough hours in the day to accomplish

what he wished to do with the pressing obligations from the press, publisher, website—not to mention his art. After the release of the *Ring of Betrayal*, David and Logan Neudor had spent some time rehearsing his responses to the obvious questions that would come his way in interviews. David had spent a day in Logan's office being interrogated by Logan preparing him for the media's rabid questions.

They both felt that his fame would only increase if they limited his interviews to one or two reporters, both who would give it their best shot to tear him down. But David sailed through them. He'd successfully replied to all of their questions with the cool sincerity of Lance Armstrong after every race.

David drove to his small, albeit, wildly expensive studio apartment in the Mission District and gratefully found a parking space nearby. He got out of the truck and walked to the three-story building next to a liquor store and stopped at his building's front door—a locked iron gate. He opened the gate and slammed it shut and ran up the flight of stairs to his second-floor studio.

The studio had become exactly that—a working studio. Canvases, crates, paints, boxes, packing materials, easels—the room was a dedicated work space with a small twin bed pushed up against a wall. He stopped a moment to enjoy the lingering smell of the paint, turpentine, and smoke, sadly mixed in with last night's dinner of tortilla soup. His entire life, all he was worth, was lying around unsecured in his studio. It gave him the shivers sometimes when he was away from it, worrying that something might happen.

He threw his keys on a makeshift desk area and glanced at an open box containing about a hundred copies of his second best-selling book. He picked up a copy and stared into the eyes of his daughter and then to his latest work-in-progress of her on a canvas in the middle of the room. He tossed the book back into the box and considered whether or not he should pack it for the trip. Probably. Why not? It was a money-maker and a part of his package. But he knew there would once again be the inevitable questions.

During all of his interviews, David had successfully kept to his script. He was an artist— frustrated and overwhelmed with his life's pressing concerns. He did what he had to, what his heart told him, in order to do what his calling demanded of him. He made some mistakes, he had terrible regrets for what he did as a passionate youth. He had suffered— and yes, he hadn't been completely forthcoming (never lying), in the first book, but only to protect his daughter from the shame of his actions. It was the Carrows who had done that! Every day, through his art, in his Petunia series, was a *cry for forgiveness*, for understanding, for compassion. He denied trying to blackmail the family for more money and claimed it was the Carrows way to discredit him and shame him further. Life was short! His life was short! It was a precious gift and he had many painful times, painful junctures that presented tormenting challenges, an agonizing labyrinth of life altering decisions, temptations that he could not ignore. With every canvas, with every stroke of his brush, he was finally being his true self— an honest man, a flawed man, contritely begging for compassion.

Oddly it worked. Strangely as well, the Carrows family had not been able to stop the publication of either book nor had they attempted in any way to collect any money from him or his profitable industry. It was all coming together. He was a working artist, a sought-after celebrity with a bit of money in the bank and a bright future ahead. He and Logan had plans to capitalize the hell out of his hot moment. He wouldn't fall victim to the fifteen-minute rule. He was David Cordoza, and he would be around for a long, long, time.

David picked up the phone and brought up his contact for Marcel Broussard, an exuberant gallery owner in New Orleans who'd been the first to contact him with interest in a commission and then a show.

Frustrated when he got the voicemail for the gallery, David left a message confirming his itinerary. A two to three-day drive across the country. On the one hand he was loathing it, on the other, cheerful about why he was going.

The Broussard Gallery, in the heart of the French Quarter, was a perfect debut for David, and he'd spent thousands of his hard-earned dollars framing his artwork to perfection. He bent to examine a few of the pieces, carefully encased in bubble wrap and placed a few by the front door.

If Marcel were to be believed, and David could think

of no reason not to believe him, he would be sold out of inventory by the end of the three-day event. David had hungrily devoured the email of press clippings and copies of advertising that Marcel had strewn across the city and country to attract people to attend the ballyhooed affair. Marcel Broussard was a wildly excitable Cajun whose enthusiasm over David's art was intoxicating. It felt very right.

David walked a few steps to his walk-in closet with sliding mirrored doors and pushed a side open. He grabbed a couple of his better jackets still in plastic from the cleaners and held them up against various trousers and jeans. He'd need to choose his clothing for the gallery show carefully. First impressions and clothing were important, a lesson he learned long ago from his onetime girlfriend, Charlotte Carrows. One of the only good things about her that he retained. Well, that and the kid. She'd been worth a bundle. He smiled as he considered his image. It was all coming together.

Chapter 30

David walked along the hardwood floors of the Broussard Gallery and stared at the cream walls, now adorned with his artwork. The adjustable track lighting on the ceiling was positioned over each piece to enhance its beauty. The beam angles, the intensity of the lights, each were individualized to showcase his children. Ironically, in the case of much of his subject matter, literally.

Marcel Broussard was no rookie to adjusting the lighting plan to showcase the art and the mood in the room. David had been to many galleries and art shows in his life, and he appreciated the professional result Marcel had achieved. He looked down to the far end of the gallery where a bar was being set up for the six p.m. opening. Tonight, Sazerac cocktails and champagne would be complimentary to the invited attendees. Tomorrow, the gallery would be open to the public and they would serve free ice cream and coffee. The third and final day, people traditionally brought their own go cups as they wandered in from the street. Broussards was located on Royal Street, one of the many galleries on a street where for over a century, artists had been showcasing their work, building New Orleans into a southern mecca of cool. Serious collectors, as well as those enthusiasts in search of art which spoke to them, often spent days traversing the long street, appreciating each of the galleries and boutiques for their diverse collections.

David glanced up as he heard Marcel laughing and watched him enter the gallery from the back. Walking toward him with his assistant, David was mildly relieved to see the young, dreadlocked kid named Laurent cleaned up. Not that he was that young or dirty, but on David's day of arrival, Laurent had a large, distasteful stain on his shirt when he helped David unload his van. The young man seemed capable though and would be on hand over the next several days to help customers with their purchases.

Marcel had also changed, but this time into some long white mumu with a Greek influence. David blinked, slightly shocked at the hugeness of the man. His hair was newly-styled too—all twisted and spiky, coming out of his head like a short-haired medusa. Marcel was large and exotic, and while his look might be a bit over-the-top— possibly tilting toward fine, he was unfortunately carrying his dumb dog, Steve.

David was not overly fond of dogs and he didn't trust that stupid Steve wouldn't take a nervous wiz in front of his guests and ruin his show. David curled up his lip slightly thinking about it but put a smile on his face as Marcel, with one arm extended approached.

"Mr. Cordoza, tonight will be spectacular. You are happy, yes?" Marcel gestured around the room.

"Yes. Thank you, Marcel. It's very clean, the lighting is just right."

Marcel nodded as they strolled down the wall together and looked at the art. "David, you will sell tonight. I guarantee it. There is a bravery I see in your work. You've left a part of your soul the canvas and people will respond to it."

They stopped before a particularly large painting, the showcase piece, the one most used in his advertising. Marcel continued, "I've showcased many artists, David. Talent may be a dirty word to some, but I don't care. I'll use it. It is indefinable, it is something which cannot be taught. In this painting, you can feel her innocence, somehow a life not yet lived. There is potential on the canvas, a feeling for her and the young woman she will become. She is at once unknowable, yet before us, brave."

"Thank you, Marcel." David glanced into his eyes. He saw a sincerity which gave him confidence. "I only wish I had more. I kept back several works on my Petunia series, I thought some of my other pieces were important as well."

Marcel turned his head and looked at the other side of the room lined with a mix of impressionist images of modern-day scenes. "Yes," said Marcel as he stroked Steve's head, "you need more inventory. I have a friend who is a contributor to *Artforum* stopping by this evening. You will want to take some time with him."

Artforum, the *Vogue* of the artworld, was a magazine

David had devoured for years. He felt a small surge of pride thinking of his name, his collection possibly mentioned in it. He was exactly where he should be. Definitely not hawking his art on Jackson Square like so many of the struggling, dirty masses of artists in the French Quarter who could never hope to achieve his level of success.

"Will you have family, anyone special to introduce me to this evening?" Marcel asked.

David shook his head. "No. Most of my friends are on the west coast. They'll attend my gallery showings back there."

"I see," Marcel said, stroking Steve. "Well, tonight you meet the monied, interesting, edgy, best of New Orleans. My friends. They'll read your work, David. And believe me, the commissions and demand for more will roll in."

David smiled. He believed him.

Chapter 31

Cheryl Davis stared at a picture of David Torres Cordoza, the man she was being asked to destroy. She saw a handsome, sly face with an olive complexion. Very white teeth and nicely groomed, he had a model-like slimness which made him look good in his clothes, but he reminded her of a fox. She'd watched a television interview he'd done after the release of his first book and was fascinated by his unflappable smoothness and confidence, even though on some level he had to know that what he was selling was total bullshit. Their fates were on a collision course, and he didn't know that Cherrie Corona was coming.

Cheryl clicked on the image and closed the app. Nearly two a.m., she heard the booming music of the bar through the walls of Lacey's and wondered if she'd miss being here. She put a hand out and touched the small Tiffany-style lamp she'd bought years ago after she'd invested her hard-earned money and became a partner in the bar. At the time, she thought the lamp might class the place up. But the reality was, it was always going to be a strip bar. No matter how much glitter you threw on it.

She knew her lifestyle and surroundings were about to radically change. She was no longer going to be Cheryl Davis, and definitely not Cherrie Corona. Her new name, her latest alias, would be Geneva Crawford.

She got up and went to a mirror. She pulled the baseball cap off her head, released her pony-tail holder and let the newly blond tresses fall. She ran a hand through the soft wave in the hair, expertly installed with the help of the Carrows' high-end stylist. The multi-tonal color job was exceptional. She, Charles, and Angelica had decided that the newly minted and fashionable Geneva Crawford should present herself in London as a beautiful soft blond. The hair-stylist had been her first appointment after agreeing to the job. They needed pictures of her to send to Alex Macchi so he could get to work on her new identification papers.

She held the pony-tail holder in her teeth as she pulled her hair back up and re-banded it. She put the Cubs baseball cap back on and returned to her desk, pulling over a box which held a few of her things. She hadn't told her partners that she was going forever, only that she was taking a long vacation. A sabbatical, she'd told them. She thought it would be easier that way.

They hadn't been happy, but she knew it was because they realized they'd now have to do the heavy lifting of managing the dancers and staff. She didn't think she'd miss her partners, but she'd miss the girls. She felt protective over them and hoped that after she left, things wouldn't go to hell. It may only be a strip bar, but it was *her* strip bar, and she was proud of it.

"Cherrie," a young dancer, named Mandy, said as she pushed open the door. The loud music reverberated into the office from behind her.

Cheryl smiled.

"We're meeting for breakfast at Cindy's, right?" the young girl asked in reference to the late-night deli down the street.

"Yeah. I'll close up."

The young girl put out her bottom lip. "We're going to miss you sooooooo much. I can't believe you're leaving."

"It's just a sabbatical." Cheryl smiled. "It'll be okay."

"Yeah, I guess." The girl frowned. "So we'll see you over there."

"Quick as I can." Cheryl nodded.

The door shut. Cheryl returned to her packing. She put her laptop and a few other items in the box and put a hand out again to grab the lamp. She thought better of it. It was a part of the room now. And where she was going, she definitely wouldn't need it. She wondered if she'd ever use it again.

Chapter 32

While Cheryl was being transformed into Geneva Crawford and saying goodbye to her life in Los Angeles, Charles and Angelica flew back to London to secure an offer on their new home in Curzon Square, in the exclusive Mayfair district of West London. Not far from the casino, their new home was a spacious two-bedroom apartment situated on two floors moments away from Hyde Park and in the immediate area of some of London's best restaurants and boutiques. With an elegant white gothic front alcove, the black door opened into a spectacular drawing room with high ceilings, full sash windows and an ornamental balcony overlooking a garden. For six million dollars, it was a beautifully intimate property perfectly suited to their needs while they were living in London and building the next grand piece of their legacy.

They had also purchased a much smaller, albeit charming, one-bedroom apartment in another part of Mayfair across the street from the Ritz London hotel.

Occupying the site of the former home of Britain's first Prime Minister, a developer had turned it into five luxury apartments with private entrances and twenty-four-hour concierge service. Charles and Angelica felt Carey would be very comfortable in the three-million-dollar apartment but were surprised by her response when she arrived.

Standing in the tastefully decorated apartment, Carey looked out the window to the Ritz across the street. She turned to Charles with a flat, deadly look. "I don't think so. I'd rather live over there."

The siblings stared, challenging one another until Charles broke and rolled his eyes. "Fine, Carey. We'll use the apartment somehow. Maybe Cheryl Davis will like it even if you don't. Get yourself a junior suite at the Ritz and stay there when you're in town."

Carey gave him a wide smile. "Thank you, sweetie. You want me to be happy, don't you?" She walked over and gave him a quick hug. "I just can't see myself managing my own laundry and cooking and there isn't even a gym in this tiny place. You want me to look my best while I'm canoodling with the potential investors, don't you?"

Charles turned to leave. "I do. It was my mistake not realizing that you needed round the clock catering. Just keep the services below the crazy mark or it will cost me as much as this apartment."

Carey followed him out the door and waited while Charles locked the door. "Once I come into my inheritance you won't have to put up with me, Charles, then you'll miss me."

"I won't miss you. You'll be around; it just won't be

on my tab. I'd try to ride your tab onto the building of the casino, but I don't want the cost of your services to scare away the investors. Your wardrobe alone would make them think we were nuts."

The two of them walked to the elevators. "I'm worth every penny and you know it, brother. While I'm in town, I plan on making a very big social and media splash and keep that Carrows name in front of the hungry press. They'll just gobble me up. Angelica and I are in for loads of fun while I'm over here."

"I'd appreciate it if you'd keep her away from the more lurid moments on your path to celebrity. I would like her image to be slightly above that of a party girl."

"Got it. I'm the party girl, Angelica's the queen bee, and then we have Cheryl Davis. How do you see her role?"

The empty elevator opened and the two of them entered. "As nothing. I don't want her in the press at all, ever. I don't want her face to appear next to yours or anyone associated with the Carrows family until David's heard the metal doors being banged closed on his sorry ass. You protect her, Carey. Help her to acclimate, shop, have fun, but do it quietly until this is over. I know Cheryl can probably hold her own anywhere, but she needs some exposure to higher society, some tips on how to behave at Hambley Hall. She's not exactly an innocent lamb that needs protection, more of a Pygmalion who could use your help. But don't let her know you're helping her, I don't want her feelings to get hurt or anything. I'm sure she has the party girl part in the bag, it's the lady of the manor part that needs your help."

"When does she arrive?"

They got off the elevator and Charles waved to the doorman as they walked out onto the busy London street. "In a few weeks. We're letting the David show in the States build some more momentum before we convince him to come to Hambley Hall to paint the Countess' portrait. Is Harley coming over any time soon?"

"No. Harley is going to sit this one out. He has his own interests to attend to right now, and besides, I'd rather swing around London as a singleton. Sounds like much more fun."

They caught up with the pedestrian traffic and emerged onto the crosswalk. "So what's the deal with you and Harley? Is he going to get upset if he sees you in the press hooking up with some good looking Brit?"

"Maybe, but I don't care. He doesn't own me, Charles. Nobody does. Sometimes I just want to have my own kind of fun without worrying about what he thinks."

"Do you love him at all?" Charles asked as he took her arm as they walked.

"I guess. I mean, yeah, I love him, but I'm not ready to be tied down to one person, and I'm pretty sure he's not ready either. Maybe it'll be good for us to be apart, and maybe it'll be good for him to see that he isn't the only glamor-boy out there interested in sweet little me."

"I see. I'm sure that means that you'll put your very best into enlightening him of that fact in the press. Give our London public relations rep, Summer Ash, a call and use her to your heart's content. She's gonna love you. Just be sure to keep it clean, Carey."

"You're such an old man sometimes. I hope you realize that Angelica is just about the same age as I am and I'm sure she isn't ready to retire to her rocking chair yet either. You'd better give her some room to live it up or she's gonna regret getting tied down so young to the first billionaire to come her way."

"I love you, too, Carey," Charles said laughing. "But don't worry about Angelica. She knows exactly what she wants in life, and I'm delighted to say, it happens to be me."

Charles nodded to the top-hatted bellman at the Ritz and watched as Carey smiled and began her slow courtship with them herself. One of them took off his hat and swung it to the side as he made a slight bow in her direction. They walked up the five stairs to the lobby entrance as Carey continued, "If you say so. Tell her we're meeting for drinks this evening at six at the Rivoli Bar. Tell her to wear something sparkly. I've already called Summer Ash by the way, Angelica gave me her name last week. She knows I'm in town, and the press knows exactly where we're going to be this evening. I've even lined up a date! You're going to love him."

Charles narrowed his eyes with surprise and confusion. "Who are you bringing?"

"Wait and see. Look sharp, and remember, I'm only here to help."

"You are good at your job," he whispered.

"I love you too, Charles."

Later that evening, Angelica, stunning in a black and white sleeveless, Alexandra Vidal, cocktail dress featuring hand-beaded crystals, and an A-line skirt embellished with dyed ostrich feathers, greeted her sister in-law-to be and her date for the evening—none other than the doe-eyed Nick Maachi.

"Nick, Nick," Angelica tsked later, quietly visiting with him while Carey and Charles had their heads together. "Are you sure you know what you're getting yourself into with Carey? I know she's beautiful, but she's a wildcat."

Nick was all glorious smiles that night having a great time with the Carrowses once again. "I'm from Brooklyn, Angelica. I'm a college and law school graduate, and I'd like to think I know my way around the ladies, even if she is a Carrows."

"I know, honey. I'm just looking out for you. Even though hot Harley isn't here at the moment, doesn't mean he won't find out what's going on. I have a feeling some of Carey's plans involve making sure he's reminded that she's single. Just promise me you won't fall in love with her or anything crazy like that."

"Crazy like you did with Charles?" Nick raised an eyebrow.

"That's different and you know it. I didn't have a

boyfriend when I met Charles, and Carey does. Do what you want, but I think you should be a little bit careful. I'm just sayin." Angelica shrugged.

"Thank you. I understand what you're saying, but in the meantime, I intend to have some fun. What a crazy world I'm living in right now, over here. It feels awfully good." Nick smiled broadly, high on life.

Charles turned and interrupted. "There's a photographer over there. Probably the one that Summer Ash has following us tonight."

"Well, let's give her something to print." Carey leaned over and grabbed Nick's face and kissed him thoroughly.

Angelica's mouth was one big O as Charles tipped his glass to his mouth and muttered to her quietly. "Try not to look so surprised, honey. It's Carey's world and we're just living in it."

Chapter 33

Cheryl Davis arrived in London soon after toting her new Globe Trotter and Gucci luggage through Heathrow airport and taking a taxi to Charles and Angelica's home in Mayfair. They settled in for a chat and caught her up to speed to what was happening with the plan.

"I'm so excited you're finally here," Angelica said. "The first thing we're going to do is go shopping! I've been pouring over the shops with Carey and I know exactly where to bring you. Charles and I made a list of the things we think you'll need to pull off a rich girl from old Texas money."

"Yes, and to that end, you're going to need these," Charles said, handing her an envelope.

"What do we have here?" Cheryl opened the envelope.

"Your new identity. Geneva Cecelia Crawford. You'll find a new Texas driver's license, a passport— although you probably shouldn't use that for now, credit cards, and cash."

"Wow, a party in a bag." She smiled into it.

"We should begin calling you by your new name right now," said Charles. "You need to start getting used to it and no one in Britain ever needs to hear the name Cheryl. We'll keep your Cheryl Davis passport and credentials here in our safe, so you can use them when you leave the country. In the meantime, start using the cards and start dressing like Geneva as soon as possible. Shop quietly, girls. If you see a photographer out there, either of you, just separate immediately. We can't have you linked up."

"Geneva—" Charles paused to look at Cheryl sidelong until she nodded. "—as much as we would love to have you stay here with us, we need to move you into your own place immediately. We purchased a really nice apartment for Carey not far from here, but unbelievably, she rejected it."

"I can't wait to show you," said Angelica. "It's so sweet. I had it decorated, or I should say, we had a decorator furnish it and stock it with linens and groceries, and everything you need. I really hope you like it. I didn't know what your taste was, but I told them to make it girly, cozy, country French with some nice antiques and doodads. Carey is at the London Ritz across the street from your apartment, so you can stroll over to see her whenever you want."

"I'd text her before showing up," Charles pressed his lips together.

"Oh, man." Angelica shook her head. "Charles is just mad because Carey has been hanging out with Nick

Maachi, Alex's youngest brother. Do you know about the Macchi family?"

"Not really," said Geneva. "Charlotte is married to a Macchi, right?"

"Yes," said Angelica. "Alex. Nick is Alex's youngest brother and he's heading up the security for the hotel and casino for us. Macchi & Macchi opened a branch here in London. I'm sure you'll meet him soon." Angelica placed a sympathetic hand on Charles shoulder. "Really, Charles, it's none of our business if they want to date or carry on. Neither one of them are married and it's not like she's that much older than him."

Charles scowled. "I see. So you don't think it's a bit odd that both my sisters have a Macchi in their bed?"

"Geneva," Angelica turned to her. "Don't get dragged into these small family issues just yet. Let's focus on getting you some great clothes and jewels and get you out to the country. The sooner you get the job done, the sooner we can all get on with our lives."

"That's good advice," Charles said rubbing his head. "Soak up London for a while and get to know the town, and I'd like to spend some time with you going over the plans for the bar and the casino so you can see what we're building. Then you can decide if you'd like to join us over here after the job is done."

"Charles named the bar Angelos. It's the Greek translation of my name. It's just the sweetest thing he's ever done for me." Angelica gazed at her adoring fiancé.

"I see the two of you are still going strong," said

Geneva. "Angelos. I like it. Italian. Got an LA vibe, too."

"But mostly for Angelica," Charles smiled. "A gentleman I know, my inspiration for the casinos, has a famous bar he named after his mother called Clementine's. It's a popular place that I'd like you to visit before you leave town. The only problem is it's too public to risk us being seen there together."

Charles smirked, then suddenly smiled at the two women. "I tell you what. I'll have a friend of mine take you there one night before you leave England. I think you'll like him. Consider it my bon voyage."

"Who is it Charles?" Angelica asked.

"Just wait and see, darling. Geneva, we should get you over to the apartment, so you can see where you'll be living for the next couple of weeks. It's also the permanent apartment we will be offering you after David is in jail, and if you move to London to manage the club.

"As to David's current status, he's just finished his art show in New Orleans at our friend Marcel Broussard's gallery and by all accounts it actually had a very decent turnout. Marcel said that David left thoroughly pumped up and pleased with himself and is now back in San Francisco. I'm going to have Marcel give him a call and offer the contract commission from the Linningtons. It all hinges on whether or not David bites and is willing to travel to Hambley Hall. I have confidence in Marcel, but we'll find out soon enough."

Chapter 34

David Cordoza stood shirtless before his easel in his modest San Francisco apartment, painting like his life depended on it. *I'm a star*, he thought. God, New Orleans had been a dream come true. People admired his work, admired him, gawked at him, took his picture, asked him to sign autographs, paid actual fucking money for his art! His wildest dreams were finally coming true. He had money in the bank, and soon he would be able to afford a real studio and stop sleeping with his paints. He didn't mind it terribly; it meant that he could get up and paint any time he wanted, day or night. And since he'd been back from the show, he'd painted non-stop. He was on fire! Inspired! A Goddamned Famous Artist! He almost pinched himself he was so happy.

While he was in New Orleans, Marcel Broussard had asked him how he managed his web site and sales and took a real interest in his future plans. Startled that David didn't have someone helping him deal with the tedious administrative side to the business, Marcel had offered to help him run it from New Orleans, for a percentage. It was perfect for both of them.

Glancing now at his ringing cell phone, David was mildly annoyed to have his creative flow interrupted, but he answered since it was from Marcel.

"Hey oh, David, how're you doing, Mon?" Marcel said cheerfully.

"I'm fine. Working. It might be a good idea if we set some boundaries around what time I would be available for your calls."

Marcel continued, "Whatever you say big guy. Listen, sorry to interrupt, but something exciting has come up and I was calling to see if you were interested. I got a call from a guy in Europe who wants to commission a portrait."

"Europe?" David piqued. He grabbed a pack of cigarettes and shook one out. "How did he find me?"

"From your website, Man, and the press. Your story has officially gone abroad my friend, and get this, the guy is an Earl, in Britain."

"An Earl? And he wants me to paint what?" David sat down on his small bed and lit up.

"He said he wanted you to paint a portrait of his wife. Apparently, they have some family jewelry that they are going to be selling at auction at some point and wanted her to wear it one last time. His wife is American, and she follows the news over here. Don't take offense because he seems to have a pretty good sense of humor, but he said they thought it would be a hoot for a jewel thief to paint their family jewels. We yukked it up. He thought it would be a good story to attach to the portrait after you're finished."

David paused and considered the oddity of the request. "Really," he stated flatly.

"Hey, David. It's out there. You've explained the circumstances. The story gives you character. I say we use it. It should be a nice commission, it may open up Europe, but it's up to you."

David was silent considering the importance of the offer. He hadn't expected that people would be interested in commissioning him to paint their portraits.

"Marcel, this is untapped market for me. I can't believe we didn't think of it ourselves." He puffed and blew his smoke toward the ceiling. "You need to get that on my website. Right away. I mean, it could be a big sideline for me. Did he say how much he was willing to pay?"

"We haven't negotiated that yet, I wanted to see if you would be willing to pull yourself away from your Petunia work first. He did mention that he would pay for your travel."

"When does he want me to do this?" David scanned his apartment, smoking, considering his current inventory.

"Right away. Apparently, it was a last-minute idea his wife came up with and since she's so upset about having to sell the jewels, the earl said it would mollify her or something. They're putting them on auction at Sotheby's."

"Alright, I can do this. You call them back and negotiate a *really* good price, whatever you think is fair, and I'll do it. It'll look damn good on the website too. A portrait for an Earl. What did you say his name was?"

"The earl of Hambley, Barford Linnington."

"Barford?" David rolled his shoulders.

"Yeah, Barford and Jane, the earl and countess of Hambley out of Yorkshire, England."

"Get it done, Marcel. This is a great opportunity for me."

"You got it! Say do you have an active passport? How soon can you be ready to go?"

"I can be ready almost immediately, and yes, my passport is current."

"Okay. They also said they might be interested in some of your other work from the Petunia line and wanted you to bring some of your finished, framed pieces over with you. I guess they want something from the series to show other people who might recognize you as the artist relative to the portrait you'd be painting."

"Geez, absolutely. I've got a couple of really amazing new ones being framed as we speak. They'd be perfect for them. I picked out some beautiful ornate Italian frames. This feels like kismet."

"You bet. You're really on a roll, David. I'll get back to you after I square a price with the earl. You get back to work! I have a feeling we're going to need all the inventory we can get."

David hung up without saying goodbye and stared at the phone and smiled. *My God*, he thought, *life's getting better and better*. He lay back on his bed and smoked. He was a rock star.

After David gave him his marching orders and disconnected without saying goodbye, Marcel rubbed his hands together and dialed Charles.

"Your skeevy putz took the bait, Charles. He's barking orders at me and thinks he's the next Vermeer. He said he can shake loose immediately, so when do you want him there?"

"How about in a week or two? Did he say how much he wanted for the portrait?"

"No, he told me, his new manager and gofer, to commission a deal. What do you want to pay him?"

"Tell him ten grand in cash plus travel and that they will guarantee purchase of one or two of his Petunia portraits, assuming they are tastefully framed. Be sure to tell him to pack a variety of sizes of the framed portraits so they have some options."

"I'll remind him. I think he'll take the offer. If he doesn't he's an idiot, in which case, I'll have to convince him it's all about the prestige of the job and building his idiotic resume."

"Is he wearing on you, Marcel?"

"He is. After spending a few days with him and seeing for myself that he was a complete scumbag, I was happy to see him go. It was an interesting exhibit for the gallery and I'll say this, it brought in a different clientele.

People included a stop at my gallery as part of a party evening—having dinner, having your fortune told, getting hammered, and gawking at David Cordoza. Not a real elite crowd on the last day, not that David was distinguishing. He's blinded by the stars in his own eyes, man."

"Well, we thank you, my friend. I'm sure it was distasteful, but we really appreciate it."

"Charles, I do have a concern. Not to tell you how to conduct your personal escapades, but when I spoke with him and mentioned the earl thinking it would be a hoot to have a jewel thief paint his jewels, I got a bit of silence on David's end. I don't know, like the hair on the back of my neck stood up. Are you certain he won't suspect you're behind this?"

"We've considered that, but with all the layers, we thought we were covered."

"But you're a rich, powerful family. Wouldn't he be asking himself why you're not somehow making his life miserable?"

"You got a niggle?"

"Maybe."

"Alright, let me see if we can do something about that. In the meantime, book his flight into Heathrow, and tell him a driver will meet him at the airport to take him to Hambley Hall. It's time for David to get his comeuppance."

Chapter 35

Geneva Crawford had a black Rolls Royce Ghost packed to the limit as her driver negotiated their way out of London. A newly hired employee of Macchi & Macchi, he had instructions to get her safely out of the city, turn the car over to her in Peterborough, and take a train back. Geneva Crawford would drive up to Hambley Hall alone in her three-hundred-thousand-dollar prestigious rental.

She had been on a roller coaster since arriving in London but loved every minute of it. Her apartment was charmingly decorated, and while it would not have occurred to Cheryl Davis to decorate in such a feminine manner, it fit perfectly for Geneva Crawford and the gentile lady she would be portraying. She'd been wide-eyed shocked at the expenditures she, Angelica and Carey tallied up as they helped her fully embrace her new identity and she was glad she'd had the privacy with them as she practiced her nonchalance over the sticker shock.

Geneva Crawford wore beautifully tasteful designer

clothes, casually elegant, never casually tacky. Her only real lounging clothes consisted of riding outfits, complete with Dover boots. Kitschy skirts, classic cut dresses, cardigans, lovely linen trousers, pastels, frilly shirts, elegant dining clothes and a ton of excellent costume jewelry bulged out of her many wardrobes in the trunk of the car. She would need staff to keep it all looking freshly effortless and was assured by Charles that the countess had hired an extra maid for her personal use. She was instructed to be the eternal lady, an elegantly mannered, entertaining houseguest in front of the earl and countess, but a bad girl in front of David.

Beautiful, blond, single Geneva Crawford was an American from Texas whose mother was a friend of Jane Linnington. Poor Geneva had just gone through a bad divorce from an extremely wealthy husband who unfortunately caught her in bed with another man. *Colto in flagrante*, she would laugh when questioned.

Her very rich mommy and daddy were furious with her for messing up such a promising future with her Texas millionaire, and had been counseled by their good friend, the Countess, that it would be good for Geneva to spend some time in the country with them—recovering. Geneva's mother had thought it was a brilliant idea especially after the countess insinuated the possibility of a good match to a bright young man in England, and a fresh start to wash away Geneva's tarnished reputation at home.

Stopping the car at the top of a ridge and looking down into the valley and onto the village of Hambley, Geneva got her first glance at the magnificent estate of the earl and countess. She couldn't quite believe this was happening to her. While gazing at the house, and the gardens, the damn sheep dotting the luscious green countryside, she almost lost herself completely into character. She inhaled through her nose and reminded herself to stay focused and that she was sent there to do a job. And a dangerous job at that. Winding her way down to the stately home, poor old Cheryl Davis poked her head out and said, "Girl, get this right. They're counting on you. Get in, get out, and send that crazy bastard to hell."

That morning before leaving London, Charles had reminded her about what to expect. The earl and countess had been extremely nervous about the entire scheme from the moment their friends Henry and Julia had proposed it. It was not something they would have ever contemplated doing in the real world, but then, as everyone knew, Henry and Julia didn't really live in the real world. Apparently the Carrows family had made an offer to the Linningtons that they could not refuse.

A side of Geneva's mouth rose as she thought about the Carrowses and their knack for making offers which could not be refused. On that front, she and the Linningtons were in the same boat.

It was also helpful that the Linningtons claimed they would lose no sleep about the moral implications of what they would do to David, but they'd been very concerned about the lying and playacting which would be involved. Henry Carrows had assured them they would bring in someone who would manage it all.

Geneva shook her head. Shit. And that girl is me.

She pondered the situation as she drove down the avenue of trees toward the main house. The apple, pear, and cherry trees were in full bloom and it was a gorgeous anticipatory embrace for guests driving up to the Georgian house. When she pulled up into the circular drive of the three-story home with more windows than brick, she thought about how sad it would be if because of the forty-percent inheritance tax, the Linningtons would lose their home. She'd been told that roughly forty million pounds would be due to the tax man when the earl died, and the house had been in the family since the 1700s.

She thought it was an incredible legacy to have lived, and she couldn't blame them for hating the thought of losing it.

A butler-type guy dressed formally opened her driver's door and helped her from the car. "Welcome to Hambley Hall," he said and gave her brief nod.

Geneva thanked him and smiled at the couple standing on the wide flight of steps in front of tall, eight-panel double doors.

The butler escorted her up the steps. "May I present, the earl and countess of Hambley, Lord Barford and Lady Jane Linnington."

Geneva had been prepared for this and knew what to do, but observing Jane Linnington literally wringing her hands, she recognized instantly that they were probably more nervous than she was. But the three of them had public scripts to keep to in front of the staff. The show began.

"Lady Hambley, Lord Hambley, it's a pleasure to finally meet you! Mommy has told me so much about you!" Geneva smiled with confidence and extended a hand to the Earl.

"Yes," said the Earl, "a delight. Won't you come in? Sorsby will have someone see to your bags."

"Did you find your travels to us difficult?" Jane's voice echoed slightly as they walked through the historical, two-story hall. "I would have sent a car to collect you, but your mother told me you much preferred to drive."

"I told Mommy that I needed to get comfortable with driving on the left. Leaving London was a bit of a challenge, but nothing I haven't dealt with before in Houston or Dallas."

"We're just in here dear," Jane said as she directed Geneva and her husband into the day parlour, a cheerful room with chintz floral walls. "I thought we might take our tea in here. Sorsby will bring it shortly. Won't you have a seat, you must be exhausted from your drive." Jane turned to the butler. "Sorsby, would you be a dear and close the door behind you as you leave. We'd like a private moment with our dear Geneva before you serve."

Alone in the classically English surroundings of the posh, feminine room, Geneva watched as the earl and countess threw themselves down into chairs and each expelled a large breath. Both of them looked like they had already been through an ordeal. Geneva took a seat in a chair primly next to them and said, "As much as I would like to call you Jane and Barford, I understand that you need to give me leave to do that?"

"Yes," said Jane, "Thank you. You may call us Jane and Barford in private. It's nice to meet you, Geneva. Is that your real name?"

"No. It's not, but I don't think it's a good idea to muddle your thoughts with any other. While I'm here, and forever after, you will only know me as Geneva Cecelia Crawford. I believe Charles mailed you something with my fictitious back story to prepare you for my arrival? If you still have that around, you should destroy it. Also, Charles wanted me to remind you not to email them about anything. No written trails. No texts or phone calls. I'll do the same. I assume you told the staff that I was the daughter of your American friend from Texas, coming to stay. Did you tell them why?"

"Not exactly," said Jane. "Sorsby, our butler, has been with us forever and is more like family, but we obviously don't want to involve him in any way. He knows you are here to visit, to spend some time away from America, and that you had recently been dealt an unfortunate situation that you need to get some distance from."

"That's perfect. Did you have any other questions for me right now?" Geneva looked to each of them with concern.

"What is it we are supposed to do!" Jane put her face in her hands.

"Well, right now, nothing. Just entertain me like you

would any other guest from out of the country and when David arrives to paint your portrait next week, I'll give you instructions about anything I might need to move the plan along."

"Such as?" questioned the Earl.

"Well, I've been told that you have a son, Brandon, or Barford, the next earl and that Jane, you love nothing better than to introduce young people to one another to make matches. We believe it would be a very good idea if you thought of me as someone who needed cheering up, and someone who might be a match for your son. Someone who you were considering as a potential mate for your son and off limits to David Cordoza."

"I say, you want us to bring Brandon into this?" The earl's eyes widened.

"Maybe not. Not directly. But it might be a nice idea to invite him to dine with us while David was staying here, you know, to reinforce the plan."

Geneva could see the uncertainty in their faces and realized she needed to move slowly. "No worries. Let's think about it for a while. Really, I don't want you to worry; it's all going to go fine. I'm here to do the dirty work as they say, but I will need your help."

"Golly," said Jane, standing. "I'll ring for Sorsby now, and that tea. I'm quite sure we could all do with some refreshment."

"Tell him to bring a bottle of brandy along with it. You know, to steady the nerves," the earl said as Jane looked sharply at the earl and forcefully blinked.

"That's an excellent idea," said Geneva. "Just as long as you can continue to keep our secrets while you're in your cups."

"Oh my," said Jane, "maybe I'll have a wee tot of something, too."

Geneva realized that not only was she going to have to take charge, the Linningtons would require serious stroking as well. Cocktails were definitely in order.

They spent the next week relaxing and getting to know one another. The Linningtons found Geneva to be extremely well mannered and totally at ease in her new surroundings. They were immensely intrigued and continually asked for hints as to her real background. Geneva held her ground and gave them nothing about her real identity, any one of them.

Geneva knew the Linningtons would be extremely shocked if they knew who she really was and where she came from, so she turned her mind to task and became the perfect houseguest. She was very interested in the estate, its history, the family artwork adorning every wall, the suits of armor from their actual relatives standing in protective profile over them at the dining table. Geneva enjoyed walking in the garden with Jane and hanging out in the kitchen with Emma while she cooked them delicious meals, walking the farm with the earl and learning about the estate's holdings and the village of Hambley. She and the earl even went for pints at the Hambley Arms in the village where she was gawked at as a beautiful, young, and obviously wealthy American staying at the Hall with the earl and his wife. They left the Arms with the locals gossiping and laying odds about whether or not they had met their next countess of Hambley.

By the end of the week, Jane and Barford couldn't have been more relaxed and confident in Geneva's power to charm the pants off David and get the job done. With their son Brandon living in London, and their daughter Ashley living half way across the world in Australia, they immensely enjoyed her easy company and were almost looking forward to the prospect of the upcoming jewelry caper.

But reality set in the evening before David Cordoza's arrival as the three of them took their after dinner cocktails in the privacy of the drawing room.

Geneva sat across from Jane on a slightly worn sofa. "You do understand that I intend to seduce David? Behind your backs, so to speak, so that he sees me acting one way toward you, and quite another toward him in private. At some point, I'll need one of you to *accidently* catch us out. This will be cause for his expulsion from your home, since of course, this will be upsetting to you because you have *my* hand in mind for your only son, Brandon."

"But my dear," said Jane, "won't this be distasteful to you? You aren't really going to have a go with him between the sheets, are you?"

Geneva laughed at the sincere concern the countess had for her morals and reputation. If she only knew the tricks that Cherrie Corona was capable of. "You've been so sweet to me Jane and Barford, but please, don't worry about me. I won't be doing anything I'm uncomfortable doing—with David or anyone else. I'm just going to have to see how receptive he is to me and how far I'll need to go. Please don't take offense by anything you see me do that you might not like. I hope you know that I wouldn't want to purposefully offend you."

"Well, I don't like it," the earl puffed up. "A nice young girl like yourself. I'm not sure I can allow you to do this Geneva. Now that I've gotten to know you, I feel rather protective."

Geneva didn't know if what they were saying were only appropriate words or actual sentiments, but one thing that surprised her was how much she wished it were real. They were wonderful people, as were the Carrowses, and she was honored and blessed that they had all come into her life.

Geneva looked away, slightly embarrassed by her sentimentality, as Jane said, "After this is over, what will you do Geneva? Will you go back to America? Will we ever see you again?"

Good questions all. Geneva stared at the sweet ceramic vases of white garden roses that she and Jane had cut that morning. "I'm not sure if I'll see you again. That might be up to you, or the Carrowses, depending on how it goes. I do know that after David is arrested and charged, I'll be returning to the States. After that, my return to England will depend on the developments."

Jane walked across the space and sat next to Geneva. She took her hand. "Wherever you go, I wish you the best of fortunes. You're a wonderful person Geneva or whoever you are. I've always been an excellent judge of character, and I can tell, even though you're playing a role, I know who you truly are, and I think you're wonderful."

Geneva squeezed her hand and let go, thinking, *we'll see.*

Chapter 36

Sean Murray and his Spanish-speaking cohort from Macchi & Macchi sat in a Lexus on 110th Street in Inglewood, California and stared at a small blue home.

"This the place?" Sean said, leaning down and staring out the driver's side window.

"It's the right address," said Santiago, otherwise known to everyone as Santa.

"Fucking dump," Sean said as he buttoned his suit coat and patted his pockets.

Santa looked out the window toward the small lot with patchy grass and a broken narrow walkway. "Old Toyota Corolla in the half-ass driveway. He's probably home."

Sean turned to his partner. "Okay. So showtime. Remember, good cop, bad cop. I'm the bad cop. You're the smooth, Spanish-speaking interpreter who feels a little sorry for the guy. Got it?"

Santa turned off the car and glanced in the mirror. "I look alright?"

"You look like a slick-ass lawyer in that new suit. Just

like me. I can't believe Alex made me get a freaking haircut for this one."

Santa and Sean got out of the car. Santa pressed a button to lock it and looked both ways as Sean came around the car. "You think Alex might give us an extra day or two out here? Maybe catch a Dodgers game. Disneyland?"

Sean put on his sunglasses and shook his head as they crossed the street. "Disneyland? Alex said a quick in and out. We deliver the message to David's dad, and then get back to New York."

"Yeah," Santa said as they walked onto the property. There was a small air conditioning unit in a window in what was most likely the kitchen near the front door. Bars encased the only other small window and an iron security door was the first level of entry before the hardwood door.

"How many square feet you think this place has?" Sean said under his breath.

"Fuck if I know. Eight hundred, nine hundred, it's a box."

"All right, here we go." Sean looked for a bell. Finding none, he rapped his knuckles on the iron door. "Ow," he said changing up his pattern and using the ball of his hand.

The hardwood door opened. A small man in his 60's with a beer belly, his shirt tucked in with a large belt and buckle stared at them through the iron bars.

"Si?"

Sean removed his sunglasses. "Mr. Alejandro Torres?"

"Si."

"Hello, sir. My name is Karl Jorgenson, this is my

associate Bruce Caswell. Do you speak English?"

"Un poco."

Sean glanced at Santa who shook his head. Sean gestured toward Santa and said, "Intrepreter."

Santa said, "Intreprete."

Sean nodded. "We're representatives of Baach, McKenzie & Blake, a Los Angeles law firm, and we were wondering if we could speak with you about an important matter. May we come in?"

Santa translated.

Alejandro Torres did not open the door. Sean could see a large portrait of Jesus on the wall, and a woman, roughly the same age as Alejandro appeared behind him. The two of them spoke in rapid Spanish and the woman wrung her hands.

"What is this about?" Alejandro asked.

Santa interpreted Sean's words. "May we come in? We'd appreciate it."

"No." Alejandro said and made a move to shut the door.

Sean took a step back and said, "This is very important. It concerns your granddaughter. We'd like to discuss a financial settlement. Money."

Santa translated and expanded, ending with what Sean caught...mucho dinero, señor."

The woman grabbed Alejandro's arm, but he pulled it out of her grasp.

Sean pulled out a business card and held it up. He spoke rapidly as Santa interpreted. "We represent the

Carrows family. They would like for you to influence your son, David Torres Cordoza, to sell the rights of publication of his books to them. They'd also like for him to stop any further attempts of publicity using his daughter and to stop painting and distributing works of art which use her image. We are willing to pay you if you can help negotiate this *truce*."

"....*tregua*," Santa emphasized the last word.

"No. No lawyers."

Sean looked at Santa who responded to Mr. Torres in rapid Spanish, but in a measured, polite manner. At the end, Santa shook his head with sadness and put his empty hands out.

Alejandro looked back and forth at both of them, appeared to be considering something, then made a long-winded statement in Spanish and slammed the door.

Sean's mouth dropped open as he looked at Santa. "What the hell," he whispered.

Santa walked backwards a few steps then down the sidewalk as Sean followed. They got back into the car and Sean slammed his door closed. "What did he say? What the hell did you say?"

"I told him that we came in good faith, from the family. That they only wanted all the attention to stop. I begged him to help us." Santa paused and looked out the window, back toward the house.

"What did he say?" Sean asked again.

"He said that it wasn't his business and he wouldn't get involved. He said that the Carrows family has kept his granddaughter from him and he will not touch any blood money. He wanted me to deliver a message to Petunia and tell her that he would be happy to meet her."

Sean squished his face up. "Oh hell. That is not what the boss is going to want to hear."

Santa started up the car and turned on the air conditioning. "Are we done here, or do we go back and try again?"

Sean pulled out his phone. "Let's see what the boss wants us to do."

Santa said, "And ask him about adding a couple days. See if he'll spring for it."

Sean shook his head as Alex answered and he reported the situation. Alex decided it was enough. Santa punched him and spun his finger in a circle mouthing something about the second half of the request, so Sean asked for the extended stay on the company dime.

Their heads together near the phone, they listened anxiously as Alex paused and then said, "Yeah. You can stay, but only if you go to Disneyland. You come back and produce punched tickets on a bunch of rides, show me some pictures of you with Goofy, and I'll be happy to spring for it."

Alex hung up and Sean rolled his eyes as Santa made a fist and gave the air a soft punch of excitement.

Chapter 37

David Cordoza arrived at England's Heathrow airport and hurried to baggage claim to retrieve his luggage and extra baggage, which contained his priceless art and supplies. His driver met him at the carousel and helped him load his trunks into the back of the Range Rover that the earl supplied for his trip into Yorkshire. David had done some traveling in his time, but oddly never to Europe, or to Britain, and was now extremely excited to have finally arrived. The earl had booked his air travel in business class, and David had an extremely comfortable journey over the great pond. Now ensconced in the back seat of the Range Rover, he pulled out his cell phone and called Marcel. He lit a cigarette and caught a glimpse of surprise in the mirror from the driver. He didn't care. He puffed and relaxed.

"Marcel, I just landed at Heathrow. How are sales going over there?" he said partly to impress himself, partly to impress the driver.

David listened to Marcel's report with interest, gratified that he finally had his own reliable staff.

After Marcel had finished, David said, "Alright then, keep me posted. I should be flexible in a week or two, possibly more, depending on the earl and what he needs, so I can stay over here if you get any calls."

He hung up on Marcel, and sat back, business concluded and relaxed as the driver made their way out of London and north toward his next step on the ladder of success.

His phone rang, and David answered, surprised at the caller. "Dad?"

His dad lost no time launching into a report that some attorneys had stopped by his house asking for him to negotiate a settlement between him and the Carrows family. David was frankly stunned.

"What did you tell them?"

His dad told him and concluded by telling him that he thought a settlement would be a good idea if it meant they could see Petunia. He hung up before David could respond.

David stared out the window. Well I'll be damned. The Carrowses had come out of the woodwork. They probably thought they could use his dad in some kind of emotional play. Ares Publications was apparently really holding on tight to the publication rights. Damn it felt good to have people clamoring for your attention—especially when you held all the cards.

David was excited. He'd have to consider his options

carefully. If the Carrowses were sending representatives out, it was because they tasked the job. They wanted to save face. They wanted to make a deal, but they didn't know exactly how. And they thought they could tip the scales, if they could get his dear old dad to somehow shame him.

Well, it didn't work. The Carrows family could wait. He'd let them sweat. He smoked some more and thought about what a settlement number might look like. That could be very interesting too. Maybe he would end up getting it all!

At Hambley Hall, a butler, introducing himself as Sorsby, met the car and opened the door for David to exit. David instructed the driver to bring the bags into the hall. They walked up the steps and into the wood paneled entrance hall. Corinthian columns in each of the four corners of the room brought David's eye toward the classical reliefs near the coved ceiling. A carved marble chimneypiece and dark wood floors gave the room a serious feel, but the light from the many windows and the bright rugs and furniture made it feel welcoming.

"The earl and countess will meet you in the drawing room sir. If you would follow me," Sorsby instructed.

David obliged and gazed in wonder at the valuable antiques and paintings surrounding him. He would love spending time getting to know the background of each and every piece. Coming into the very large drawing room, the earl and countess stood and introduced themselves.

Jane put a delicate hand out toward a young, blond woman and said, "May I also introduce a friend of the family who we've had the great pleasure of entertaining, Ms. Geneva Crawford. Miss Crawford is also from America, Mr. Cordoza."

David looked at Geneva and saw a beautiful woman wearing a modest pastel skirt, and a pink cashmere cardigan that was mildly straining to contain what was obviously a magnificent chest. She wore a pink pearl necklace and she fingered the pearls as she smiled at David politely and shook his hand.

"I'm from Texas. Houston, Mr. Cordoza. Have you ever been there?" Geneva smiled.

David smiled back. "Please, everyone, please call me David. No, I can't say that I've ever been to Houston. I know it's pretty hot down there though."

"It certainly is," Geneva said smiling and rubbing the pearls at her neckline.

"David, would you like some tea, or can we get you a nip of something stronger after your travels?" The earl said as he walked to the bar.

"Tea would be fine. Your home is magnificent, sir," David said, admiring the room.

"Been in the family for generations. The first earl of Hambley was given the title in 1745 after the Battle of Culloden. Are you familiar with your British history? Do they teach you these things over there in the colonies?"

"Yes and no," David said, blinking at the reference and at his host who had puffed up, seeming amused by his attempt at humor. "I look forward to hearing about it. I'd also enjoy learning about the history of your collections."

"Right. Quite right. The grand tour. Ah, here's Sorsby with the tea. Let's get you settled in and if you're up for it we can show you around a bit before dinner. Cocktails at seven. We dine at eight."

"If you wouldn't mind showing me where you need me to set up for the portrait, I'd like to take a look at that space and the lighting after tea."

"Perhaps." said the Earl. "We'll head out and see to it that Sorsby's had our man, Timber, distribute your baggage."

They sat in companionable, slightly strained silence as Sorsby poured. It would become a familiar pattern.

At seven that evening, David once more walked through the hall to the drawing room. He'd assumed that they would dress each evening for dinner, and since he had been invited to stay with the Linngtons at the Hall, had packed accordingly for an American. He didn't pack a tux and hoped they wouldn't expect that from him, but he did bring a suit and a couple of nice jackets and ties.

Entering the drawing room, the earl walked over to him and said with a wink, "No worries about the top and tails around here, Mr. Cordoza, that suit will do just fine." David bristled slightly realizing the earl had just accepted an apology that David had not given.

Having arrived on time for the mandatory cocktail hour, David noticed immediately that the earl seemed to have made a jump start on the process, emitting quite an odor of brandy.

"David," the earl said loudly now as he walked across

the room. "Tell us what you think about your studio. Is it up to your standards for our portrait?"

David walked past a large, draped, jutting alcove containing a long chaise and harp. He smiled at the countess seated nearby. "Yes sir. Both my room upstairs and the room you have for the work have excellent light. We need to discuss the foundation of the work, however, and how you want the portrait to feel. The image you want it to portray."

"I want it to look like the countess of Hambley!" The earl barked at David.

The countess, seated on a sofa, interjected, "Dear, I believe he means what I'm going to wear. If it will be formal, or informal and how we'd like for me to sit or stand. Is that what you meant, David?"

"Yes, Your Ladyship," he said awkwardly, not exactly comfortable with the titles and etiquette.

"You can call me Jane, David." She took a sip of her sherry.

"You can call me Earl, or Your Lordship," barked the earl as he poured himself another cocktail.

David wasn't put off but glanced and awkwardly smiled at Geneva who sat silently across the room. He turned his focus back to Jane as Barford walked past him with a glass of something brown and shoved it in his hand.

David mumbled his thanks and returned his attention to Jane. "I assume you'll want to wear something formal like the ancestor's portraits I've seen around the hall. Have you had your portrait done before?" David took a sip of the drink. Scotch. Excellent Scotch. He'd give it four stars.

"Yes," said Jane. "Several times actually. Once with the earl, one with the earl and the children, and one of me alone, but never in the full HRH costume with the family jewels. For some reason, we hadn't gotten around to that one. The earl, of course, after the last earl died, had his formal portraiture made with the family heirlooms. You'll see that in the dining hall this evening. It's quite wonderful. We had an English artist paint that on specific instructions from Barford's father, but that artist has passed on and we thought it would be fun to branch out and do something completely different for my last official portrait before our son, Brandon, inherits."

David took another sip of the Scotch and glanced again toward Geneva. He felt her eyes on him as she silently sipped a small aperitif. This time his eyes lingered on her green satin evening dress. The deeply plunging neckline hugged what might be the most amazing body he had ever seen. Her nipples out and proud, Geneva rose now and walked closer to him. She smiled and said, "Jane, I think you should explain to Mr. Cordoza that the HRH is just an informal title in these halls, and not an actual standing."

"Of course," Jane said, shaking her head and placing a hand firmly on her leg. "My apologies, David, if we mislead you. The His Royal Highness title was not what I intended. The Linningtons are not actual members of the *royal* family, it's just that we go so far back in the 1700's and so many people treat us like actual royalty. I suppose we are in some circles, but technically, we are not."

Geneva sat close to Jane and gazed at her adoringly. "I'm sure he didn't think you were misleading him, Jane, but Americans don't understand some of the etiquette and titles and such. We don't have any royalty in our country. We're just a bunch of mutts compared to Your Ladyship."

Jane laughed nervously and said, "Geneva, no need for that now. We're practically best friends. Geneva's mother and I go way back. Such a sweet, pretty young girl. You remind me so much of her in that beautiful dress. Doesn't she look wonderful tonight, gentleman?"

"Yes, right, very nice," the earl said, distractedly looking out the window.

David realized it was his turn to compliment the waiting ladies and said, "You both look very pretty. I'm happy to be here."

Jane stared at the earl's back and fluttered nervously. She glanced at Geneva who seemed deep in thought looking at her glass while running her finger slowly around the rim.

David jumped in and said, "Will you be wearing the family jewels then with your assemblage for the portrait?"

"Bob's your uncle," shouted the earl, startling them all. "That brings us right to the matter, eh? David, why don't you tell us about *your* history and that famous ring of *yours*? The Fancy? A lot of mileage on that old girl, wouldn't you say? First famous for being Nicky's gift to his bride Alexandra Feodorovna, and then smuggled out of Russia, and then God knows where, and then nicked by you and I'm assuming sold? Eh? Care to tell us where it might be now?"

Although David had taken a beating in certain quarters and fielded some difficult questions about the theft of the Tsarina's Fancy, he hadn't expected it to be blurted out so bluntly in this genteel home in the middle of England, over cocktails, before his first semi-formal dinner.

"Barford!" said Jane in a shocked voice. "David, forgive him, he's just a bit under the weather this evening. Something seems to be going round. I do hope it's not catching. I believe the earl just has a fascination like we all do about your history. I don't think it's a secret since you published the facts yourself in your last book. I can report that I found it truly *fascinating*. Did you read the books, Geneva dear?"

"I haven't read them. I apologize, David, I just haven't had the time recently. Jane, do you have copies of them around here that I could borrow?"

"Yes, of course. They must be around here somewhere. I'll see to it tomorrow."

Once again, the conversation came to a halt and David was at a loss about what to say when they were saved by Sorsby announcing dinner.

"Letch get to it, then," said the earl clearly mispronouncing his word. "We're having fish, Mr. Cordoza. Trout. Caught fresh just today. Nothing like fresh trout." His words trailed off as he left the room, and then followed by the women speaking quietly with their heads together and lastly by David who wasn't sure what to make of any of it.

Dinner wasn't exactly a disaster, but David sensed a tension around the table and assumed it was about the earl's condition. The women lead the discussion, which chiefly revolved around the history of the family with the occasional loud eruption of thought from the earl. Dinner was mercifully brief, and as David was exhausted with jet lag, he excused himself as soon as decently possible with instructions loudly made by the earl to "get the knees up" after breakfast. Whatever that meant.

———————

The next morning David came downstairs concerned with being able to start work that day. He walked into the small breakfast room and found the earl alone sipping coffee and reading a paper at the head of a long oval table with seating for eight.

"David! Good morning. Join me for some kippers and eggs. Her Ladyship doesn't like them, but I hear they're mighty good for you. How did you sleep last night, eh? You look well rested. Difficult journey you had, must have wanted to take a kip at dinner. Look at that, another day of sunshine. Fine weather we're having, I must say."

Sorsby interjected, asking David if there was anything special he would like to drink, and directed him to the buffet set up along the side. David poured some coffee as the earl said, "Are you up to starting the job today, young sir? Master artist here in the hall, Sorsby, eh? I say we get this going straight away. David? What are your thoughts?"

The earl seemed happy as a clam and apparently not interested in David's response since he picked up his paper and started reading again while shoveling the smoked herring into his mouth and loudly moaning with pleasure. David drank his coffee and looked around the bright, yellow room while listening to the earl brashly masticate his food and make comments under his breath, none of which were directed to David. He was relieved when the ladies entered the room, bringing with them some civility. The earl immediately put down his paper and stood and greeted each of them with a soft kiss on the cheek and a kind salutation.

"Good morning, David," said Jane as she walked to the sideboard and examined the spread of food. "I gather you slept well. I was hoping you were an early riser. The earl and I usually get a start on the day right after the sun comes up. We're usually here as early as six or seven and then off on our morning constitutional. Of course, this morning, I thought we should all gather in the studio after breakfast and get started on the portrait. We wouldn't presume to keep you from your work as I'm sure you have many, many clients lined up to have you paint their portrait."

Jane didn't wait for a response but instead turned to Geneva, asking about her health. David was beginning to understand that it was apparently not required to respond to their questions. Most of them seemed to be directed to no one in particular. They seemed to just speak for the sole purpose of speaking. At one point he received acknowledgement of this fact from Geneva who he could see was greatly amused by the Linningtons. She smiled knowingly at him while they listened to the earl and countess argue over the value of a kipper. They eventually got through their first breakfast, and David followed them out of the breakfast room and toward the studio where he hoped to begin their work.

They walked down a hallway as Jane explained. "The room was originally a saloon, of all things. But the morning sun warms it so beautifully that I turned it into a sitting room. I receive visitors in there during the day."

She opened the door, and David saw that much of the furniture was pushed back and several rugs were rolled and standing in a corner. The full length, eighteen pane windows gave the room tremendous light.

Jane said, "We had Sorsby roll up the rugs and set the room up last night." She glanced at the hardwood floors and gestured toward some supplies. "We were told by your agent, a Mr. Marcel Broussard of Louisiana, that it would be helpful if we had several canvases available for you." She walked over to a large easel, paints, and sheets neatly folded by a chair assembled in the middle of the room as she continued. "Of course, the village doesn't have these types of supplies. We had these sent to us from London based on Mr. Broussard's instructions. If there is anything else you need, we can make arrangements to have it delivered from Petersborough."

David walked around the large room and examined the supplies. "These are perfect, Your Ladyship. You only need to decide how large you want it and I'll begin my work on that canvas. I assume you know what you'll be wearing? This morning, I took the liberty of looking at some of the portraits of your ancestors and I believe I have spotted the family jewels. Will you be wearing the entire parure?"

"Yes. I'll be wearing the necklace, the large pendant as a broach, and the earrings. I obviously won't wear the Earl's brooch, only what the other Countesses have worn for their formals."

"It's time we got you dressed, my dear," said the earl. "You'll begin painting today, won't you, Mr. Cordoza?"

"I have every intention of beginning today," David nodded. "My process would first begin with some sketching and then to the oils. I'm excited to get started. It's a wonderful project and I thank you for trusting me with the work."

Jane smiled at David then turned her attention to Geneva. "Geneva, dear, come along and help me get ready. Barford, you go get the jewels out of the safe."

Not long after, the three of them paraded back into the studio, Jane like a queen being followed by her subjects. She was striking in an extremely elaborate purple silk gown with a square cut neckline which framed the magnificent riviere necklace of rubies and diamonds. The large family pendant was positioned by a partially exposed shoulder and her short hair was pinned back to display the massive ruby, diamond and pearls earrings, which hung almost to her shoulders.

David quickly inhaled at the sight of her which he

noticed brought a smile to Jane's face. He said, "Countess Hambley, you look wonderful. It's a modern look, and yet it's so regal and elegant, it's almost like a throwback to the middle ages. The jewels are magnificent. May I see them in the light by the window?"

The necklace was a circle of large rubies that gradually increased in size to the center large rose cut diamond. The rubies were startlingly well matched but roughly cut, as was common for the Georgian period when the piece was made. What made it most exquisite was the rare, blood-red color of the rubies. God knows where on the earth they originally came from or what price was put on them when they were purchased, but David could only imagine their worth. The diamond was stunning as well, but the rubies were unlike any David had ever seen. Saying as much now, the earl said, "It's a great shame we're going to have to sell them. The entire parure. My last hope is that it will be sold as a set and that whoever purchases them will keep them together. This portrait will be the last time a Linnington will wear the real jewels. Not something we're proud of Mr. Cordoza, but times must if we want to retain the estate for the next earl."

"We had a replica made of the parure, David," Jane explained. "That way we would always have the Linnington jewels at Hambley Hall. The difference will of course be, that they won't be real. Would you like to see the replicas?"

David grimaced, slightly uncomfortable as everyone in the room knew what he had done with the replica of the Tsarina's Fancy. "Yes, but I can't imagine the difference wouldn't be obvious next to the brilliance and sparkle of these stones."

"You'd be surprised," said the earl now opening another very plain wooden box which he had brought into the room and revealing an almost identical parure.

The four of them stood near a window overlooking the pool, the jewels sparkling in the light. They stood slightly stupefied as they compared the extraordinary craftsmanship that must have gone into making the copies.

Jane softly ran a finger along the replicas. "So many of the royal families and families of title have had to do what we're doing it's almost a cottage industry. Apparently with the advances in science, and cutting techniques, they can do an amazing job making the fakes look incredibly real. Of course, any jeweller with a loupe would see the difference, but at a distance, and even in the right light, they are remarkable."

The earl walked away from the group and laughed. "The countess is the one who thought it would a smashing idea for a man with your reputation to paint them. It will lend something peculiar to the portrait. The next generations can have a chuckle and cry about it while they admire it."

An awkward silence surrounded them until Geneva jumped in and said, "Alright Barford, let's get on with this. Mr. Cordoza is here, all the way from America and I'm sure he'll do an excellent job on Her Ladyship's portrait. It's time we let him get to work. You come with me," she said leading the earl out of the room, "and Jane, David, just let us know if there is anything you require while you work. Have fun Jane, and, David, best of luck."

———————

The first day Jane sat for David in the studio for almost five hours before she declared she was ready for a break and for tea. David agreed and told her he would meet her after she had changed out of her formal attire. Coming into the green drawing room, David halted at the sight of Geneva, now wearing a tightly fitted riding outfit, leaning over a table and admiring a photograph. Her wonderfully formed backside was directly in line with his view.

Geneva spun around and smiled. "David! How did your first day go? Was Jane a good sitter?"

"She certainly was. I had a bit of a time getting her to settle in and stay silent, but we had a productive first sitting." David smiled.

"And what do you think of the earl and countess?" Geneva gave him a small smile as she meandered over to the tea tray.

"They seem to be very interesting people. Fascinating history. Their home is magnificent." David played longingly with a pack of cigarettes.

"Ah yes, their home. It is magnificent. But what do you think of *them*?" she said as she walked closer to him trying to tease out a confidence. She put a finger on the cigarettes and pushed them down.

"They're great. Very nice people. I'm happy to be here to paint the portrait, and I have high hopes that it might be my best work."

"Your best work? I haven't actually seen any of your work. I was told that you were going to bring a selection for the earl and countess to look over. Did you bring something to show us?"

"I did, I just haven't had a chance to bring them out. When do think the best time for that might be?"

"How about now? Why don't you run along and get them and we can look them over during tea? I'll let Sorsby know not to pour until you get back."

"Okay then," he said as backed out of the room just as Barford and Jane made their entrance.

"Hold up there, wrong way, teas in here. Never be late for tea or cocktails, young man," said the earl.

"I'm just going to get some of my work. Geneva thought you'd be interested in seeing some of my collection."

"Right. Off you go then. Make it quick, don't want to upset Sorsby and the routine, you know."

David ran through the hall and out a side door. He puffed on a cigarette with relief and then threw the butt to the ground. Running up the stairs to his room, he grabbed a large portfolio and then returned to the drawing room out of breath and with the large hard-sided case containing several of his favorite framed pieces.

The earl, by the bar, said loudly, "We couldn't wait. I had Sorsby pour." He held up a crystal decanter and said, "Care for a drop or two in your tea?"

Still catching his breath, David declined the offer as he unpacked the pieces and arranged them delicately on a sofa for display. There were five of them, all of Petunia.

Proud of the pieces, David stepped back and let his admirers come closer to examine them.

Geneva said, "Oh my, they are awfully good. So interesting what you did with each one of them and the various themes of color."

Jane jumped in enthusiastically. "Ooh, I saw this one on your website! Isn't that the most exquisite framing? Wherever did you have that done, David?"

David smiled. "In San Francisco. I have the most imaginative partner who understands that the framing of the portrait will give it the grandeur and call attention to the details of the painting with a subtle yet demanding harmony. See how the mood and color of each one in the series is captured exquisitely in the frame? They were imported from his supplier in Florence. He only works with the very best materials."

They each took their time examining the framing and the pictures, Geneva picking them up and holding them various ways to the light and examining the backs.

"Do you see anything that strikes your fancy, Countess?" said Geneva.

"Oh yes, they're all wonderful. I can see that the artist has really captured a vulnerability, a sadness in each of them, but in an entirely different way. David, you are a very talented young man." Jane shook her finger at him and smiled.

"Thank you for the compliment, Your Ladyship." He bowed his head slightly.

"Yes, I suppose we could squeeze one of two of these

into our collection," said the earl as he walked back to the brandy and poured more into his tea.

"May we keep them out, David?" asked Jane. "I'd like to admire them while you work so we can decide which ones we would like to keep."

"Of course."

"What do you think, Barford?" Jane said gesturing toward the group of portraits.

"Whatever you wish, my dear, this is your project." Barford walked to a window and looked outside, the large crystal decanter still in his hand.

Jane furrowed her brows and turned to David with a smile. "In that case, I think we should keep them in the studio and I can consider them while we spend time together. Isn't that a splendid plan, Barford?" She turned to where he'd last been standing, but the earl had left the room. David and Geneva glanced at one another when they saw the obvious concern on Jane's face.

Geneva stepped toward her and put a gentle hand on her arm. "It might be a long evening, Jane. But no worries. David will be here to keep us entertained." Geneva gave him a sidelong look with a devilish smile.

Once again unsure of how to respond, David gathered his art and re-packed them into the portfolio to move them to the studio for display.

The four of them fell into a routine of breakfasting together, and after, the countess and David would retreat to the studio to work on the portrait. When Geneva occasionally visited, she stood close to David and the canvas while she cooed at his progress. Today she entered, this time wearing a modest wrap and carrying a large, casual bag.

"Good morning, again," Geneva called as she walked to the window. She looked out onto their view, a long rectangular pool, enclosed on four sides by the house and a high wall for privacy. "It's glorious out. Jane, you should allow David a small break today to smoke. You know how much he adores it. A good suck on something intoxicating will keep the creative juices flowing. David, come outside by the pool in about an hour or so and tell me how it's going."

Geneva walked past him as David looked at the countess for her reaction. Jane was looking down, fluffing her shirt as she said, "Quite right. We'll take a break then soon, shall we?"

Geneva left them with air kisses and David got to work. But shortly thereafter, he became highly distracted when Geneva came into his view outside. She took some time positioning her chair to catch the best sunlight, and once satisfied with her arrangement, she shed the wrap to reveal a body of perfect proportions almost indecently displayed in a tiny, flesh-colored bikini.

David tried to focus on the painting but couldn't stop himself from glancing out the windows. Geneva took an agonizingly long time applying lotion to every part of her body, eventually flopping on her front and removing her small top. She was basically naked, and on full display in David's line of sight, while the countess sat oblivious across the room in her regal gowns. David had a long day ahead of him and was now very thankful that Geneva had put in a word about a smoke break. He willed himself to focus but glanced again out the window and wondered how she would look if she flipped over. It could happen—they were in Europe, girls went topless all the time.

It was a maddening morning, and for good or bad, Geneva never showed more of herself than was already on display. David tried hard to control himself from running outside when he and Jane agreed to take a break. As he got closer, he slowed his roll and strolled up to Geneva. Oddly, during his run for the break, she had chosen that time to sit up and reattach her top. She lay on her back now, the bikini covering her.

"How's it going, David?" She smiled at him.

David lit up a cigarette as he stood staring at her. "Fine. We're making progress."

"It's really taking shape. You should be proud of yourself, Mr. Cordoza, you're a fast worker."

David gave her a smile and was about to feel out her intensions when there was a rap on the window. Jane was at the studio window, smiling and waving.

"She's wonderful, don't you think?" Geneva asked, one hand shielding her eyes and waving back with the other.

"She is. As a matter of fact—"

Geneva popped up. "She's calling. I better see what she needs."

David smoked and kicked at a few leaves in the grass

as Geneva sauntered her way inside. He wondered if she'd resume her sunbathing once he was back in the studio. She'd spent enough time on her stomach, maybe this time, she'd spend it on her back. But then again, he'd never be able to concentrate if she did. He smoked some more and thought about it though.

——————————

That evening, Geneva arrived at cocktails in a dress which revealed far too much for what David assumed was proper for a semi-formal dinner, but the earl and countess made no comment. On the one hand, Geneva presented perfectly polished manners and interest in every word uttered by her hosts; at the same time, every word she said might be a double entendre. By the time dinner was served, the earl was once again well on his way to a silent or angry drunken stupor while the countess prattled on about anything and everything. To David, it sometimes seemed that he and Geneva carried on a different, silent, and private conversation. He thought of Jane and Barford as oafish and obtuse. At any given time, they danced to both those tunes and he remained unsure what to think about any of them.

David did come to understand, through Jane's ramblings, that the countess clearly thought that her *dear* Geneva would be a perfect match for her only son and the next earl, Brandon. Apparently, the next earl would be gracing them with a long overdue visit that weekend. He would be coming to the manor to finally meet dear Geneva.

At dinner each evening that week, the countess grew more and more animated by the thought of a match, which she practically pronounced a fait accompli. David understood that dear Geneva came from old oil money in Texas and was fabulously rich. He'd been told that the Rolls Royce by the garages was hers.

The countess impressed to both Geneva and David, however, that her monied status did not matter. David also picked up that Geneva had suffered from some difficulty in the States having to do with her ex-husband. From the wink that Geneva gave David behind the Countess's back while she shared vague details of the *difficultly*, David assumed that it was Geneva herself who had caused it. And she was making it very clear that she was willing to go at it again.

David didn't know what to do with the growing sexual tension Geneva was creating with him while the earl and the countess weren't looking, but he knew that Jane had set her sights on making Geneva the next countess of Hambley. He knew he should tread very carefully, but Geneva was making it harder by the day. The few times he'd been with her alone had been maddingly brief. He thought it was time for that to change soon.

The work on the portrait was coming along nicely, but the earl had started bickering with Jane that it was too much trouble to return the jewels to the safe each afternoon when the sitting was through. Against her strong objections,

Jane eventually did as her husband instructed and left them in the velvet crested box, in the studio each day next to the wooden box containing the replicas.

David was initially astounded that they would leave the priceless heirlooms unsecured, but he realized that the home itself was largely understaffed and remote, and that the earl, typically drunk by tea, couldn't be argued with. The rich were different, and the earl and countess of Hambley were no exception.

Chapter 38

David wondered what Brandon, the next earl of Hambley, would make of his mother's high-strung plans for his capture. He didn't think Brandon would stand a chance against Jane and her intentions, and with the painting incomplete, he'd be around to witness Geneva launch her special form of seduction on Brandon. It would be amusing to watch another male squirm.

At cocktails that first evening, however, Geneva surprised him. The first surprise was that her dress was the most modest one she'd worn to date, the second, that she was only politely solicitous with Brandon. The third may have irritated him the most as she completely ignored him. He simmered in a corner and watched the three adults listen and gaze at Brandon Linnington like he was the most interesting man in the world.

Another oddity popped when for the first time since David's arrival, the earl was not completely drunk at dinner. David was stunned that the man had the ability to say no. The five of them sat in the formal dining room grouped on one end with the earl at the head. David tried to look interested in Brandon's conversation, but found him lacking. In his opinion, the thirty-two-year old heir to the manor, the hot shot, was passably good looking, but a bit unsophisticated and predictably stuffy for a lawyer.

In contrast to his own opinion however, Geneva Crawford seemed interested in his every word. She sat next to Brandon, and David sat across from her and next to Jane. He watched the two of them carefully. They looked at each other often with what seemed respectful chemistry and spoke in polite, interested tones.

"I'm looking forward to seeing the work you've done on my mother's portrait, David," Brandon glanced at him with simpering curiosity.

"David wanted to wait to show it to you and your father after it was completed, but I convinced him to give you a peek at it this evening after dinner." Jane gave her son a girlish shrug of her shoulders.

"How do you find England, David? Have you been over here before?" Brandon asked, not bothering to look up, but instead engrossed in his soup.

"No, oddly, I've never been to Europe before, only Saudi Arabia and South America," said David, glancing past Brandon and over to a livered footman standing next to two suits of armor situated on each side of the earl. David thought it was ridiculous that a footman was brought in especially for *Master* Brandon's dinner. He certainly hadn't made an appearance before.

"Oh, Ho Ho!" said the earl loudly, smacking the table. "Now there's a clue if I ever heard one, eh? We've been joking with him, Brandon, over the week trying to get him to tell us the whereabouts of that Fancy. Pretty sure the young lad let something slip there."

David inhaled with patience. That they constantly made light of the theft was wearing on him, but at least they seemed to have a sense of humor about the whole thing. From the constipated look on Brandon's face—he did not.

"Since you brought it up, Dad...As a Barrister, I must say, I'm quite surprised that they let you off the hook on that one over in the States. Not so sure the crown would have allowed you to get away with it, David."

"Brandon!" Jane scolded. "That's a rather personal situation. It might not be something that David would like to discuss."

"I don't know why not," said Brandon, laying his soup spoon down. "He wrote a book about it. After my dear parents surprised me last week, informing me that they had hired you to paint my mother's formal and telling me they already had you ensconced in the Hall, I took it upon myself to have a go at your books. Quite a life you've led, Mr. Cordoza. Quite a remarkable story. My parents told me that you have also brought some of your other work with you for our perusal, from the Petunia line. The portraits of your nine-year old daughter, Petunia, is that correct?"

David looked at Geneva for support, but she took that moment to gaze at waitstaff who had entered with the next course. He met Brandon's challenging glare and sat up straighter. What did he care? His life, his crimes, those books, his daughter, and his art was what brought him to this bastard's table in the first place, and after he left, his reputation would only grow. "Petunia is my muse. My inspiration, and yes, my long lost daughter. Circumstances have prevented us from being together and it is my great hope that one day, through my art, she will see how devoted I am, the only way I know how."

"Isn't that beautiful?" Jane said, smiling. She reached out a supportive hand and patted his arm.

Brandon coughed into his hand and sat back. "So you think by painting her picture and selling them worldwide for a nice profit, you will earn your daughter's respect? Is that it?"

David put his chin up. "Precisely."

"That may be a load of rubbish, Mr. Cordoza." Brandon cocked his head as Geneva looked down into her lap.

"Brandon!" said Jane who reached out and gave a quick air pat in her son's direction across the table. "Please, that's quite discourteous. I believe a change of subject is in order. Let's listen to our dear Geneva's affection for our estate and hear her impressions of the Hall. You'll be very impressed with the enthusiasm she's displayed over our history, Brandon. Geneva, do tell us what you thought about the hens and the horses."

Brandon looked at Jane sideways. "Mother, we don't have any hens and horses."

"That may be, Brandon, but we used to have hens and

horses, and Geneva has asked about them. Isn't that so, dear." Jane tilted her head and gave an encouraging smile to Geneva.

All eyes turned to Geneva at this abrupt turn in conversation. She smiled and said, "Yes. Hens, I've learned, can distinguish between more than one-hundred other chicken faces and can tell one another apart. They have full color vision, and they dream just as we do, although about what I'm not sure, and they have a complex social structure known as a pecking order."

"Well done, Geneva. Now tell us about the horses." Jane crinkled her eyes and nose and smiled at Geneva with admiration.

Heads swiveled back to Geneva who shrugged with modesty and gave a demure smile to the earl. "Horses can sleep either lying down or standing up. Horses height is measured in units known as hands. One hand is equal to four inches. You can tell if a horse is cold by feeling behind his ears, and Brandon's favorite horse while he was growing up was named Doggie, because he thought if he named it that his father might mistake him for one and let him sleep in his room."

"Very true," Jane smiled sweetly and gave Brandon a slow nod as he stared at Geneva who had hung her head and blushed.

Jane clapped her hands like a small child. "Brandon's always had a soft spot for animals. He would have had a menagerie in his room if we'd have let him."

"When you inherit, Brandon," said the earl softly

laughing, "I hope you'll hold up the image and keep the horses and goats outside where they belong. Although I imagine the hall will be crawling with dogs. What kind of dogs are you thinking of breeding now?"

"I'm not going to be breeding dogs, Dad. I just thought it would be nice to have a few running around the place."

"Geneva dear," said Jane, "how do you feel about dogs?"

David shook his head and longed for a cigarette.

Geneva put a finger in the air. "Well, I know that dogs love to chase the hens, so you should consider that combination carefully, Brandon, before you build your wildlife park."

"Do you have a dog back home, Geneva? Were you raised with dogs?" Brandon turned his entire body toward her in preparation to receive the exciting answer to his mundane question.

"No, I've never been fortunate enough to have a dog and my mother had allergies. If I ever had one, however, I would like a Great Dane, and I'd take him with me wherever I go."

Brandon pulled up slightly as Jane held her hands up before her. "Brandon, I promise you I did not tell her it was your dream to have a Great Dane. That's entirely our Geneva."

Geneva turned her head and met Brandon's eyes. "Is that so?" she almost whispered in a reverential tone.

Brandon shook his head with wonder. "I've been partial to them all my life. Maybe it's the lord of the manor thing, but they're extremely noble beasts."

The discussion lingered on dogs for some time as David stewed in his corner. From that point forward, over each course, the boring conversationalists chose not to seek his opinion on topics he would have no opinion on anyway. Not that any of them seemed to care.

After dinner, however, he was back in the spotlight when they all marched to the studio, and David reluctantly uncovered his unfinished portrait of the countess. He wasn't keen to show it unfinished, nor would he be interested in Brandon's prosaic opinions.

After some inspection, however, they all decreed it to be a wonderful likeness and even Brandon grudgingly gave his approval of the work.

"What's this, Dad?" Brandon marched across the room and grabbed up the velvet box containing the family jewels.

"The parure, of course," the earl said as he sauntered over and picked up the simple wooden box containing the replicas which had been sitting next to it.

Brandon opened the box and held it up. "I know that. What is it doing laying out here?"

"Brandon, now lad, it's just too far to the cellar," the earl puffed up. "And that fake bookcase they're stored behind has become so heavy that I can't be bothered with it."

The earl patted his son's back and pulled up to full height. "Now, now, I'm sure they're perfectly safe here in the house. Sorsby is the only other person who has been in here, and I should think you wouldn't be worried about him."

David watched with interest as Brandon turned to his mother and gaped at her. Jane pursed her lips and gave Brandon a cautionary look. Whatever objections he was about to offer were interrupted when the earl opened the wooden box and held it next to Brandon's.

"There now, have a look at these. Something to gaze at, eh?"

Brandon's head swiveled from side to side until Jane walked over and kissed her son's cheek. She closed the parure and gestured toward the door. "Take the paste ones with you, darling. You should examine those in the drawing room alcove in the morning light."

Jane placed the parure back on the table and smiled at Geneva. "Geneva dear, would you be a lamb and escort our Brandon back to the drawing room for a nightcap. I'm afraid that Barford and I are quite done in."

Jane clasped her hands before her. "Come now, Barford, the hour is late, and I'm certain Brandon would like to hear Geneva's observations on cricket. David? Will you be turning in early?"

David wanted to laugh at Jane's transparent attempt to get Brandon and Geneva alone. A task which David had maddeningly tried to accomplish himself with very little success. But she was the client, and he'd go along. He nodded. "I am."

Jane returned his nod with approval and left.

No one looked at David's steaming eyes as he followed

them out of the studio. He heard Jane saying loudly to Geneva as they left, "Geneva dear, you should also be sure to tell Brandon what you know about the gardens."

David rolled his eyes and couldn't wait to get the job done and get the hell out of Hambley Hall.

———

Thankfully, Brandon left the next morning for London, and David was glad to see the back of him. The four remaining adults met for their nightly cocktails in the drawing room before dinner and it was almost as if Brandon had never been there. Everyone picked up right where they left off. The earl got terribly drunk, Jane pattered on about how wonderful it was to see Brandon and how wonderful he was and wasn't it marvelous that they had so much in common, blah, blah, blah, and Geneva began to once again shine her light solely on David. It felt nice to be on the receiving end of her affections again, but he was unsure if he could trust them as sincere. He also noticed the wooden box containing the replicas of the parure was now laying casually in the drawing room, next to the bar.

Chapter 39

David could sense the earl getting anxious for the portrait to be complete. He'd begun making it a habit to ask him each morning how much longer it would take. And while David had never been put to a timeline before and was uncomfortable rushing his work, he felt it safe to say that if they worked hard, it would probably only take another week. He told the Linningtons that toward the end he wouldn't need Jane to sit for him and that the finishing touches could be done without her.

Another change that occurred after Brandon left was that the earl seemed to take more of interest in him and became extremely buddy-buddy over the evening cocktails. Once or twice, he even demanded that they have a walk around the estate. David began to feel comfortable in his company and, even though there had initially been strain between them, felt they may have overcome their differences.

The Linningtons had also finally picked out the two

Petunia paintings that they wished to purchase. This also went a long way toward David warming to the family, especially when the earl didn't blink at the price and wrote a check on the spot. They left their chosen paintings in the studio, telling David they would need some time to decide where best to hang them and then helped him to carefully repack the rest of the portraits for his return to the States.

David's biggest concern now was Geneva's increasing interest toward him and his awareness that any relationship between them would piss the Linningtons off. But Geneva was brazen in her attention to him when the Linningtons were not in the vicinity and once made a pass kissing him boldly while they were alone in a hallway. It felt like heaven, but damn it to hell, it once again led nowhere.

Not long after the lusty kiss, Geneva arrived in the studio before the mandated cocktail after Jane had left to change. David, alone in the room, was finishing up when Geneva walked in, wearing another clingy dress with a zip-up front. She closed the door and pressed her back to it. "Look at you, all handsome over there. I don't think I'll be able to bear your absence when you're done, David. Maybe we'll just have to leave together." She gave him a coy smile.

David looked at her with skepticism, cleaning some brushes. "What about Brandon? I thought you were the designated intended. Jane's made that perfectly clear."

"God, David, he's sooo British. So upper crust, I'd be bored out of my mind. I mean, it would be nice to be a countess and all that, and I know Mommy and Daddy want me to go for it, but my gosh, I just don't know if I can do it." Geneva walked to the window and then leaned against it, her arms folded under her chest.

"This sounds a lot like a high-class problem, Geneva. Don't you have any real worries? Any goals or responsibilities other than marrying into the right family?" David grabbed his cigarettes and shoved them in his pocket, ready to get outside for a quick smoke before changing.

Geneva walked toward him slowly. "I have only one goal right now, David, and you know exactly what that is. I've seen you watching me out by the pool. Do you think I spend all that time touching my body, rubbing my body with oil for my benefit? I do it for you. I like you, David. It takes a lot of balls to do what you did, stealing that jewel all those years ago, running away, starting over. It's exciting, and I like a man who knows what he wants and goes after it. Aggressive, strong, determined. You've got all those qualities, and you're not bad to look at either."

Geneva stood in front of him as he warmed to the idea of somehow going for it. He said in a low voice, "What exactly do you have in mind, Geneva? The earl and countess know where we are all the time, and she would be furious with both of us if she knew we were thinking about hooking up."

"Hooking up? Is that all you want?" she pouted. "Do you only want me for my body, David?" Geneva slowly rolled down the zipper which expelled relief as the dress opened, exposing her breasts.

David inhaled and stood speechless, his pulse quickened. "Geneva, shit. We'll be late, you know we can't do anything here." He reached out to touch her.

Geneva smiled and retreated, teasing him as she zipped the dress back up. "Oh, I know you're right, but I wanted you to have an artist's view at what you might be missing. Give me your honest opinion, David. What did you think about what you saw? From a professional point of view."

David ran both of his hands aggressively through his hair and doubled over to breathe. "Jesus, Geneva. Stop toying with me or I'll never get through the evening."

He straightened, as she walked back to him. He put his hands up to ward her off but couldn't resist as she kissed him lightly on the lips and touched his nose. "Another time, baby," she whispered. "We'll find it. Don't worry, I'll make sure of it."

She walked out of the studio. David groaned with frustration, dreading another tediously predictable cocktail hour and staring at Geneva in that dress.

Chapter 40

It was time. Now that David no longer had the need for Jane to sit for him and the painting was nearly complete, it was time to move the jewels. On cue, Barford took David for a long walk, but this time down to the Hambley Arms where they'd be away all afternoon.

Geneva needed complete assurance of privacy in order to plant the real necklace into the back of one of the Petunia pictures that David was taking home with him to the states. She would put the fake necklace in the velvet box with the rest of the real parure in the studio in case he checked to see if they were there.

It was a quick affair and even though Geneva knew the earl was completely capable of keeping David away, and Jane watched for an unannounced return, she was nervous. She carefully unpacked the works from David's luggage and inspected the backs of the frames. She had spent as much time as she could with them and knew she would have to do some delicate work with a variety of tools and tape in order for it to look unmolested. She had previously gathered the items she would need to do the job and took her time to be very careful with the delicate operation. It wasn't as easy as it looked, but in the end, she got it accomplished. All they needed now was for the police to find them in David's luggage and have him arrested.

After she was finished, her heart still beating fast, she closed the door to David's bedroom and walked quickly back to the drawing room. Rubbing her palms together, still sweating, she ran into Jane who searched her face for an update.

Geneva nodded. "There's no turning back now."

Jane paced by the window in somber reflection as Geneva went to the bar and poured herself a brandy. She gestured at Jane with her glass. "Jane, would you like one too?"

"No. Thank you."

Geneva walked over to and stood next to Jane at the window. "Hang in there, Countess. We're almost home." She gave her arm a squeeze and then reclined on a sofa and drank her brandy.

Shortly thereafter, the earl's loud singing announced their return from a successful trip to the pub. Jane and Geneva went to the window and watched as the earl and David walked up the drive arm-in-arm.

"My goodness," said Jane. "It looks as if the Earl has really put his back into it. It'll be a relief to see him sober again after David leaves."

"Tomorrow. If all goes as planned, he'll be gone."

———————

The next day after his morning session with Jane was over, Geneva entered the studio smiling like she had a secret, and most definitely an agenda. "Daaavid," she said as she closed the door and put a finger to her nose. She sashayed her way over to him. He met her with his mouth. They kissed passionately, and David dropped the brush in his hand to the floor and at long last began to use them to explore. She didn't resist but pushed him gently back and quickly unbuttoned her blouse, revealing her astounding assets supported by a garment whose only purpose was to enhance them.

David drank in the site of her and reached out, firmly cupping them when the door suddenly opened. The countess walked in.

"Davi—" Jane stopped cold. Her hand went to her mouth and she said softly, "Geneva." The countess turned and left the room.

"Oh shit!" David stamped his foot and pushed Geneva away from him.

"Oh shit my ass," Geneva said coming back at him for more.

"What are you doing?" he said as he fought off her advances. "We've been caught, she's going to be furious. The earl's probably going to be busting through that door any moment and throw a drunken fit!" David was fuming as he scrambled out of her grasp and backed away.

Geneva rolled her eyes. "David, I don't know what *you're* so worried about. It's not like it's *you* they want to marry their son. This will be my problem." She wearily began to redress. "What do you care what they think?"

David stopped cold to consider this. She was right. It wasn't really that important what they thought of him as long as they paid him, and he could use them on his resume. David threw an arm in the air. "But, I'm not done with the painting and we still have teas, and cocktail hours, and stupid dinners to plow through. Imagine how fun those are going to be now if they're mad at us? I'd also like them to speak highly of me and my work. Why aren't you more upset? Jane looked really hurt. She's going to be pissed."

"I doubt it. She'll get over it. I mean I really care about her, but Brandon and I were never going to work anyway. She'll understand that once I explain it to her. For God's sake, David, we're single adults. It's not like it's the end of the world or something."

"Well you go talk to her. I'm not going to do any awkward hanging around with them until you let Jane know that Brandon wasn't ever going to happen. Shit. The earl and I were just starting to get along too. He told me yesterday at the pub that he liked what I was doing so much he wanted to commission another portrait of the estate from the hill. I don't know what will happen with that now."

Geneva walked toward him and put her hands on his shoulders. "David, look at me. It's all going to be okay.

We're okay, they're okay, we've done nothing wrong. I'll go talk to Jane. Really. I'm sure once I explain, everything will be just fine."

But it wasn't. Not even close.

Some hours later, the earl tried to pep David up as he helped him pack his things, "David my boy, I'm on your side. A nice young filly like that, you both single? Can't say that I haven't had a thought or two run through my head since she's been here as well, but don't tell the countess I said that. No worries, it will just be easier this way. I've called my man at the Arms, and they have a wonderful set of rooms waiting for you. Wonderful light! You'll see. You'll be well taken care of over there, my boy, I can assure you of that. Special guest of their lord from the Hall. I told Mr. Page over there that we were having a bit of a rodent problem in the studio. Thought it best for everyone if you finished Her Ladyship's portrait over at the Arms. They'll love it. You'll be a celebrity over there, I can tell you. You just relax, finish the work, take it easy, have a few pints with the lads, and I'll smooth things over with the missus."

"Thanks for all this, Barford. I appreciate your support."

"No problem at all. Let's get you packed up and over there. They're waiting for ya."

Jane and Geneva watched the earl and David load his bags into the back of one of the cars and their day man, Timber, drove David and the most valuable piece of their ancestral heritage away to the safety of the village inn.

Geneva went to her room and pulled out a burner phone. She paced the room and called Charles on his cell. "It's done. David has moved out of the Hall. The necklace is hidden in the back framing of one of the Petunia pictures just like we planned. God, I can't believe this is happening."

"Good job," said Charles. "You should relax a bit now that he's gone. Are you alright?"

Geneva looked out the window from her room onto the pond and the rolling hills beyond. She'd grown extremely fond of her idyllic countryside scene, but the job was now pounding for center stage attention. She took in a breath. "Yes. I'm fine. Jane and Barford are pretty shaken. We all are, really. But it's done."

"Yes. For a good cause—several of them, Geneva. Remember that. I'll be thrilled to call my family with the good news. But the first call I make is to Oliver Baach. It's time for him to launch his prepared campaign of legal shock and awe against David and his assets."

Geneva ended her call with Charles and sat on the edge of the bed to steady herself. There was work left to be done, and the earl and countess needed her strength. She got up and grabbed a light cardigan out of a drawer and pulled it over her head. She almost wished it were an old, familiar comfy sweatshirt, but she'd left all of them in Los Angeles.

She opened the door and headed downstairs. Jane needed to call Sotheby's. She'd help her with that one.

It was time for them to send someone to collect the Linnington parure to put up on auction. And time was of the essence on all fronts. The walls were closing in.

Geneva stopped on the stairwell landing and looked up at a portrait of one of the Linnington women proudly wearing the fated parure. In her wildest dreams, that woman couldn't have ever imagined that an ex-stripper from America would one day plant them on a double-crossing weasel and save Hambley Hall for the next generation. Geneva smiled. Their histories were now firmly intertwined. She liked that very much.

She continued her walk toward the drawing room where the next exact set of instructions would be reviewed. Over the next several days while they waited for Sotheby's to arrive, the earl, the countess, and Geneva would make certain that no one from Hambley Hall left the manor. No one from Sorsby to Emma to Timber would set foot outside of the property, and the three conspirators would somehow make sure their presence was, at all times, carefully accounted for.

After everything else they'd done? Totally doable.

Chapter 41

Mr. Benedict Peak and his capable assistant from Sotheby's arrived at Hambley Hall like the undertakers they were. Mr. Peak knew that taking custody of the family jewels, which hadn't left an estate since the 1700s, would be a task that needed to be handled with grave dignity and delicacy. Sadly, he and his assistant spent more and more time on these assignments as one home after another across England were selling their valuables to pay the tax man. Sotheby's was profitable, but on the front lines, it was indecently sombre work.

"A quick in and out, like ripping off a bandage," Mr. Peak privately tutored his assistant as they arrived at the hall. "You never want to linger." With that in mind, Mr. Peak and his assistant entered the Linnington drawing room, accepted the jewels, and declined the offer of tea.

"I'll just need you to look over these papers and sign the releases that will allow us to transport the jewels to our London office for safe keeping. Lloyds of London has insured the transfer and you have our assurance of their discretion." Mr. Peak handed over the documents and a pen.

As Barford looked through the papers and signed, Mr. Peak said, "There now. I'll just need to take a quick look at the jewels in your presence and we'll be on our way."

"They're still in the studio down the hall," said Barford. "We've finally had the countess's formal portrait done wearing them by an artist from the States. He's staying at the Arms right now, putting on the finishing touches. I say, you should have a look at the replicas of the jewels when we're done. I'm quite certain you'll find them impressive."

"That won't be necessary, Your Lordship. Just a quick peek at the real ones and we'll be on our way."

Geneva stayed in the drawing room leafing through her magazine, as Barford and Jane led Mr. Peak and his assistant into the makeshift studio then gave him the velvet box. "We've excellent light in here for this," said Mr. Peak with approval as he opened the box and pulled out his loupe and began to examine the pieces. He held up the pendant for inspection, then the earrings. He muttered softly—expressions of "lovely, very nice," until he came to the necklace.

Mr. Peak didn't look well as he held the necklace out in his hand. "This is most irregular...but I'm afraid these stones are not rubies and diamonds. You said you have a duplicate? I don't believe this is the original."

Jane cocked her head as the Earl said, "What's that? Not the real thing?"

"No, this necklace is not the piece which will be put

on auction which I've come to collect," Mr. Peak said, beginning to perspire. "Perhaps it got mixed up with the other one by mistake?" he said offering a solution. "Maybe if I take a look at that we can be on our way."

Barford and Jane looked at one another like lost chicks looking for direction. Jane said, "I think we left them in the drawing room," and walked out.

Mr. Peak and his capable assistant followed Barford and Jane back to the drawing room where the countess walked the length of the room and said with a puzzled expression, "Barford, weren't they in here? By the bar?"

"Hello," said the earl looking around the bar with her. "I believe so. Don't know where they could have gone off to?" He dropped his head and looked at the floor and around the area.

"Geneva dear, did you happen to see the box with the replicas around here by chance?" Jane asked.

Geneva went to them and joined in the search. "The last time I saw them they were by the bar."

At this point Mr. Peak watched as the three of them separated and began looking high and low, under cushions, behind furniture, and on the shelves. After a while the Earl stopped and said, "Maybe I've lost the plot here, but I could have sworn I saw them last in this room! Jane, where do you think they could have gotten to?"

"Let's ring Sorsby, perhaps he moved them." Jane said as she moved to a small button on a wall and pressed it.

Mr. Peak was unsettled that the family seemed to have such a loose recollection about the whereabouts of something so valuable but felt confident that certainly the butler would set things in order.

"Here he is." Jane gestured at the butler and sighed as Sorsby entered the room. "Sorsby, do you happen to know where the box with the jewels is? We seemed to have mislaid it."

"Your Ladyship is referring to the family jewels which are being painted by the American?"

"Yes. Well, no, not those. Those are the originals. We had copies made and they were in that unremarkable wooden box that I could have sworn we left in this room?"

"Yes, I recall seeing a box of that description in here by the bar area several days ago."

"Did you move them by any chance, Sorsby?" Jane asked hopefully.

"No, my lady, I did not."

"I see. Of course. I don't suppose one of the day maids would have moved it, do you think?" she pressed on.

"No, my lady. They have mostly kept to the kitchens assisting Emma, and the upstairs assisting Miss Geneva and keeping the family rooms tidy. I have been the sole person attending to the downstairs rooms and drawing room."

"I see. Yes. In that case, we seem to have a bit of mystery. You see, we can't seem to locate the box and Mr. Peak is here especially from London to have a look at them. I don't suppose you would be able to assist us in locating it? I believe you are familiar with the box in question?"

"Yes, my lady. May I suggest that you look in the studio

where the American was painting your portrait? Perhaps it is in there?"

"Yes. Thank you Sorsby, we'll go back in there and do another once over." At that, the countess and the rest followed her back to the studio where they immediately spread out in search of the plain wooden box.

"Blimey!" said the Earl as they reached the end of the search in all the obvious places. "This is a cock-up. Where the bloody hell could they be?"

"Barford," Jane admonished softly. "There's no need for that. I'm sure they'll turn up directly. We should simply split up and search the downstairs rooms. Sorsby, if you would continue searching in the dining room and breakfast room, the Earl and I will start in the library, and Geneva dear, if you would be so kind to search in the common areas, the hall, etc., I'm sure we'll uncover them shortly."

The group split up and began their search. They eventually regrouped in the drawing room—empty-handed.

Mr. Peak raised a brow of concern but immediately corrected himself to remain calm. He looked down and brushed an imaginary nothing off his jacket as he waited discreetly for the Earl and Countess to sort through their personal predicament.

"Barford," said Jane, "did you by any chance put them in the safe?"

"Why would I do something like that? If I didn't put

the real jewels back into the safe, why would I lock up the fakes?"

"It's an excellent question, dear, but is there any chance you could have been confused, perhaps being fatigued after a long dinner?"

Mr. Peak tried gazing elsewhere as he saw the Earl's colouring flare with anger.

"I wasn't tight enough to do something as idiotic as that, but why don't we have a look, shall we?"

Mr. Peak, now slightly panicked himself, blinked back alarm as the countess turned to him and blushed. She gestured after her husband's retreating back and said, "Would you follow us, please? I'm sure we'll have this mystery solved in short order." With that, she and the rest of the group followed Barford through the hall and down through the kitchens where the cook and maid gaped with wonder as the six adults trooped past them and into the cellars.

After Barford made a great effort of moving the hidden wall and opening the safe, he announced it empty.

"Well then," said Jane. "It seems it must still be upstairs hiding from us. Shall we?" She indicated for them to follow her back up.

Mr. Peak scratched his head and caught a questioning look from his assistant trying to ascertain the appropriate next move. He replied with a nearly imperceptible shake of the head. They would be patient.

They followed the countess back into the drawing room where they began the search again and Sorsby said,

"My lady, did you want me to ask for the assistance of the day maids in the search, or did you want to continue searching for yourself?"

"I'm not sure, Sorsby. I'm a little disturbed by what could have happened to them," she said with a wringing of the hands and a worried look.

"Well, I'm not going to take the blame for mislaying them," barked the earl. "Damn ridiculous that we can't find them!"

"If I may, Your Lordship, is it possible that the American painter took them with him in order to complete the work on her ladyship's formal portrait? Could he have them at the Arms?" Sorsby offered.

"But that wouldn't explain why the fake necklace is in the box with the rest of the real parure." Jane said, staring at Barford.

Geneva walked over toward Jane with her arm extended. "Are you saying the real necklace is missing and you think it's in the box with the rest of the fake parure?"

Jane looked about to cry as she put her hand over her mouth. "I'm afraid that's the gist of it. It seems as though the fake ruby necklace is now laying in the family's crested velvet box in the studio with the rest of the real parure. We seem to be missing the real necklace."

Geneva inhaled, and Sorsby looked at the group aghast.

Mr. Peak felt this was going very badly as he watched the Earl go to the bar and pour himself a large glass of brandy. His assistant lowered his head and shuffled his feet. Mr. Peak shot him a quick glance directing him to contain himself.

"My Lady," said Sorsby clearly upset at his mistress' distress. "Perhaps we should simply ask Mr. Cordoza if he has the necklace. That might solve the mystery instantly."

"Just a moment, Jane," said Geneva. "I don't think it's a good idea to just phone him up and ask him if he happens to have accidently, without telling you, mind, that he took the necklace with him to the Arms. I mean, who does that? And he put the fake one in the box with the real ones? Did he think we wouldn't notice that?"

Jane sat down heavily on a sofa and said, "Why would we notice it? They're clearly almost perfect replicas and we hadn't returned them to the safe because we knew that Sotheby's was coming by to pick them up!"

"Did David know Sotheby's was coming by to pick them up?" Geneva sat on the edge of chair across from her.

All eyes were on Jane while she quietly contemplated. "I know he knew we were going to put them on auction, but I don't believe we ever told him when we were going to do it."

Mr. Peak could no longer play the bystander in the big game of Clue and jumped in. "You said he was an American staying at the Hambley Arms?"

"Yes," said the Earl, gesturing with his drink. "He's over there right now. Finishing the portrait. Or at least I presume he's still there. I assume I would have gotten a call, naturally, from our man Mr. Page. He would have let me know if he checked out."

Geneva moved over and sat next to the countess. "Jane, Barford, I really don't think we should be the ones to ask Mr. Torres Cordoza this question. We should have someone in authority around here do it. I mean, what if? What if he does have it? I suppose that would be okay, because then we could just get it back. But you have to stop and ask yourself— why would he have it? I think we should call the police."

The word echoed in the room until the capable assistant spoke for the first time and said, "Mr. Torres Cordoza you say? The American painter, Mr. David Torres, Cordoza?"

All eyes turned to him. He had the decency to blush from the attention before he continued. "Do you mean the American jewel thief? The one who stole the Tsarina's yellow diamond, the Fancy?"

Geneva put a hand out for Jane's, who looked like she was going to be ill, and said, "That's exactly the one. He's at the Hambley Arms, and I'm betting he has the Linnington necklace."

"But why would he do that?" Jane pleaded. "He'd know we'd eventually discover that we didn't have the real necklace, or perhaps we actually still do and it's in the box with the rest of the replicas. Calling the police seems like an unnecessary step, Geneva."

"I suppose you may be right, it might be in the box we can't find, or maybe Sorsby is right and David has the box with him at the Arms. But Jane, when you wore the necklace and the other jewels for the sittings, did you ever put it back into the wrong box? No! And why would

David even touch it! He has no business touching the jewels, not without your permission. And why would he take them with him without telling us, assuming he has them? Because think about this, if he does have them, he clearly shouldn't. I don't think any of us should just *ask him* about it either. It's unacceptable for him to have the fakes, or for God's sake, the *real ones* at all."

Jane shook her head and looked at Barford with fear. "Well we can't just call the police and have them storm the Arms looking for them. David's feelings will surely be hurt if we do that."

"His feelings," barked the Earl, marching toward them red in the face. "Do you know how bloody much those jewels are worth! We need to find them right now. And if he doesn't have them, maybe he can tell us where the other box is located. Good God, his feelings are the least of it. And I'm not going to sugar coat this thing any longer, Jane. The man is an admitted jewel thief, whether you find that disturbing to discuss or not. You thought this would be a fine idea. Something the children would get a kick out of. Well no one's laughing now."

The countess looked horrified that her husband had admonished her in front of so many strangers. Mr. Peak felt strongly that they should leave, but he couldn't find the impetus to move.

The atmosphere was filled with tension until Geneva said, "We all understand that this is terribly stressful, and I don't think anyone is to blame for it. The facts are that we need to find that second box and we need to find the real necklace. We've looked in the obvious places and it's not there, so now we need to dig a little deeper. It's logical, not accusatory, to ask David if he has the other box or the necklace. If he does, mystery solved. Bad planning on his part, but no harm, no foul, we'll just get it back and be done with it. If he doesn't have it, perhaps he knows where it is. Again, there's our solution. The only problem would be if he denies having the box or the necklace and claims to have no knowledge where it could have gone. In that case, our only alternative is to search again. Deeply search, because it has to be somewhere. Whether it is in the hall or at the Arms with David, we just need to find out."

Geneva looked at the faces around the room. "So, if we can all calmly agree with that, let's decide who we should send to ask him. This needs to be done in person, not in a phone call. We need to gauge his reactions."

Everyone was quiet as they went over the options. Mr. Peak couldn't help but swivel his head among the candidates, judging for himself who would be best to question Mr. Torres Cordoza. It was ludicrous. If it were up to him to decide, the police were the only sane option.

"I'll take the silence to mean that we don't have a proper candidate in the room," said Geneva. "Sorsby, would you please ring the police and ask them to pop by regarding a delicate situation."

Jane opened her mouth to protest, but Geneva stopped her and said, "This could be a big deal, Jane. We need credible witnesses, and not a member of the family. Let it go. It's what needs to be done."

She nodded and Sorsby left the room to call the authorities.

Mr. Peak was terribly unsure what his role was at this time. Should they stay and wait for the outcome in case they found the necklace in which case they could finally be on their way, or should they leave now and come back another day? This was thankfully answered before he could ask it by Geneva, who, once again, seemed to be the least emotional of everyone and taking charge.

"Mr. Peak," she said. "I won't presume to tell you what to do, but if I might advise you, I'd say you should wait to see what happens at the Arms with David. That way, if he has the necklace, you won't have to make a second trip."

Mr. Peak, while uncomfortable with the unprecedented situation, was extremely curious about the outcome and relieved that someone gave him leave to stay.

"Of course," he nodded with deference. "If you think it best."

"I do. I'll just go to the kitchen and see if Emma would be kind enough to serve an early tea. We could all do with some refreshments while we wait for the police to arrive."

Mr. Sheffield, the local Hambley constable, arrived within minutes. Extremely earnest, he entered the Earl's drawing room and immediately felt the tension in the air. His Lordship's colouring was off, and the always affable Countess was bundled into the corner of a couch and did not rise to greet him. Several other strangers were amongst them, one, an attractive blond woman, gave him the broad outline of the predicament.

Constable Sheffield scanned the faces of the earl and countess who appeared anxious but in agreement with the plan. "I see," said Mr. Sheffield. "You just want me to ask the American if he happens to have left the Hall with His Lordship's priceless family heirlooms. And on the off chance that he does have them, you're hoping that he'll just give them back?"

"Precisely," Jane nodded.

Mr. Sheffield looked around the room and ascertained that the peculiarity and gravity of the situation required shrewd judgement. As a sworn officer, he knew that he had a job to do and he better do it well. "My lord, I don't think it's a grand idea for me to go marching over to the Arms alone. I'm afraid this requires some further assistance from Petersborough. If I may suggest, I'd like to pop out and give them a call and see if they can spare a couple of coppers to help me sort this out."

The countess visibly deflated into the sofa's corner as the earl snapped. "That's fine, Sheffield. Get to it, we haven't got all day. Bring in the coppers."

Mr. Sheffield breathed an inward sigh of relief that the earl had confidence in his decision. He felt much more confident in his position now that he would have some backup with him for the inquisition of a jewel thief currently ensconced at the local pub. He left the room to make the call.

———————

About an hour of uncomfortable conversation ensued while Police Constable Sheffield enjoyed the tea that Jane insisted he share with them while he asked them other questions regarding their unfortunate situation. At the bell, they waited silently until Sorsby escorted two Petersborough police into the drawing room.

The officers introduced themselves as Officer Gunner and a detective named Christopher White. Mr. White and Officer Gunner declined the offer of tea and had a seat while the Countess, once again, reviewed the circumstances of why they were all gathered.

"So you see," she said, "we don't want to create a scene or unduly embarrass Mr. Cordoza, but we just felt that we might be out of our depths here, legally, I suppose, and felt that a bit of a professional presence was needed to get us all sorted out."

Detective White pursed his lips. "You did the right thing. We'll need to investigate this. It must be quite startling to have such valuable jewelry missing from your home."

"As I said," Jane waved her hand through the air. "There's a chance it's not even missing at all, perhaps just mislaid."

Detective White looked at their faces to see if he could understand how that could possibly happen. "So I'm to understand that you don't make it a habit to lock up these priceless jewels at the end of the day?"

"No," said Barford. "And I resent anyone telling me what's proper and improper in my own home."

"I meant no disrespect, Your Lordship, I only wanted to make sure I understood correctly. But you need to understand that you invited a jewel thief into your home and then openly left your most priceless pieces under his nose. Did you really believe they were safe?"

"Of course we did," said Jane rising to her husband's defense. "We had no reason to believe he would do it again. It would be too obvious! Why would he do that and think he could get away with it?"

"Maybe he thought that you wouldn't notice until he had left the country. Maybe he thought you would blame someone else. Maybe he thought that he could prove he didn't do it because you left the jewels out for any number of others to take them?"

"This is all just a silly misunderstanding," Jane's hands shook. "I'm sure once you speak with Mr. Cordoza we can find out what happened."

"Right then," said Detective White shaking his head and standing. He patted his leg and said, "We'll just be on our way over there to ask him. We'll be in touch shortly." The police left the room.

Barford went back to the bar and the rest of them sat uncomfortably until Geneva said, "So who wants to hear about what I've learned about the sport of Kings?" She didn't wait for an answer but launched in. "Polo. Did you know polo ponies are actually not ponies...."

Chapter 42

David Cordoza was lost in thought at the Hambley Arms, standing in his studio, thoroughly admiring the just-completed portrait of the countess Hambley, Jane Linnington. My God, I'm good, thought David, pulling out his phone and taking pictures. The light perfectly reflected from the jewels, and Jane's face had a remarkable likeness of the woman he knew. This avenue of portrait painting was going to be huge for him. One look at this, and all the European aristocracy and rich folks from around the world would clamor for his services.

David lit a cigarette, thrilled that the Hambley Arms allowed him to smoke indoors. The earl had been right about one thing, the main proprietor, Mr. Page, was extremely attentive. He'd said he was excited to have a celebrity in the Arms, and happy to please His Lordship. David had had to contend with a gaggle of philistines each night, but hanging out with the proprietor and villagers had been a relief after the tension at the hall.

He contemplated his next moves. He'd forward the pictures of the portrait to Marcel and have him get them on his website. In the future, Marcel was going to have to do more of the heavy lifting for him, especially if he wanted to remain his agent. He'd have a talk with him when he got home. It would be great to get back to the States, but David had to admit that he had enjoyed himself in England. The people were a little crazy, certainly the Linningtons were off their rocker, but then a lot of wealthy people were odd. He'd just have to get used to it if he was going to be spending time with them.

One important lesson he learned from the Linnington experience was that it might be a bad idea for him to live with his customers. Too much of his time was taken up with the socialization. It drew him away from his passion, his creations. While it might be a good idea to socialize for networking opportunities, there was something to be said about too much of a good thing. He wouldn't live with the families on his future commissions.

Then there was Geneva. My God, what a head trip she was. Women had always been his problem. Charlotte, Dawna, Petunia, Jane Linnington, and lastly Geneva. Who knew how her problems with the family were going at the Hall. Well good luck to her. She was going to need it.

All that was left was for the earl to pay him and arrange transportation back to London to catch a flight home. The earl had paid for an open-ended round-trip ticket. David picked up his tablet to check on the return flight availability. He scrolled and smoked. Maybe he'd stay in

London for a few days before returning home. He could see some museums and churches. Marcel texted him this morning that he had no new commission requests, so he was basically free to enjoy himself.

David hummed happily while searching for flights when a knock sounded on the door. He opened it, surprised to see three police officers.

"Mr. Cordoza?"

"Yes, I'm Mr. Cordoza." David pulled his head back.

"Right then, would you mind if we came in for a moment? We have a couple of questions we need to ask you."

David stood aside for them to enter not closing it behind them. "What's this about? What's going on?"

"Yes. Exactly. I'll make the introductions. I'm Detective White, this is Officer Gunner, and the local Constable, Officer Sheffield. We've just been to the Hall and have some questions that you might be able to help us answer."

"About what?"

"Precisely. Mr. Cordoza, you're an American here to paint the Countess of Hambley's portrait, yes? But of course, I can see that for myself," Detective White smiled as he walked over to the large canvas in the room. "My, my, what a lovely likeness that is of her, don't you think, Mr. Gunner, Mr. Sheffield?"

The three policemen gathered around the painting and murmured. David, still wide-eyed, put his hands out in confusion. Why were they there? "Excuse me, what's going on? Has something happened to the countess?"

Turning back to him, Detective White said, "No, no, don't alarm yourself. The countess is perfectly well. We just have a question or two," he said, seeming to be in no particular hurry to ask them.

David stared at their backs as they resumed their examination of the portrait until his mouth dropped open, and he impatiently yelled, "Well, what then? What do you want to know?"

Turning slowly around, Detective White said, "How long were you planning on staying with us here in England, Mr. Cordoza?"

"How long? I don't know. I just finished the portrait and was looking at flights back to the States before you came in. Why?"

"Just curious. So the portrait is done?" he said gesturing toward it and pulling out a notebook and writing something down.

"Yes. I just said that."

"Quite. Have you enjoyed your time with us in England Mr. Cordoza?"

"Have I enjoyed my time here? I've been working. I don't understand what you want."

"No need to get yourself upset, sir, just making pleasantries."

"Okay, well, if you would get to the point I would appreciate it."

"Of course. It seems there is a situation at the Hall, and we were called to investigate."

"What sort of situation?" David walked across the

room to one of the officers who had picked up his iPad and had a finger poised over it to swipe. He grabbed it out of his hand and gave him a dirty look.

"Yes, apparently, it's a bit embarrassing, but they seem to have mislaid a box. A plain wooden box, which contains what I am to understand are some replicas of the Linnington jewelry. Would you happen to know the whereabouts of the box, Mr. Cordoza?"

"The box? No. Last time I saw it, it was in the drawing room by the bar. They can't find it?"

"Apparently not. A bit of a predicament."

"Well, I'm sorry, I can't help you. I don't know where it is." David gestured to the door for them to leave.

"Ah, that's too bad. We were hoping you might have it with you and we could be on our way."

"Well I don't. It was in the drawing room the last time I saw it, several days ago." David placed his iPad on a table and crossed his arms.

"Well, it's not there now. Do you have any other ideas of where it might be laid?"

"How should I know? The earl probably picked it up and moved it one night while he was drunk. Put it somewhere safe and now can't remember."

"So you're suggesting the earl drinks a little more than he should?" Detective White stared at him.

David threw out his arms. "Yes. All the time. Ask anyone, he sometimes starts after breakfast and runs one all day. By dinner he's usually totally wiped out."

"And you think the earl moved the box, but just can't remember?"

"That's probably what happened." David searched the sober faces but got nothing.

"Do you have any other property over here at the Arms that belongs to the Earl or Countess?"

"What? No! I mean other than the portrait. Did they want the rest of the paints back? I mean they can have those. It's not like I'm going to pack this stuff up and bring it back with me."

"I'm not referring to the portrait or the paints."

"Well what then? I don't have anything belonging to them. What are you insinuating?" David felt his temper rise.

"Not insinuating anything, Mr. Cordoza, just following up with questions. Now, back to the missing box. You do understand what it contains?"

"Yes, it's the replicas of the family parure. The jewelry. You can see the countess wearing it in my portrait." David gestured toward the painting.

"Did the family tell you why they wanted the portrait painted at this time?"

David stopped before he answered, for the life of him trying to figure out why these questions were important. "They said that they'd never had a formal portrait done of the countess wearing the family jewels and they wanted to have one done before they sold them at auction. I supposed they had the duplicates made for sentimental reasons. So they could still pretend to own the real ones or something."

"I see. Did you ever have a chance to compare the real jewels with the replicas?"

David wanted them to leave. He took in a patient breath. "Yes. When I first arrived—we all did. We held them up to the light and looked at the differences."

"Did you find them to be incredibly different?"

"They were very good copies."

Detective White walked around the room touching some of David's things and eventually sat in the one good chair while the rest of them were left standing.

"I understand you're familiar with jewels, and paste copies of jewels, Mr. Cordoza."

David's face darkened. He'd had enough. "What is it you want? I don't have to answer any more of your questions." He walked to the door and pulled it open wide.

"Ah," Detective White said, hanging his head and pouting.

"The problem, Mr. Cordoza, is that it was discovered this morning by the representatives from Sotheby's that the necklace in the velvet family crested box is a fake—the duplicate. The real necklace seems to be missing."

David's mouth hung open, while Detective White continued, "We were hoping that the real necklace was put into the wooden box with the rest of the fake jewelry by mistake. We were hoping upon discovery of the wooden box that we would happily discover the real necklace and we could all call it a day. The problem, however, is that the wooden box cannot be located. So, the real necklace remains missing."

David paced in the small tight space, his face hot. "And you think I have it? I don't have it! I don't have any of it. When I left there, the real ones were in the velvet box in the studio and the fake ones in the wooden box in the drawing room. That's the last I know about them. Now you can all get the hell out of here." David again threw his arm toward the open door.

"Mr. Cordoza, calm down." Detective White patted the air. "We're not accusing you of anything. We only know that the box is missing and simply wanted to ask if you knew where it was."

"I said I don't, so leave." David tried to control his breathing.

"But, you see, I have a problem here, Mr. Cordoza. I need to be thorough in my job. I need to be certain that I've done what's necessary to make sure this all gets sorted properly. Now, as you say, the earl drinks." Detective White turned to one of the other cops and shook his head gravely. "Pardon me, Constable, I know you're close with him. I saw it for myself just now when we were visiting with them. Lovely couple, but you could tell the earl was already halfway to tight."

The cop nodded acceptance of the apology as Detective White continued to speak with David. "I think it's very likely what you suggested, Mr. Cordoza, that they simply mislaid it, or the earl put it somewhere for safe keeping but now can't remember where he stored it. And I shall suggest to them that they do a better, more thorough search when I report back to them."

Detective White cocked his head and squinted. "But the problem I have, is that I need to leave no stone unturned here, with you, Mr. Cordoza. You must be under no illusion that your reputation precedes you. I can't go back to the station and tell them that I simply asked you if you have the jewels and you told me, 'No, I don't have them, Detective,' and I just took your word for it? They would laugh me back to being a flatfoot. I don't want that, Mr. Cordoza. The thing is, we need to see with our own eyes that you don't have the box or the necklace, and then you will be in the clear. I will be in the clear. I can put in my report that you don't have any property of the earl's, and we'll be on our way. So what do say you, Mr. Cordoza, may we have a nip around the room, look through your things, give us all some peace of mind before I go back to the Hall and tell them to look again?"

David knew that he didn't have anything to hide. He pulled up to full height and gestured around the room. He was sick of this. "Go ahead. You can look everywhere, but you won't find them because I don't have them."

"That's just fine," Detective White said, getting up and nodding to the officers. "We'll be out of your hair in no time, Mr. Cordoza. We appreciate your cooperation. Now, why don't you have a seat over there while we get started. May I start with your luggage? Let's see what we have here."

———————————

Back at Hambley Hall, the natives were getting restless. There were only so many casual topics of conversation you could run through while sitting on pins and needles. When the hall phone rang, they waited until Sorsby entered the room, announcing that Constable Sheffield was on the line. They all followed the earl into the hall to listen as the constable began breathlessly, "Your Lordship. Sorry for the delay, it's just that we've had a bit of excitement here at the Arms. I'll not belabour it, Sir, but I'm happy to report to you that the ruby and diamond necklace has been recovered. It seems Mr. Cordoza had hidden it in the back of a portrait. Rather cleverly disguised, it seems, to throw off the scent of the customs officials, but nevertheless we discovered it, Sir. The American was checking for flights out of the country when we arrived. No sign of the wooden box or the other missing items, but I knew you'd want to know as soon as possible that your necklace was safe."

"My God, Sheffield. What a shock. Good work all-around. What a relief you've found it. Is Mr. Cordoza in custody then?"

"Yes, they've taken him to Petersborough, and he'll be processed there. Kicking and screaming, he was. I can tell you there'll be a few lads at the pub tonight with some stories to tell."

"What, he couldn't have denied it, surely?"

"He did though! Said he had no idea how the jewels got pasted into the back of his painting." Constable Sheffield chuckled a bit. "Queer really. But then, he's American.

Rather pompous, too. Said quite a few unflattering things about all of us."

"Fantastic, Sheffield. Steady on and keep us posted. I don't suppose you could run the necklace over, so we can give it to the lads waiting here from Sotheby's, eh?"

"I'm afraid not, Your Lordship. They'll need to be held as evidence until we get a judge to release them. I shouldn't think they would have need of them for too long, however."

"Good. Good. Well done, Sheffield. The countess and I couldn't be more relieved to know it's all been managed so well. Keep me posted."

The earl hung up the phone and announced to the waiting party, "So it seems your jewel thief couldn't be trusted with the family jewels after all, my dear. Seems he nicked the necklace and hid it in the back of a painting and was checking for flights out the country when they arrived. Sounds like we managed to avert a disaster."

Jane put her hand to her heart and sat down hard in a hall chair. Geneva ran to her. "Are you alright, Countess? Jane?"

"Yes, yes, my God, Barford, what a shock! I can't believe he would do something like this. Under our very noses. Why would he do this to us, I thought we were getting along so well?"

"Good God, woman, he's a jewel thief! It's what he does. Thank God he was found out."

"Did he have the wooden box with the rest of the fakes then?" said Geneva.

"No, only the necklace. Don't know where that lousy box is after. Good God, this calls for a drink." The earl left them.

Mr. Peak shook his head. "I don't suppose the police will want to hand over the jewels to us today, Countess. Perhaps it would be better all-around if we reschedule this. Just give us a call when you have them, and we'll pop by to pick them up," he said as he made ready to leave, but then stopped to bow. "Thank you for a memorable afternoon. So sorry for your trouble, but very relieved it worked out. Just give us a shout when you're ready."

Sorsby showed them out.

Geneva looked at the countess and allowed herself a very small smile of triumph. She pulled Jane into her arms for a hug and whispered, "Well done, Jane. Very well done."

Chapter 43

David Torres Cordoza sat in a small concrete prison cell and had a breakdown. He knew he'd been set up because he knew he didn't steal the jewels. For the life of him, he couldn't understand why someone did it. The cast of characters wasn't very long, and he spent all his time fantasizing about which one of them planted the jewels on him. It had to be someone at the Hall. But why? For fun? For more notoriety for the jewels so they would sell them for more money at auction? He was going crazy.

The cops didn't believe a word he said about being framed. Their self-congratulatory attitudes sickened him as they laughed and back-slapped their way around the station thinking they solved the crime of the century. He immediately asked for a lawyer and was appointed some idiot newbie who wouldn't listen to or maybe simply didn't believe him. He was charged with grand felony and intent to transport stolen goods out of the country and was facing twenty years in prison. What he needed was a good lawyer who would help him prove he was innocent and find out what devil framed him. But investigators cost money, and good lawyers cost even more, and David nearly had a heart attack when he found out his bank funds were frozen pending litigation in the States by the Carrows family. Apparently, they finally wanted the money for their ring, and they got a judge to freeze his assets until it was decided. How the hell did that happen? He thought they were interested in a truce! Now he needed an attorney in the States as well, but he didn't have any money to pay them either.

He finally made a call to Marcel Broussard. He felt sure his agent would help him, but Marcel had been almost hostile over the phone telling him that he wasn't going to be associated with a career criminal. David begged him to keep the website going so he could make some desperately needed income, but Marcel told him to take a flying leap and do it himself.

How the hell was he going to run his website from a prison cell in England? He called his friend and publisher, Logan Neudor in Los Angeles, and begged him for money and help as well, and even though Logan said he would do his best, there was something in his voice that said otherwise. David practically cried on the phone pleading with Logan to believe he was innocent. Someone had framed him.

"And why would someone frame you, David? You know, it was one thing to listen to your bullshit when it was making me money, but it's another when you think I'm going to be pulled into it, too. You need to start smelling what you're shoveling, David. I'll do what I can, but I'm not sure we can spin this thing out any further."

David needed a miracle. And money. And a really good lawyer, and a sympathetic jury, but it didn't look like any of it was coming his way.

Chapter 44

Some weeks later, the Countess of Hambley sat quietly in the drawing room after dinner with the Earl. Leafing idly through *Hello!* magazine she said, "And thank goodness you're sober now, Barford. I'm not sure your poor liver could take much more of that abuse."

"I quite agree," said the earl with a large smile. "But I think I was rather good playing a drunken boor."

She gazed fondly at him. "A little too good, dear. Who knew you were such a dedicated actor."

"Yes, well, in for a penny, in for a pound." The earl leafed through his own newspaper.

Jane flipped through the pages of the magazine. "I know the trial will be strenuous, but I do feel as though the difficult part is behind us, don't you?"

"I quite agree. Having that man in the house made my playing a drunk quite easy. Half the time I just wanted to kill him knowing what a bloody bugger he was."

"But now that it's almost over, I must tell you, Barford,

I really miss our dear Geneva." Jane put her hands in her lap and looked over to the earl with sadness. "Truly, such a wonderful girl and to think that we may never see her again. I wonder if she's gone back to the States or if she's still in the country."

"I suppose we could find out. I could give Henry a call."

"No, we stay well clear of the Carrowses, darling. At least for some time." Jane looked out the window to the green rolling lawns, the blue sky, her beautiful home. She was grateful for it all.

She kicked her leg in her husband's direction to gain his attention. "It will be such fun to spend time with Brandon next week when we go to London for the auction. Don't you think? I've such mixed emotions about the jewels now. And the portrait. I'm so glad we decided to leave it at the Arms. I don't ever want to see it hanging in our home. The memories! My goodness. That would be too much." She resumed flipping.

"You should stop over there, my dear. See the place of honour it has in the front entry. Exceptionally grand! One thing I'll say for David is that he could paint. You look very majestic."

"Maybe sometime after things cool down and after the trial. Do you think we'll be called as witnesses, Barford?"

"I should think so. At least one of us. Perhaps Mr. Page at the Arms, or Sorsby too. I wouldn't worry too much about it. It'll be fine."

"What about Geneva? Do you think they'll want to

call her?" She looked over to him as he peered over his spectacles.

"They may try, but not if she's in the States. Doubt it's necessary. They found the jewels on him, darling. He's like the boy who cried wolf now. No one believes a thing he says."

"Sweet Geneva. So fortunate she was able to find that box for us before she left. Quite extraordinary that it slipped under that bookcase over there. Good thing she's such a thorough young lady." Jane smiled with the recollection of that scene being play acted for Sorsby's benefit.

Jane suddenly straightened and screamed, "Barford!"

He looked up startled and saw she was still staring at her gossip magazine.

Jane jumped up and ran over to him pointing to a large picture. "Look! Look who that is? It's our dear Geneva and look who she's with!"

They read the caption. "Leaving the famous Clementine's, George Clooney escorts a mysterious blond. No sign of Amal!"

The Linnington Jewelry auction was one of the most watched auctions in Sotheby's recent history. The perfect Georgian parure was cleaned and shimmering grandly when the bidding began. Seated in the first row, the earl and countess, and their son, Brandon waited anxiously as the bidding opened at £1,000,000. In short order it made its way to four and after that, the bidding ran solely between two bidders. One bidder, who they could not see, was apparently at the back of the room, and the other bidder was working through a sales agent of Sotheby's by phone.

The intensity in the room built, the hushed oohs and ahhs became louder as the bid went higher and higher, and the normally reserved audience members barely repressed their excitement. The Linningtons watched their son, Brandon, mystified as the numbers continued to rise. Finally, for the round price of £10,000,000, the magnificent Linnington family parure was sold to the anonymous caller on the phone.

Brandon and the earl and countess joined the standing ovation. The three of them each searched to get a look at the bidder in the back of the room. A woman, it turned out, smiled at them. Brandon, startled by the sight of her whispered to his mother while the room roared with continuing applause, "Mother, do you see who the other bidder was!"

"My heavens, Brandon, if it isn't our dear Geneva."

About the Author

Annabelle Lewis lives in Minneapolis with her husband and children.

You can reach Annabelle at:

https://www.theannabellelewis.com

Follow Annabelle on Facebook at:

https://www.facebook.com/AnnabelleLewisAuthor

Acknowledgements

I'd like to thank my family and friends for their support. Throwing random pages at them for review and listening to my problems as the characters in the book often did whatever they liked rather than what I'd planned, was invaluable. Thank you for giving me the time and space to romp with the Carrows.

To the Western Suburb's Writing Group, thank you for your wonderful advice and friendship. The sessions are a highlight of my week.

To my editor and friend, Susan Stradiotto, thank you for staying in the trenches with me and slugging it out even when I couldn't see the forest for the trees, and vice versa. I deeply appreciated your patience and professionalism.